The
PUMPKIN
PRINCESS
and the FOREVER NIGHT

The PUMPKIN PRINCESS and the FOREVER NIGHT

STEVEN BANBURY

ILLUSTRATED BY MATT ROCKEFELLER

LITTLE, BROWN AND COMPANY

New York Boston

Copyright © 2024 by Steven Banbury

Illustrations copyright © 2024 by Matt Rockefeller

Cover art copyright © 2024 by Matt Rockefeller. Cover design by Gabrielle Chang. Cover copyright © 2024 by Hachette Book Group, Inc.

Interior design by Gabrielle Chang.
Interior art credits: Branch frame © Eroshka/Shutterstock.com

Little, Brown and Company
Hachette Book Group
1290 Avenue of the Americas, New York, NY 10104
Visit us at LBYR.com

First Edition: September 2024

Little, Brown and Company is a division of Hachette Book Group, Inc. The Little, Brown name and logo are registered trademarks of Hachette Book Group, Inc.

The publisher is not responsible for websites (or their content) that are not owned by the publisher.

Little, Brown and Company books may be purchased in bulk for business, educational, or promotional use. For information, please contact your local bookseller or the Hachette Book Group Special Markets Department at special.markets@hbgusa.com.

Library of Congress Cataloging-in-Publication Data
Names: Banbury, Steven, author. | Rockefeller, Matt, illustrator.
Title: The Pumpkin Princess and the forever night / Steven Banbury ; illustrated by Matt Rockefeller.
Description: First edition. | New York : Little, Brown and Company, 2024. | Series: The Pumpkin Princess ; book 1 | Audience: Ages 8–12. | Summary: "A runaway orphan is adopted by the fabled Pumpkin King and whisked away to a land of undead creatures." —Provided by publisher.
Identifiers: LCCN 2023048482 | ISBN 9780316572989 (hardcover) | ISBN 9780316572996 (paperback) | ISBN 9780316573009 (ebook)
Subjects: CYAC: Kings, queens, rulers, etc.—Fiction. | Orphans—Fiction. | Monsters—Fiction. | LCGFT: Novels.
Classification: LCC PZ7.1.B36435 Pu 2024 | DDC [Fic]—dc23
LC record available at https://lccn.loc.gov/2023048482

ISBNs: 978-0-316-57298-9 (hardcover), 978-0-316-57299-6 (pbk.), 978-0-316-57300-9 (ebook)

Printed in Indiana, USA

LSC-C

Hardcover: 10 9 8 7 6 5 4 3 2 1

Paperback: 10 9 8 7 6 5 4 3 2 1

Printing 1, 2024

To my wife, Ashley, and our dog, Bingo.
One of you made writing this book possible,
the other just kind of stared at me
the whole time.

CONTENTS

CHAPTER ONE
An Escape Most Daring 1

CHAPTER TWO
A Home of Her Own 12

CHAPTER THREE
Hallowell Station 31

CHAPTER FOUR
Grumble Grumble, Soil and Shovel 52

CHAPTER FIVE
Banished 72

CHAPTER SIX
The Be-Spelled Bookcraft 89

CHAPTER SEVEN
Friends and Fangs 107

CHAPTER EIGHT
The Harvest Festival 130

CHAPTER NINE
Haunted Holidays 153

CHAPTER TEN
A Sleepless Sleepover 175

CHAPTER ELEVEN
The Clock Tower 193

CHAPTER TWELVE
The Wailing Water Wheel 205

CHAPTER THIRTEEN
The Grimm Pine Woods 228

CHAPTER FOURTEEN
Terrors in the Night 244

CHAPTER FIFTEEN
Smoke and Chains 264

CHAPTER SIXTEEN
The Gift of Life 284

CHAPTER SEVENTEEN
The Pumpkin Princess 306

CHAPTER ONE

An Escape Most Daring

SHE RAN.

As fast as she could move her legs, she ran.

A sparse forest loomed before her, its dark trees wrapped in moonlit mists. If she could just make the tree line . . .

Behind her, she could hear barks and men shouting; the faint glow from their flashlights was getting brighter, telling her they were closing in.

She knew they would eventually catch her. They always did, after all.

This was by no means her first escape attempt from the orphanage, and judging from the sounds of nearing dogs, it unfortunately wouldn't be her last either.

Clearing the tree line, she mentally checked off Part 4a of her six-part escape plan. Overhead, silver moonlight gleamed through scant branches, strobing across her face as she dodged from tree to tree in the deep blue of a cold autumn night. Suddenly, a flashlight found its mark directly on her back, casting her shadow perfectly ahead onto a mossy boulder.

She cut right, circling behind a tree covered in heavily peeling bark. Catching sight of a dew-soaked trench, she jumped down, sliding wetly to the bottom. She found a nook within the earth, hidden under a rotted-out log, and crammed herself as best she could under it.

Not off to a bad start, she told herself.

Only twice before had she even made it as far as the forest itself. Escape attempts one through three (or was it four?) had all been thwarted before she could even cross the tree line. It wasn't wasted effort, though. Those attempts taught her that she would need to delay the adults if she ever wanted to stand a chance at getting away. She had hoped if she could just make it to the forest before they did, then she could use her size and nimbleness to evade capture. And when she finally *did* make it to the shelter of the trees—two failed escapes ago—that plan had worked . . . for a brief and hope-filled moment. But it was the ever-keen guard dogs, Watcher and Curfew, that caught her in the end. The first chase through the woods, they sniffed her out under a log not too dissimilar from the one she currently hid under. The second, they caught her on the run, tackling and pinning her to the ground.

Not this time. This time she had a surprise for them.

Pressing her back against the log's decaying bark, she squeezed herself as best she could underneath it, trying to make herself invisible to anyone above. Hunched over, her long black hair hung to either side of her face, the tips swimming in a puddle that reflected her hazel eyes back at her. Mud now fully covered her thin pajamas, clinging to her tall and lanky frame and causing her to shiver.

Overhead, chunks of wet dirt tumbled down the side of the embankment, followed by a cone of yellow light that searched inches from her nose. She forced herself as far into the moldy bark as she could, scrunching her nose against the musty smell, and that's when she heard it: the unmistakable sound of a hound sniffing.

Time to test the next part of her plan.

She knew that if this escape were to be any different from the last, then she would no doubt have to solve for the dogs in some form or fashion—which is why she had concocted a strategy to deal with them.

From one of her pajama pockets, she pulled out a rolled-up pair of particularly nasty, ridiculously smelly, well-worn socks. It had been Part 1c of her plan and had required her—to the dismay of many—to wear the same socks for months on end. The process of which was not a pleasant one, as the smell had begun to get so bad that the orphanage's headmistress started making her shower twice daily. From her other pocket she withdrew a small, two-pronged slingshot that she had swiped off a younger boy when he wasn't paying attention.

With as little movement as possible, she nudged the hair from her face and carefully loaded the balled-up socks into the slingshot. Then, making sure to stay hidden, she drew back on the sling as far as her cramped arms would allow, aiming it out of the ditch and back the direction she had come.

With a *twang* that made her hold her breath in fear of being heard, the socks launched into the darkness and away from her hiding place.

There was a sudden bark and the quick cracking of a leash pulled taut as either Watcher or Curfew took the bait and went after her *especially* fragrant socks. With bated breath, she waited until she could hardly make out the sound of them running through the fallen leaves strewn about the forest floor; then, as fast as she could, she leaped from under the log and picked up her flight away from the orphanage.

The trees seemed to multiply as she made her way deeper into the forest, blocking path after path and forcing her in their own devious directions.

Encouraged by making it farther than she ever had before, she pushed on, till her nose was red and her fingers numb from the cold. It was then that she began to wish her intricate plan had included a jacket, for the evening chill was piercing through her mud-damp pajamas with minimal effort.

Suddenly, a deep bark cut through the October night from somewhere to her right, and to her left another bark answered, both far too close for comfort.

Apparently, her sock ploy wasn't the lengthy distraction she had hoped it would be.

Desperate for anything else she could throw that might smell like her, she kicked off her slippers and tossed them in random directions, hoping that maybe, just maybe, that might draw the dogs' attention and slow them down.

With no tricks left up her sleeves (or in her pockets), she ran for it. The forest closed in all around her as if it too was in pursuit, making it harder and harder for her to move. Thorns of grasping bushes latched on to her clothes as she pushed, clawed, and struggled forward. Broken sticks nipped at her bare feet, and an ever-increasing chill deepened until her breath was forming around her like the exhaust of a steam engine.

She came upon a wall of bramble and fought with all her might to force her way through. Still, the forest pushed back, and she found she couldn't go any farther. Desperately, she turned to run in another direction, but her foot caught on a vine, and she tripped and fell heavily forward.

Here, only the merest trace of moonlight was able to penetrate the black canopy above, shining a lonely ray of light onto the leaf-covered ground. Darkness closed in from everywhere else, surrounding her and trapping her for the dogs.

She lifted herself onto her knees, defeated.

So much for this attempt, she thought. Time to start planning the next. At least the orphanage would be warm, and possibly, if she apologized enough, they'd let her take a hot shower *before* locking her cold and wet in the detention room.

A nearby bush shook, and the two hounds burst through the trees.

Curfew and Watcher stood noses down, a slow rumbling growl coming from each as they backed her up against the bramble wall. Their leashes hung loosely behind them; either their handlers had let go or the dogs had forcefully broken free after her. Regardless, she was caught.

Curfew lifted his broad head to howl victoriously—

But an unexpected whimper came out instead.

She watched bewildered as both of the large dogs began to slowly back away, their intimidating growls replaced by low, fearful whining. Then, to her surprise, both turned and ran back the way they had come, their tails tucked between their legs.

Um...what? she thought. She had never seen Watcher or Curfew scared of anything.

"Your turn to run," a low voice growled from behind her.

She tried to whip around on her knees, but in her haste stumbled onto her back, facing the brambles.

There, obscured by thorns, were two triangles of warm light, each tilted at an angle and glowing orange like burning embers.

"Is someone there?" she called, unsure if she had imagined the voice and even more unsure of what she was looking at.

For a moment, there was no reply. Then, slowly, the vines began to twist and slither away, seemingly of their own accord.

A head emerged from the bramble, or at least what appeared to be a head. What it really was, and she had no idea how, was a massive pumpkin, with a face like that of a glowing jack-o'-lantern carved into it. The two lights she had seen became sharp, angular eyes that moved and squinted her way; underneath was a triangular nose that seemed to sniff at her, and a wide, jagged mouth shifted to a thin frown as it judged her where she lay.

A cloud passed overhead, cutting off the lone moonbeam that had been able to penetrate the treetop. She was thrown into complete darkness, save for the light emanating from the face staring down at her.

She found herself speechless, trying (and failing) to make sense of what she was seeing. Had she hit her head when she fell? But then what were the dogs running from?

"You have seen me," the face rumbled. "Now would you wish to run?"

Where anyone else would have felt fear, she did not. Instead, she glanced back over her shoulder the way she had come. The only way *to* run was back toward the orphanage. "Um . . . ," she stammered, thinking there was no way she was going back if she didn't have to. "Is there a second option?"

"Hrmph," the being grunted, and one of his eyes grew wide in curiosity. "Who are you?" he asked, with a voice like deep roots inching through soil. The hollow nose sniffed again, flickering in its own light as it did. "Your kind have always feared me. Why do I not smell that on you?"

"I'm just an orphan," she answered cautiously. "And you don't smell fear because I'm not scared. Also, well, because fear isn't really a smell. Should I be, though? Scared, I mean."

"Yes," he growled, and his pumpkin face split into a wide, threatening grimace. Steam poured from his jagged mouth into the cold air as he spoke. "For from my wakening breath comes the storming winds of fall. My opening eyes cause the leaves to turn color in fright. My voice chases the sun from its perch and allows the shadows to grow. I am the bump in the night, the monster under your bed, the trick in the darkness, and the treat of it all. For I am the Pumpkin King."

The face loomed farther out of the branches and closer to her own, revealing a dark, pointed collar atop a pitch-black cape that covered the creature's broad shoulders.

"Do you find yourself scared *now?*" the Pumpkin King asked from behind a twisting smile.

She studied the otherworldly face, wondering how any of this could be even remotely possible. Yet, so far he hadn't given her any reason to feel in danger, and until he did . . .

"Nope. Still not scared, sorry," she answered.

The smile disappeared from his face.

If he was hoping to frighten, he chose the wrong person, she thought. Fear was something she no longer let herself feel; she had buried that particular emotion away years ago.

When she had first arrived at the orphanage, and through most of her childhood there, she had suffered from terrorizing nightmares brought on by an almost constant state of being scared. Eventually, she bottled all that up, locking that fear in a little box and hiding it somewhere deep within. Ever since, she decided things could only scare you if you let them, and had trained herself to never, *ever* let them. She would not be scared again. Not of the nightmares, not of chasing dogs, and surely not of a large, talking pumpkin.

"Besides, I'm pretty sure you don't make fall happen," she added simply. "The rotation of the planet causes seasons, not your breath."

He tilted his massive head to the side, and if a pumpkin could look intrigued, he did.

"What is your name, orphan?" he asked, his tone far less menacing than before, and much more . . . well, mainly less menacing.

"It's—I don't have one," she lied. She never liked the name the orphanage gave her. It was of a life that wasn't hers.

"Hrmph," he grumbled, considering her with eyes that cast a warm, amber glow over her.

She met his penetrating gaze with a curiousness of her own, and for a moment, not a sound could be heard within the forest, save for the rustle of the leaves in the wind.

Finally, he gave a small nod, as if he had come to the end of some unspoken decision.

"Do you know what tonight is?" he asked.

She knew what night it was well. In fact, it had been an integral part of her escape plan.

"It's Halloween," she answered.

"Yes, All Hallows' Eve," he said. "Thus, I shall call you Eve."

She pondered this, wondering why he felt the need to call her anything. *Eve* was pretty, though, prettier than her other name.

"Short for Evelyn, I like it," she said.

"Then it shall be your name," the Pumpkin King growled, almost proudly. "Eve, how would you like a new home? One where men and their hounds do not chase you through the woods? One where, should you want, you could leave at your leisure, though I hope you find reason to stay."

From deeper in the forest, she began to hear the rustling of footsteps followed by the reluctant whimpers of scared dogs. No doubt her pursuers had finally narrowed down her location and would soon be upon her.

She looked up at the illuminated face and gave a slight shiver. Not from fear, no, not her, but rather from the cold that was biting through her damp clothes.

She knew the offer was one that currently didn't make sense, but given more time, she thought she might be able to work out whatever *this* was. Talking pumpkin heads were not something that should exist, at least not from what she had ever seen from the confines of the orphanage or the surplus of books she read to busy herself while there.

"I would like that," she finally answered, knowing at the bare minimum it would be a different life from the one she had, the one she was so desperate to escape.

"Good," the Pumpkin King answered with a nod. "Then you shall come back with me, and I shall adopt you as my own child, where you will be the Pumpkin Princess."

"Wait, wha—"

But before she could finish her question, vines reached out from the towering wall of bramble and grabbed her legs.

With a sudden tug, the dogs were left with nothing to find as the orphan they searched for was yanked from a world she knew and into something different, for the Pumpkin King had gone, and with him . . . so had Eve.

CHAPTER TWO

A Home of Her Own

EVE LAY WITH HER EYES CLOSED.

She had woken from a dream that she didn't want to leave, and hoped she could will herself back into it if she didn't get up. It was a dream where she had finally escaped the orphanage and had felt so real that even her legs were sore from the imagined running. But it couldn't have been more than a dream, because in it, she was adopted by the made-up and entirely fictional Pumpkin King. Something that Eve knew wasn't possible.

The Pumpkin King was just a scary story used to frighten children at Halloween, and nothing more. She probably only conjured him into her dreams because Halloween had just happened.

Yes, surely that could be the only explanation, she told herself.

It was the only logical outcome, and Eve prided herself on being a logical person.

Which, and this was the most unfortunate part, meant that when Eve did open her eyes, she would open them to the stained ceiling of the orphanage. Even lying in bed, she could practically already hear the headmistress's impending scolding for once more trying to run away: *She was being an ungrateful burden and should be thankful anyone took her in at all after the death of her parents, blah, blah, blah....* But despite having the speech memorized, the words never cut Eve any less, and were why, even now, she was already plotting her next escape. Desperate not to just run away, but to run *to* something: to the happiness she had always read about in books and wanted so badly for herself.

But then, just beside Eve's bed, an unexpected voice spoke in a scratchy tone that was *most certainly* not the headmistress's, followed by something prodding at her shoulder.

"Time to wakes up, Prin'sis," rasped the voice. "Yours food is getting cold."

Did someone just say "Princess?"

Eve's eyes shot open.

There, inches from her face, two mismatched buttons stared back at her, one blue and one white. They were sewn onto a stuffed burlap sack with a cross-stitched x for a nose and a moving, rough tear for a mouth.

"Oh good, you'res awake," said the makeshift head, and

13

a smile formed across his burlap face, revealing a mouth full of straw. Over his sticklike frame he wore an oversize coat so old that it was more patchwork than original, and at the cuffs, wooden posts gave way to hands gloved in equally old gardening gloves. "We's made yous firstmeal downstairs."

Okay, definitely still dreaming, Eve thought. Otherwise, she was fairly certain there was a scarecrow talking to her.

Eve glanced out a nearby window draped in thin curtains, to where a yellow moon peeked between soot-gray clouds. She was in a quaint bedroom, dark save for the light of the moon and a tall wax candle the scarecrow was holding. A dust-covered reading chair sat in the corner, kept company only by a small dresser and the bed she lay in.

What is going on? And had she somehow slept through an entire day?

"Where am I?" asked Eve. "This isn't the orphanage."

"Orphanage? No! This is the Hall of the Pumpkin King!" the scarecrow said proudly. He threw back the itchy sheets that covered Eve, revealing her mud-soaked pajamas. "Come, come, we's have a surprise for yous."

Eve didn't move. *The Hall of the*— "Wait, the Pumpkin King is real?"

"As real as me's!"

"That—I don't think that helps the way you meant it to," Eve pointed out, trailing off as the scarecrow headed for the bedroom

14

door. "Wait! Come back! I don't understand—" She slipped from the creaky bed frame, her feet landing on a threadbare rug so thin it hardly covered the wooden floor.

Rushing after the scarecrow with a head full of questions, she exited out onto a narrow loft overlooking a long wooden hall with vaulted ceilings. Lit by candles and torches, the air was warm and cozy, and smelled of fresh baking full of cinnamon and spices. A stone chimney spread up the middle of the wall opposite them, rising from a hearth that blazed wildly on the floor below. Peering over the wooden banister, Eve found herself speechless as a dozen more scarecrows bustled about a handmade table that stretched the length of the Hall.

Suddenly, all the scarecrows stopped and stared up at her, each as different as the next.

"Nows!" shouted one, and two scarecrows hobbled in opposite directions, unfurling a hand-painted banner.

Across it, written in letters both upside down and backwards—and taking Eve a second to decipher—were the words WELL-COMES PRINSIS! All the strange scarecrows smiled up at her.

"We's didn't know what yous might like to eat," said the scarecrow beside her, leading her down from the loft. "So we's cooked up everything."

Eve descended to the ground floor of the cavernous Hall of the Pumpkin King, where she had to basically force her eyes to stop staring at all the moving and talking scarecrows, briefly taking in the food-covered table instead. The scarecrow wasn't kidding when he said they'd cooked everything. There was so much to eat that hardly an inch of the table's surface could be seen at all.

Scarecrows rushed over to welcome her and to try to hand her food. Some had gardening tools for hands, others gloves or bunches of straw. Some walked directly on postlike legs; others wore boots or waders.

"Didn't know if yous wanted butter or jams on your toast. Here's both!"

"Try our sweet potato pie!"

"The oatmeal has fresh berries in it, picked thems myself!"

Eve was in such a shock that all she could do was mumble flustered thank-yous or "Um, this looks nice," talking to each of the scarecrows in turn.

Suddenly, an arched door at the end of the Hall swung open, and with it, a cold gust of autumn air billowed inside.

In loomed the Pumpkin King.

He no longer had a black cape draped over his wide shoulders, but rather a deep blue, colonial-style coat from shoulder to knee, adorned with heavy brass buttons. A stiff collar surrounded the bottom of his pumpkin head, and below the jacket, dark pants were tucked into the tops of mud-covered boots the color of pumpernickel. He was much bigger than Eve remembered, easily twice as large as any adult she had ever known and far more imposing. In the massive Hall, only he looked the right size. Eve, on the other hand, felt comparatively tiny.

"Hrmph! So this is where you all are," he growled. "You left me to herd the apricot trees all on my own."

"We's wanted to prepare a welcomes party for the prin'sis," said the scarecrow with blue and white buttons for eyes. "We've been cooking."

The Pumpkin King's eyes wandered the length of the food-laden table before finally landing on Eve.

The orange blaze of his carved, angular eyes softened, and his mouth twisted into a frightening smile—one that would have caused any human *but* Eve to melt from fear.

"Good, you're awake," he said. "I was not sure how long humans slept, if it was measured in hours or days."

Eve found she was unable to reply. Instead, her jaw hung loosely open.

What. Is. Happening?

"How do you find your new home?" asked the Pumpkin King, as if nothing abnormal was going on whatsoever.

Eve looked up and down the Hall, catching the mismatched eyes of all the scarecrows watching her.

Did he say . . .

"My home?" she repeated, her voice hardly more than a whisper.

She had never had a home before. Let alone even heard of a place like this. Candles flickered along the walls, tossing shadows in every direction, and from what Eve could tell, there wasn't a trace of electricity or powered lighting at all.

"Do you not like it?" he asked, and Eve could see worry form on his face.

"It's not—I'm just—" she stammered. "This isn't a dream?"

"Hrmph," he grumbled. "This is no trick of the night, of that I can assure you." Heavy on his boots, he stomped over to the table and reached for a thickly buttered biscuit.

With hands nimbler than Eve expected, a scarecrow's glove shot out and pulled the biscuit from him.

"Those are for the Pumpkin Prin'sis," said the scarecrow.

The Pumpkin King's eyes blazed. "She can't eat all this. Look at the size of her. Besides, you never cook this well when it's just me!"

"We's don't know how much shes can eat. And yous is boring. All yous ever want is oats in warm ale."

"I definitely can't finish all this," Eve agreed. "If any of you want to eat, you're welcome to." If she was being honest, she wished they would. Then maybe they'd all stop staring at her.

"They do not eat," mumbled the Pumpkin King, taking a biscuit and swallowing it down in one gulp. "Are you ready to go?"

"Go? Go where?" Eve asked, her mind desperately struggling for any foothold it could find.

"You and I are going into town," he answered. "We need to get you some new clothes. You are far too underdressed for

18

evenings here. Is it common for humans to not wear shoes in the cold?"

"Um . . . no—sorry, what town?" asked Eve, her confusion more pressing than her cold, bare feet. There were no towns near the orphanage.

"Wait, you'res not taking her already?" said a suddenly worried-looking scarecrow. "Are yous sure she's safe there?"

"Safe *where?*" Eve tried. "Wait, am I not—"

"Of course she is safe," growled the Pumpkin King. "She is the Pumpkin Princess." He turned and headed for the door.

The scarecrow hurried after him, and Eve hurried after the scarecrow. She couldn't help but notice he didn't look as sure as the Pumpkin King did.

The scarecrow gulped. "But yous haven't told thems about her yet," he said nervously. "What if someone tries to—"

"Hrmph!" The Pumpkin King's grumble was loud and definitive, and with it, steam billowed from his mouth. "She will be fine. Now, you all have work to get back to. Eve and I must depart. We have a long night ahead of us."

"All right, fine," said the scarecrow, resignation in his voice. He gave Eve one last concerned look. "But not like that shes doesn't. She'lls freeze to death." The scarecrow ran off through a side door before returning and wrapping Eve and her thin pajamas in a blanket that could cover a horse. "Okay, now yous can go."

19

The Pumpkin King made for the door, but before he opened it, he turned to the scarecrow. "Remember, the peach trees need their boots. Leather only. The older the better."

"I's know, I's know," answered the scarecrow with a bored wave of his hand.

"Excuse me," Eve interjected, nowhere near as nonchalant as the scarecrow. "Did you say boots for the trees?"

"For nourishment, not wearing," the Pumpkin King answered simply. "The leather helps their bark."

"Oh . . . okay, sure." She could maybe find logic there.

"And the boot strings give theirs roots something to do," the scarecrow added with a smile.

"They—wait, what?" Eve asked, slack-jawed. There was *no* logic there. Where in the world was she?

The scarecrow ushered them out the door and closed it behind them, and if Eve thought she was confused before, it was nothing compared to when she stepped out into the night.

She was definitely nowhere near the orphanage anymore.

They were atop a wide hill, draped so thickly in vine-wrapped pumpkins that she could hardly see the ground. The Hall itself was covered in black brambles and thorns, clawing their way up the tall walls to its angled roof. Around them, as far as she could see in the light of an abnormally large and equally bright moon, were acres of endless and torchlit farmland, all of it dressed in the hues of fall, more colorful than Eve could have ever imagined.

Golden fields of grain gave way to bales of hay marbled with greens and tans. Orchards of fruit trees stood in perfect rows, their leaves every shade of orange and red, while fruit bushes popped with berries so vibrant that Eve could see them even in the night.

A crisp chill wrapped itself around her, swirling damp leaves about Eve's bare feet and carrying with it notes of earth and dew, of wood after a heavy rain. A shiver ran from her cold toes up to her goose-pimpled arms, and she hugged the blanket tighter around herself.

The Pumpkin King began to walk down the hill, and before him, the vines and pumpkins parted and rolled from his path. He beckoned Eve to follow.

But in that moment, Eve realized she had gone as far as she could without some kind of explanation.

"Not till you tell me what's going on," she said, rooting herself to the spot.

"I told you. We're going to town to get you some clothes and whatever else you'll need to live here," he said, turning to face her. "I don't know much about being a father, but hrmph, I imagine clothing my daughter is one of the responsibilities."

Daughter.

The word echoed through Eve's head like a bell being rung, knocking out any other questions that were there.

She had always dreamed of finding a family, one that wanted

her as much as she wanted them. It was the sole thought that sustained her at the orphanage, a lone flame that kept her going through years of feeling cold and unwanted.

She had come close, once or twice. Would-be parents looking to adopt and hoping the orphanage might have a child for them. But it always ended the same. The headmistress would show them Eve's file, the words *Suffers from debilitating night terrors* scratched across it like some kind of black mark. Even long after she had overcome them, the file stayed the same, just like the inevitable decision of the potential parents when they adopted a—how did the headmistress put it?—"an *easier* child, one that wasn't *broken*."

The Pumpkin King must have sensed her hesitation, because he slowly climbed back up the hill and knelt before her. Even then he was double Eve's height. She felt the orange glow of his eyes fall on her. "Is this not what you wanted?"

Eve found herself unable to meet his gaze. She suddenly felt far too vulnerable. Instead, she hugged herself deeper into the blanket, staring at one of the buttons of his coat.

Could the Pumpkin King really be what he claimed—what she had always hoped for? Family? A . . . father?

"Are you sure it's what *you* want?" Eve asked, and though it was her mouth that asked the question, it came from somewhere far deeper.

He considered her for a moment, and in his silence Eve nearly blurted out all about her past nightmares. But just as quickly as the urge came, Eve pressed it down. She finally had a chance to be with someone who wanted her. Why would she risk that over something that no longer gave her issues?

Why risk him becoming like all the others?

She shifted nervously on her feet instead, watching as one of the vines coiled away and made room for her.

"Yes, I am sure," he finally said, his voice less gravelly than before. "I would not have brought you here otherwise. I have longed for a child, a prince or princess who could one night take over. Yet, I cannot have one of my own.

"Then, by pure chance, I met you. An orphan fearlessly looking for a home. Someone to be the Pumpkin Princess. So, yes, my offer stands. Though should you desire, I can, hrmph, arrange for you to be taken back. But . . . I ask that you give me a chance."

Eve looked up, trying to convince herself it was the wind making her eyes water.

He watched her silently, waiting for her response from behind the stare of his hollow eyes.

It wasn't that Eve was hesitating; her gut knew the answer. She just had to give her brain a fraction of a second to catch up.

She. Was. Talking. To. A. Pumpkin. And earlier a scarecrow had woken her up. Two things that should not be able to move on their own, let alone bake and eat biscuits.

23

"I'd like to stay," Eve answered all the same, deciding that the illogicalness of the world she found herself in wasn't currently important. "But . . . I don't know what it means to be the Pumpkin Princess." Suddenly, Eve became worried that might change his mind and break the deal.

To her relief, a smile curled across the Pumpkin King's face.

"And I don't know what it means to be a father. But I will teach you to be the Pumpkin Princess, if you will, in turn, teach me back. Do we have an accord?"

A smile spread across Eve's own face. The first in a very, very long time. "Deal," she said.

"Good!" he boomed. "Now, to town, before we lose too much of the moon." Without another word he turned, parting the patch of pumpkins lining the hill with every step.

Eve hurried to keep pace with his long stride, not sure if the vines closing behind them would wait for her or not.

He led her to an old barn, its walls fresh with recent red paint. Bats fluttered out of its eaves and into the night, diving at insects that hovered around the farm's blazing torches.

The Pumpkin King heaved open a heavy, rolling door, and out poured the stale smell of animals kept in close quarters. Inside the barn were several stalls, currently home to two horses that couldn't look more different.

One was a black stallion with darting eyes and twitching muscles, as large as it was fierce. The other, not so much. It was brown and round, and looked a bit like a potato with legs. Eve loved him instantly.

The Pumpkin King headed inside, and after single-handedly rolling out a wooden cart with a bench on the front, set to strapping in the black stallion.

"Atta' boy, Gleysol," the Pumpkin King mumbled. "Peaty, over here."

"Gleysol and Peaty?" Eve asked, watching as Peaty didn't budge but rather continued to graze lazily at the hay strewn across the floor.

"Yes, named after soils," the Pumpkin King growled, his eyes blazing as he stomped over to pull at Peaty, except Peaty pulled back.

"You *would* like dirt," Eve thought out loud. He was a walking, talking pumpkin, after all.

"What was that?" the Pumpkin King grunted, struggling to drag Peaty to the wagon.

"Nothing!" Eve hurried, blushing at her own slip of tongue.

It wasn't until he bribed Peaty with an apple that the stocky horse allowed itself to be harnessed to the rather annoyed-looking Gleysol.

"You next," said the Pumpkin King, and before Eve could protest, she was lifted easily up and onto the seat at the front.

The wagon then groaned and tilted precariously to one side as the Pumpkin King climbed in beside her. He leaned over and grabbed at a lamp that hung from a post, and with an exhale of hot breath, the candle inside caught, circling them in its warm light. They started to pull away from the barn, but before they got far, a voice croaked out behind them.

"Prin'sis! Waits!"

The Pumpkin King pulled on the reins, and both he and Eve turned to see who was calling.

Behind them, tripping and running down the side of the hill that led from the Hall to the barn, was the scarecrow with blue and white buttons for eyes. Something he carried in his gloves left a trail of steam behind him in the cold night air.

"This is for the roads," he panted once he reached the cart. "In case yous get cold or hungry."

He reached up and handed Eve a mug of hot chocolate, the warmth of which spread welcomely into her hands.

"Um, thank you," said Eve, taken aback.

The scarecrow beamed back at her with a wide, straw smile.

"Where's mine?" asked the Pumpkin King.

The scarecrow's smile disappeared.

"Ers, I forgot about yous," he said abashedly.

"Forgot about *me*? Hrmph! I created you, you know." He grumbled something fierce, and with a flick of the reins they set out, the scarecrow waving happily behind them as the wagon wheels churned against damp soil.

"Did you just say that you *created* him?" Eve asked while the horses led them down a path curving around an apple orchard.

"Of course. How else do you think they can talk?"

"Well, yeah, that. Or also, you know, walk and cook," murmured Eve.

"I make the scarecrows and then I breathe figments of myself into them. And they wake. It's as simple as that."

"Just like that? You breathe into them, and they come to life?" asked Eve, thinking in no way did that make sense.

"That's what I said." The Pumpkin King eyed her suspiciously. "Are all humans this slow to understand?"

Eve was affronted. "Excuse me, it's not often I have conversations with Pumpkin Kings or talking scarecrows. This is all new to me, remember?"

"Yes, hrmph, yes. Better become used to what you're unused to. There will be more of that before the night is through."

One thing at a time, thought Eve.

"Do they have names? The scarecrows?"

"Names?" he grumbled. "No. I create them to help me with my duties, not to be my friends."

"What kind of duties?" Eve asked.

"Anything and everything. Our homestead requires much upkeep, far more than I can manage by myself. The foremost of which is preparing for the upcoming Harvest Festival. As Pumpkin King, I am to oversee it, and as my daughter and the Pumpkin Princess, you will too."

There it was again, the word *daughter*. Eve felt a foreign

27

feeling in the pit of her stomach, and it warmed her more than the hot chocolate in her hands ever could.

They traveled for some time before the cart eventually found its way out of the Pumpkin King's farmland. Here, the fields of corn ended and turned to hills of wet, dark grass. Far in the distance, beyond the horizon and covered in an eerie fog, were jagged black mountains that stabbed at the night sky, like the broken teeth of some monster trying to swallow the world.

All around, rolling knolls gave way to hidden hollows and pockets of dark and twisted trees. The path the horses led them down continued to turn and wrap around itself until Eve had lost all sense of direction. It took them near a hill covered in crooked, moss-ridden tombstones, through knotted oaks filled with squawking crows, over creeks of babbling dark water, and even under a stone bridge where Eve was sure she heard snoring coming from the shadows.

"Where is this place?" Eve finally asked, practically having to wrench her eyes away as her curiosity got the better of her. "I don't recognize any of this."

"You wouldn't. We are in the Hallowell Valley, far from the world you knew and the woods I found you in," he growled in his slow, rumbling voice. "Hrmph. Ahead is the village of Hallowell Station."

Eve frowned. Not because of his answer (though she definitely didn't understand that either), but because of the *way* he answered. She worried all his growling and grumbling was a sign that she was already annoying him.

Beneath them, a thick fog was amassing across the ground, hiding the legs of the horses and the wheels of their wagon. Soon, not even the light from the cart's lamp could penetrate it, and all view of the ground was lost. It was like they were sailing through a sea of mist.

"The valley and the town are both called Hallowell?" she asked, a little more nervously now.

"Hrmph, yes. The town is named after the valley."

Finally, Eve couldn't help herself.

"Can I ask you something?" she pushed, testing the edges of their newfound relationship.

"Isn't that what you've been doing?" he grunted.

"Um, yeah . . . about that. . . . Why do you grumble so much? Am I . . . bothering you?"

"*Bothering*—wait, what?" He appeared taken aback by the question, bordering on worried. Quickly he turned a now very serious look on Eve. "Do not worry that you bother me. For you do not, nor could you ever."

Eve was pretty sure her heart smiled. Pumpkin King or not, he was no headmistress.

"Hrmph, besides, I do not grumble!" he grumbled.

"You kind of . . . well, literally, just did," Eve contested, her confidence growing. "Wait—what do you think grumbling is?" Did grumble mean something different in Hallowell?

"Grumble grumble," the Pumpkin King growled.

"No," Eve said with an unexpected and rare laugh. "That's just saying the word *grumble*. That's different."

He grumbled something else that Eve wasn't able to make out, then turned the horses down a fork in the road split by a tilted wooden post. Boards shaped like arrows hung from it, with words that Eve struggled to read in the dark as they rode by.

Eve thought she heard wheels clunk against cobblestone, but all she could see was an ocean of fog. Then, just faintly, lights began to flicker ahead; shimmers of purples and greens, oranges and yellows, danced in the distance.

"Is that—" Eve began.

"Welcome to Hallowell Station," the Pumpkin King said proudly. "Home to the undead and all those that go bump in the night."

CHAPTER THREE

Hallowell Station

AHEAD, THE VILLAGE OF HALLOWELL STATION BEGAN TO RISE from the blackness, its foundations rooted in the very mist that swallowed the bottom of their cart. It was a congested wooden village, with sharp, angular buildings teetering precariously over one another. Zigzagging between its tightly packed roofs and over its narrow streets were ropes lined with multicolored glass jars, each of which was pulsing with candlelight and casting ominous hues into the night. As they approached, the glow of firelight could be seen through many a window, and smoke of all colors billowed up through iron pipes that jutted from the rooftops.

Riding into the village, Eve soon found herself surrounded by all manner of huts, hovels, homes, and odd shops. Some were short and squat, others tall and leaning over the main street itself. Storefronts sprang up along either side of the lane, with large panes of glass showcasing steaming cauldrons, cobwebbed cages, barrels of insects, trays of what appeared to be fingers and toes marked LOST AND FOUND, and a market selling what Eve guessed could only be food, though nothing she would choose to eat. Dark figures moved about in the shadows, stepping aside and making way for the Pumpkin King's cart. It was then that one of the villagers stepped into the light of a black iron lamppost, and Eve was able to see right through her.

"Was that a ghost?" she asked disbelievingly.

"That's Mrs. Shuttersby," the Pumpkin King stated simply, as if that answered her question. "She runs the Dead and Breakfast."

Eve took a harder look at the villagers they were passing. Suddenly, she realized that the translucent Mrs. Shuttersby wasn't the only ghost, nor the only abnormal villager. In fact, one quick glance around the busy lane told Eve that *she* might be the abnormal one here.

In the nearby light of a floating blue flame, a wrapping-clad mummy conversed with a giant talking spider, their words drowned out by a group of short green and orange goblins arguing over a magazine titled *Boos and News*. From the front of a particularly odorous shop, a lady with a hooked nose and pointed hat haggled with a furry-looking man who had sharp, wolflike eyes. Two pale figures waved at the Pumpkin King, and as they smiled, their pearly fangs glinted in the lamplight. Then their gaze fell on Eve, and their smiling faces morphed into expressions of complete shock. They weren't the only ones either. Every head in the lane was turning their way.

"Mr. Pumpkin King, sir," boomed a mountainous gray troll, as tall as even the Pumpkin King sitting atop the wagon. It gave a curt nod as they passed, and Eve saw its eyes grow wide when it spotted her.

She was about to ask why everyone was staring, when the Pumpkin King turned them down a lane marked CHAFFER ST. and brought the horses to a stop.

"Here we are."

The cart leaned uneasily to one side as the Pumpkin King labored out. For a brief moment, Eve found herself frozen, her mind stuck somewhere between disbelief and awe of everything she was seeing. But then the realization that every eye around was still pinned on her snapped her back to reality (or whatever weird version of reality this now was). Deciding it would probably be best to stay close to the Pumpkin King, Eve quickly hopped out, watching as the fog swallowed her legs.

Ahead of them, sandwiched between two darkly painted buildings (one seaweed green, the other deep purple), was a narrow two-story shop. A sign overhead read THE LOOMING LOOM, and underneath was a yellow-stained window showcasing elegant Victorian dresses and suits covered in lace.

"It's pretty late. Are you sure they're open?" Eve asked, confused. "Won't they be sleeping?"

"Sleeping? The sun isn't even up yet. Why would they be sleeping?"

The gears of Eve's mind turned, and she thought about all the villagers in town, and the scarecrows back at the farm just starting their work.

"Wait, so day is night and night is day here?"

"No, hrmph. Day is day and night is night."

"No, I—no, I get that," Eve retorted. "But everyone sleeps during the day here and is awake at night?"

One of the Pumpkin King's triangular eyes grew and the other shrank, and he considered Eve strangely. "What other way is there?"

The normal way, Eve thought. She added *reverse schedule* to the things she would have to get used to in her new life, right there under talking scarecrows and trolls that say hello.

The door gave a jingle as the Pumpkin King pulled and held it open for Eve. "After you," he grumbled.

Eve entered, finding herself surrounded by more clothes than she had ever seen in one place.

Billowing ball gowns hung from the ceiling while suits, vests, and jackets of every color, size, and even shape crowded half of an entire wall. The other half was filled with blouses, skirts, robes, and dresses, all spilling out onto the shop floor clustered with racks of more clothes.

The Pumpkin King shouldered his way to the front counter, behind which a tiny staircase rose up to the second floor.

A mannequin seemingly made from a human skeleton was sprawled with its arms and head across the desk. It was wearing a puffy green blouse and had on a purple turban adorned with rubies the size of Eve's fist.

Eve peered around the shop, searching for signs of a shopkeeper, when suddenly the Pumpkin King grunted loudly.

"Hrmph!"

To Eve's astonishment, the skeleton behind the counter shot up, sending threads of fabric and sewing needles spilling onto the ground.

"Dearest me!" the skeleton said in a clattering, surprised voice. "My apologies, I haven't had my evening tea. Still sleeping off the All Hallows' Eve celebrations, you know?"

Eve stared wide-eyed, then quickly added *skeleton seamstresses* to her rapidly growing list about Hallowell.

"Good evening, Ellie," the Pumpkin King said nonchalantly. "Here for some clothes for my new daughter."

Ellie stifled a large yawn, then yelled up the staircase behind her. "Franklin, the Pumpkin King is here! And he brought—" Her empty eye sockets dropped to Eve, and she yelped with excitement, covering her mouth with heavily ringed finger bones.

"Oh my! It's a human!" shouted Ellie, shooting around the side of the sales counter.

Eve took a cautious step toward the Pumpkin King, whose gloved hand rose protectively in front of her.

"Move your arm, you big brute!" Ellie said, slapping the Pumpkin King's hand aside. "I want to *see* her, not eat her! Oh, she's precious—FRANKLIN! Get down here! There is a *living* girl here!"

Eve would have stepped back if she could, but the skeleton had her in her bony fingers, pinching her cheeks and prodding at her arms and sides.

A clacking sound came from the floor above.

"Ellie, what's all this nonsense about a living girl?" yelled a grumpy old voice.

"Get down here and look!" Ellie shouted back.

"There can't be a human here!" returned the voice from upstairs. "If there was, a troll would have eaten them. Or a vampire would have gotten to it. Not to mention the—"

"HRMPH!" the Pumpkin King grunted loudly, cutting off whatever dangerous thing was about to be said next.

A nervous realization began to take hold in Eve. "I don't understand," she began hesitantly, worried she already knew the answer. "Do all the other, um . . . *living* humans . . . live and shop in a different village nearby?"

Ellie shot the Pumpkin King a surprised glance. "Oh, honey dear, everyone here is undead, or close to it. There are no other humans. You're the only *living* in all of the Hallowell Valley!"

The only one in the WHOLE valley? Eve repeated nervously in her own mind, now understanding all the stares. The Pumpkin King had left that little fact out of his adoption pitch. (Not that Eve would have let it change her answer, but still, her being the only *living* girl felt like a notable thing to leave out.)

Eve looked up at him with raised eyebrows.

"Hrmph, what? Some of the animals are living," he offered, as if that helped. "As are the crops we harvest on our land."

If he had meant to be reassuring, Eve didn't quite find the idea of being in the same category as *food* entirely comforting.

There was creaking from a loose step, and another skeleton emerged from the stairs, dressed in a black pinstripe suit that did nothing to conceal his bony hands or skull of a face.

"My husband, Franklin," Ellie said to Eve.

Franklin stopped where he was as soon as he caught sight of Eve, his jawbone falling open with a clank.

"Um, nice to meet you," offered Eve in hopes of being polite. Meanwhile, her mind was still whirling over being the only one *living* in what was to be her new home.

"Franklin." The Pumpkin King nodded. "This is my daughter, Evelyn. The Pumpkin Princess."

Franklin looked up at the Pumpkin King, his jaw still astray. "You had . . . a child . . . with a human?"

The whole of the Pumpkin King's face turned a more crimson shade of orange.

"Adopted daughter," Eve added hastily.

"Oh, what's the difference?" said Ellie. "Just look how cute she is! How old are you, dear?"

Eve didn't answer. Instead she turned expectantly to the Pumpkin King.

"What are you looking at me for?"

"Oh, um, sorry. I don't actually know my age," Eve muttered. "At the orphanage they were always telling me to act more like the other kids, but they never really knew my birthday."

"Hrmph," grumbled the Pumpkin King. "Then your birthday shall be All Hallows' Eve, the night I found you."

Ellie practically swooned. "Isn't that just the sweetest thing you ever heard? I'm bringing out the good fabric for this. I do get to dress her, right?" Ellie surveyed Eve's muddy pajamas, looking as though she might have a heart attack (if a skeleton could have a heart attack, that is).

"That's why we're here," said the Pumpkin King. "We'll take whatever you have that will fit her now, and anything that you need to make, I can have one of the scarecrows come pick up when it's ready."

"Oh my, this is so exciting!" Ellie bubbled. "We have some skirts and dresses that will look wonderful on her!"

"No skirts!" Eve blurted before she even knew what she was saying. Her hand shot up and covered her mouth, surprised and embarrassed by her own outburst. "Um . . . sorry. It's just that I'm kind of sick of skirts."

38

She hoped she hadn't offended the seamstress, but she had spent every day of her life dressed in the orphanage uniform's black skirt. If she had a chance to try wearing something different, she was going to take it.

"And no dresses," added the Pumpkin King. "She's the Pumpkin Princess, not the spoiled daughter of a baroness. Give her something she can wear around the farm."

Ellie looked rather put out. "All right, fine, no dresses or skirts," she agreed begrudgingly. "But don't think for a second I'm not going to make you pretty," she said with a kind smile to Eve. "Deal?"

Eve nodded happily, and the Pumpkin King growled under his breath, and Ellie took both as a yes.

"Then it's settled! Franklin, go get my measuring tools. They're behind that eight-legged dress I've been working on for Mrs. Tula." Ellie then turned her attention back to the Pumpkin King. "This could be a bit. I'm sure you're quite busy with the upcoming Harvest Festival. If you want to go handle business in town, I'll take good care of Evelyn here. So run along, Mr. Important."

"I will stay," answered the Pumpkin King. "All Hallows' Eve was last night, and the Harvest Festival can wait another. Right now, I will be with my daughter."

An odd feeling spread through Eve's chest, and she couldn't help but note the surprise on Ellie's face, though she wasn't entirely sure of its meaning.

39

"All right, suit your big self," said Ellie. "There is a chair in the corner. You can wait there."

The Pumpkin King shoved his way past several racks of coats before finding what was far too small a chair for him. Eve fought back a laugh as she watched him pick up the chair with one hand, growling at it as he examined it. Then, resigned, he set the chair down and squeezed into it, his hands patiently resting on thighs the size of tree trunks.

Meanwhile, Ellie busied herself in a whirlwind of fabrics and clothes. She had Eve step onto a stool that spun, and once Franklin had returned with a pack of needles, tape measures, and various other particulars, the two set to work.

Together, they tossed outfits over Eve's pajamas almost as quickly as they traded them out for others, rapidly interchanging tops, bottoms, and shoes before Eve could even look in a mirror. Whether because the darkness outside never seemed to change, or because of the constant spinning that Ellie and Franklin were subjecting her to, Eve eventually lost track of time. All the while, the Pumpkin King sat patiently in the corner. The shadows across his face might have looked menacing if the warmth in his eyes wasn't busy making him look so proud.

Finally, after what felt like more outfit changes than Eve had ever had in her lifetime, she and the Pumpkin King walked out of the Looming Loom weighed down by several boxes and bags each.

Over her new black shoes, Eve was wearing slender yet hardy wool pants held up by a series of silver buttons just below her navel. With them, she had tucked in a simple blouse with black buttons, a frilled chest, and sleeves that billowed and tightened just above her elbows, leaving her room to get her forearms dirty in the soil if need be (a Franklin suggestion). Ellie in turn had been quite insistent on a long collar as well, not at all discreetly wanting to hide Eve's neck. Something Eve didn't exactly find comforting.

Outside, the clouds had gone away, and a large moon shone down brightly on the town of Hallowell Station.

"Thank you for my clothes," Eve said awkwardly. She'd never had someone take her shopping and didn't quite know how to express her gratitude.

"Do not mention it," said the Pumpkin King. "Now, why don't you begin loading all this into the wagon while I see to some new sheets and bedding for you?" Without waiting for a response, he set the boxes and bags down beside the cart and proceeded across the lane, his wide stride sending ripples through the mist.

It wasn't long before Eve had finished packing her clothes into the back of the wagon, only to realize that despite the villagers moving about the lane, she suddenly felt very, very alone. Thankfully, Peaty was some comfort, and Eve found herself subconsciously petting his nose to help distract herself.

Overhead, the light from a nearby lamppost flickered and burned out as a brisk gust of wind cut through the street, tossing leaves and papers about the air and sending shivers down Eve's spine.

She told herself it wasn't fear she was feeling, but rather her body telling her to be cautious in this new, strange place.

She scanned the lane, hoping to see the Pumpkin King emerging from a shop and returning to their wagon, but she only saw more and more heads turning her way, each leaning and whispering to one another. Eve tried not to stare back, instead fixing her attention on an orb of floating blue flame the size of a baseball. Eve watched as it hovered slowly in her direction, and that's when she spotted someone else, someone who wasn't paying her any mind at all.

Across the way was a young boy about Eve's age. He was shorter than her (as most her age were), and his hair slightly less dark. A tad on the thicker side, the boy's neatly trimmed vest and black pants were stretching ever so slightly at the buttons.

Eve came to a decision: If this was going to be her new home, her new life, then she didn't want to feel as alone as she had at the orphanage. There, she had never had any friends, just her books. She was the "jinxed" girl that no one ever adopted, which meant that no other orphan ever wanted to risk befriending her, in fear of catching whatever she had that made no parent want her.

But Eve wanted this life to be different from that one. She wanted friends who weren't just the fictional characters in stories.

Steeling her nerves and swallowing years of introversion, Eve decided to introduce herself and hope for the best.

She gave Peaty a pat. "Wish me luck. Neigh if you see a troll about to step on me," she said, then headed fearlessly across the street.

"Hi there," Eve offered politely as she approached the boy. He had human features, with skin that was pale save for the rose-colored hue of his round, freckled cheeks, and he wore circular glasses that he was currently using to stare at a tray of what looked like moldy cupcakes in the store window. Eve was fairly certain she saw a worm moving through one. "Those look . . . tasty," she added.

"Yeah," he said, more sadly than Eve had expected. "Wish I could have one."

"Why can't you?" Eve asked.

The boy merely sighed, then looked at her, confused. "Because I'm a—"

He went wide-eyed. And he suddenly leaned in toward her and sniffed.

Eve instinctively pulled away. "Uh, hi? Yeah, human," she said, waving shyly at the boy.

"Whoa," he breathed. "I've never met a—" He must have realized he was still leaning toward her, because he recoiled back, looking quite embarrassed. "Sorry, uh, so sorry. Um, vampire," he added, raising his own hand and waving awkwardly back at her.

A smile broke across Eve's face. Contact made and she was still alive. So far he seemed kind, vampire or not.

"No need to be sorry," said Eve politely. "If it makes you feel any better, I've never met a vampire either."

"Then you're definitely not from around—wait, are you the one who rode in with the Pumpkin King?" he asked. "I thought I heard talk that he had someone strange with him."

"Well, I wouldn't call myself 'strange,' but, yeah, that was me! He's my—he adopted me," Eve said, unsure why she couldn't bring herself to say the word *father*. "I'm Evelyn, by the way, but you can call me Eve."

"Wow, so you're going to be living here?"

"Looks like it," said Eve. "So, do vampires have names?"

"Oh! Sorry! I'm Vlad Jr. the 12th Jr. Jr.," he said, bowing politely.

"Um, that would make you the . . . ?"

"Honestly, I've thought long and hard about it, and I have no idea," Vlad answered.

"Well, I'm sure there's a logical explanation, like a family tree or something," said Eve. "Maybe I can help you work it out sometime."

Vlad seemed surprised. "I'd like that!" he said with a stunned smile across his face, through which two pointed teeth revealed themselves.

Ignoring the fangs, Eve turned her attention to the suspicious-looking cupcakes in the window. "So, Vlad Jr. the 12th Jr. Jr., how come vampires can't have cupcakes?"

At this the smile left Vlad's face. "We can't eat normal food," he said sullenly. "Although it always looks so tasty. . . ." He drifted off for a moment, appearing lost in a dream. "But if I do, I'll get sick. Like, really sick. Trust me, I've tried. A lot."

"What can you eat?" Eve asked, hoping the rules about vampires here were different than from the stories in her world. She subconsciously adjusted her collar.

"Not much," he answered. "It's a lot of—oh no."

His eyes widened from behind his glasses as he noticed something over Eve's shoulder.

"And who's your friend, cousin?" came a drawling voice from behind Eve.

Eve turned, finding herself face to fang with two identical girls. They appeared a couple of years older than Eve, with matching snobbish faces and dark red hair. Each wore intricate narrow dresses that ended just above their pale knees.

"Look, Corina, a *human*," said one of the twins with a wicked smile.

"Hello," Eve said warily. She didn't like the look of either one. "I'm Evelyn."

"Ooo, Elisabetta. She even has a name. How quaint," said Corina. "Tell me, *Evelyn*, who brought you here? And will they care if you go missing?"

"Surely not. Just look at her," Elisabetta said with a laugh. Stepping forward, the vampire lazily lifted Eve's long black hair in her hands and sniffed. She sighed dangerously.

"Elisabetta, stop it," Vlad pleaded, stepping forward and trying to put himself between her and Eve.

But in a hardly noticeable movement, the other twin stuck out a foot in the fog, causing Vlad to trip and stumble heavily into the shop window.

The glass shook, a cupcake fell from its stand, and Vlad landed densely on the cobblestones below.

"What was that for?" Eve said, pulling her hair from Elisabetta's fingers and kneeling to help Vlad up. While she gave Vlad a hand in dusting himself off, Eve couldn't help but notice the only reflection in the shop window was her own.

When she finally turned to face the twins, there was now another vampire with them. As beautiful as she was imposing, she stared down at Eve with disdainful eyes. She had flawless, radiant skin, lips stained a shade almost as dark as her hair, and she wore a snug dress that was a shimmering crimson, deep as blood.

"So, the rumors are true," she whispered from behind Corina and Elisabetta. "I didn't think even he could be that stupid."

"Excuse me," said Eve incredulously, feeling Vlad give a slight tremble beside her. But where Eve probably should have felt fear, she felt only indignation. She *hated* bullies. "Is there something I can help you three with? If you're looking for somewhere to get an even tighter dress, the Looming Loom is over there."

"The mouth on her," said Corina.

"You'll do well to show respect to the baroness," spat the other twin.

The woman merely laughed a slow, dangerous laugh. "It's okay, daughters," she said. "This one won't be around long enough to matter."

She took a step toward Eve, followed closely by the two twins.

Eve stepped back, but found she met an unexpected resistance.

An orange glow fell across the three vampires, and a gloved hand found Eve's shoulder.

"Hrmph. Evening, Malvina," growled a powerful voice.

Eve looked up and saw the wide head of the Pumpkin King staring over her and directly at the vampires.

The twins retreated behind their mother.

"Oh, hello, my *liege*," mocked the woman, before feigning a hardly noticeable curtsy. "And it's Baroness La'Ment. Or had you forgotten?"

The Pumpkin King grumbled something that Eve couldn't quite make out.

"I see you brought a souvenir back from your little trip," she

47

continued. "Trying to *liven* up your farm, I presume. How goes it down in the mud? It looks so dreary from high up in our castle."

Each of the twins snickered from behind their mother.

"All goes well," grunted the Pumpkin King, his hand still firmly on Eve's shoulder, meanwhile meeting the baroness's stare dagger for dagger. "In fact, we have a healthy showing of garlic. I'll be sure to send some your way."

The evil grin left the face of Baroness La'Ment and both her daughters.

It was Vlad who finally broke the tense exchange.

"Hello, Mr. Pumpkin King, sir," he said with a bow of his head. "How was your All Hallows' Eve?"

The features of the Pumpkin King softened as his gaze fell onto Vlad.

"Better than any year, young Vlad," he answered. "For this year I found a daughter. One who is to be the Pumpkin Princess." The Pumpkin King shot the baroness a knowing look and was met with eyes as cold as ice in return.

"Oh? But for how long will that last, do you think?" Baroness La'Ment sneered. "Now, come, girls. We have better uses for our time." She turned and marched away.

The twins each looked Eve over one last time, laughing darkly before following behind their mother.

They hadn't gotten far, however, when Baroness La'Ment turned.

"Vlad, come along! We don't have all night."

"Yes, ma'am," Vlad said drearily to his feet. He then looked back at Eve with a smile. "Nice to meet you, Eve, but I'm afraid I must be going." He gave her a polite bow, then ran after the other vampires.

Eve stared confusedly after him, watching as Vlad ran to catch up, only to immediately be shoved forward by one of the twins.

"What was all that about?" Eve asked.

"Much," the Pumpkin King responded. "Yet very little all the same."

"'Much' that you're going to tell me about?"

"Not now. Now, we go home. It's already middling-night and we still have to ride back, and you have plenty in the wagon to unpack."

"It's just some clothes . . . ," Eve started to say, only to trail off when her eyes landed on a now heavily burdened wagon.

It was covered in enough blankets and pillows to supply a town.

There was every pattern imaginable, not to mention every thickness and fabric as well. Fuzzy wools, puffy downs, thin cottons—Eve wondered why anyone would need so many.

"I, erhm, didn't know what you would like," stated the Pumpkin King. "So I bought all of it."

"I can see that," Eve said, stunned. "Thanks?"

"You are welcome," he said proudly.

Peaty, however, did not look so happy. While the black stallion appeared eager for the challenge of pulling what had to be all the world's blankets, Peaty looked very much to be dreading it.

"Sorry," said Eve, patting the horse's nose. "I'll try and steal you an apple later."

This seemed to cheer him up slightly, and after Eve stepped around the hovering blue flame that had drifted nearer (giving it a wide berth so as to not scorch her new clothes), the two horses began to slowly pull at the cart, carrying them back through town.

As they made their way, Eve once more found herself staring at all the shops and strange villagers heading in and out of them. A hundred questions formed in her mind, but when she opened her mouth to put words to them, she faltered. The orphanage was still fresh in her memory, and Eve suddenly worried that if she pulled too hard on any one thread, the whole veil of her new life might unravel, leaving her right back where she never wanted to find herself again.

So instead, a different, unexpected question came out of her open mouth. Yet one critical to her new life here all the same.

"Does Hallowell have anywhere to get books?"

"It does. Why do you ask?"

"I like reading," Eve answered truthfully. Though, saying she "liked" reading felt like an understatement. Back at the orphanage, books had been all she had—each one offering her a more interesting life than her own to disappear into.

A thoughtful grunt was all she got in response.

Next to her, the swaying light of the lamp combined with the motion of the wagon was slowly causing Eve to nod off. She fought to remain awake, but unused to staying up all night, she was quickly losing the fight.

Seeing her drift off, the Pumpkin King reached back and pulled forward one of the countless new blankets. Gently, he placed it over Eve.

"Thank you," she said with a yawn.

He grumbled something in return.

"We need to work on your grumbling," she murmured, half-awake.

"So I've been told."

The Pumpkin King guided the cart on, leaving the lights of the village behind as the horses pulled them down winding paths and over barren knolls. The gentle rocking was quickly putting Eve to sleep, but not before she thought she saw a bony claw reach out of the dirt and wave at them. . . . Or had she dreamed it?

Finally, she couldn't fight it any longer. Her head drooped slowly against the Pumpkin King's wide shoulder, and bundled in one of her new blankets, Eve felt her eyes fall shut; otherwise, she would have seen the Pumpkin King smile.

CHAPTER FOUR

Grumble Grumble,
Soil and Shovel

EVE WOKE TO A RUMBLING SNORE SO LOUD THAT SHE THOUGHT
there might have been an earthquake.

She was back in her room within the Hall of the Pumpkin
King, covered in an inch of sweat and about a dozen blankets to
justify it. She had the faintest memory of being carried up the
stairs late in the night, or had it been early morning? Through
her bedroom window, the faded gold of a late-afternoon sun
warmed the back of her moth-eaten curtains.

She still wasn't adjusted to Hallowell time, and based on the
snoring coming from two doors down—which had the distinct

cadence of the Pumpkin King's grumbles—Eve figured she must be the first awake.

With a deep, arching stretch, Eve tossed aside the covers and rolled out of bed in search of some less sweaty clothes.

Instead, all she saw were stacks and stacks of blankets, comforters, sheets, throws, pillows, pillowcases, and way more of each than she could ever properly use. After swimming her way over to her dresser, she changed out of her outfit from the night before and into another Ellie had prepared for her, then threw on a jacket with more pockets than she had things to go in them. Beneath her feet, the room's old rug did little to contain the cold touch of the floorboards, so Eve decided to cover the entire floor of her bedroom using a few of her new blankets.

Eyeballing the remaining stacks, a strange urge came over Eve. She had never had a room of her own, never had colors to choose from for her bedding, or walls to decorate how she liked. She spent her entire childhood staring at the same hideously green bedspread and the same monotonously boring white walls. So here, alone in her *own* room, next to a bed she could pick a comforter for, surrounded by wooden walls she could make look however she wanted, Eve felt the need to do just that, to make the room how she wanted it, to make it *hers*.

Using a box of nails and a hammer that she found stashed in the closet, Eve set to hanging sheets and blankets across every surface she could. She found glee in picking which went where, knowing that no headmistress was going to come in and tell her to rip it all down, or that it went against the rules. Eve highly doubted the Pumpkin King would care what she did with the room; it had been obviously neglected when she first arrived. So she continued hammering away, so caught up in decorating her first-ever room that she hadn't noticed the snoring filling the Hall had stopped, not until—

"Hrmph, what are you doing?" grumbled a slumberous-looking Pumpkin King. Both his eyes were narrowed to barely there slits, and his mouth still had a little drool on one side.

"Oh, sorry. I didn't mean to wake you," Eve said embarrassedly, holding her hammer mid swing. "I'm, um, decorating my room."

"But it's—hrmph, never mind. I'm going back to bed."

He lumbered off back down the loft and Eve heard his door shut. Soon the snoring started up again.

Eve smiled. No headmistress had told her no, or put her in detention for "falling out of line."

Standing atop her dresser, Eve finished hanging the last sheet over her head, then stepped down to admire her work.

Mismatched blankets now lined every possible surface. Plaid here, flannel there, stripes this way, polka dots that way. In no shortage of supplies, Eve had even draped them from the ceiling. They hung loosely above her, dipping low and just above her head in several spots.

She couldn't have been happier with it.

With nowhere left to hang blankets, Eve decided to slip on her shoes and tiptoe downstairs.

The Hall was empty save for the room upstairs failing to contain the Pumpkin King's snores. Downstairs, the hearth had yet to be lit, and cold, blackened wood lay crumbled within it from the night before. She found the kitchens in a room adjacent to the fireplace, filled with wooden shelves and countertops covered in sacks of grain, baskets of freshly picked fruit, and jars of spices. She rummaged through an oak cabinet before finding a loaf of recently baked bread. Cutting herself off a slice, Eve nibbled on it as she made her way out of the Hall and into the fresh, crisp air outside.

From atop the pumpkin-covered hill, all the colors of the farm stretched out around her, veiled in the fading daylight of early evening.

Figuring she had time to kill before others would wake, Eve decided to use the opportunity to explore her new home. Her curiosity was mounting, and after decorating her bedroom, she was excited to make the homestead her own as well.

She walked to the edge of the vines that twisted about the pumpkins and surrounded the bramble-covered Hall; slowly, she nudged a toe forward to see what they would do. To Eve's relief, they parted for her, allowing her a way down the hill, only to close once more behind her.

Making her way past the red barn heavy with the smell of hay and horses, Eve picked a direction (between a field of barley and a cherry orchard) and ventured out.

All across the farm, scarecrows hung sleeping from tall wooden posts, and Eve wondered at what point they would rise for the night and set about their work. She walked by one that sleepily scratched at his button nose, completely ignoring the two crows perched on his shoulders and pecking at the straw poking through his woven head.

Some scarecrow, Eve thought, smiling to herself.

She continued on, following meandering trails that took her through rust-colored groves and gingery thickets, around shimmering ponds and rows of robust gourds. She found herself enjoying the little alone time she'd had since arriving. It allowed her to sort through her thoughts, which were equal parts hopeful and uncertain. She had no idea what awaited her as the only *living* in Hallowell, but she knew it was a chance at something better than she had, and that was all that mattered.

In the distance, the sun began to drift behind the sharp mountains surrounding the valley, and long shadows started to reach across the farm. A butterscotch-yellow moon peeked over the horizon, and with it a chill wind swept across the homestead, rustling the fields around Eve. She paused to take it in. Each ounce of this new place felt so different from what she was used to, and it made her appreciate it all the more.

Nearby, a post shuddered as a scarecrow twitched from his sleep, and Eve watched it drop to the soil below. It wore a torn straw hat and had a sickle for one hand and a rake for the other, which it used to wave excitedly at Eve.

Eve waved back, watching as it disappeared into a field, and once again trying as hard as she could to pretend all this was normal.

Eventually the farmland began to fade, and Eve came upon a fence made from round wooden posts, about torso high.

Resting her arms on the top rail, Eve found her eyes being drawn beyond the fields of black grass before her and instead to the sea of purple mists swirling in the distance. In their violet depths, Eve could just make out the tops of hills, like tiny islands poking out of the strangely colored fog. Squinting, she saw specks of light coming to life among the hills.

"What you see before you is the Misty Moors," grumbled a voice behind her. "Home to a coven of witches. Among other things."

Eve turned and saw the Pumpkin King sitting atop his black stallion, Gleysol.

"How did you know where I was?" she asked.

"I know all that happens on my land." Hopping off his horse, he tossed the reins over a post and leaned on the fence beside her, causing it to groan and sink under his weight.

Eve looked up at him. "The scarecrows told you where I was, didn't they?"

"Hrmph . . . yes," he grunted, staring off into the distance.

Eve waited for him to go on about the coven of witches or maybe the farm, or anything really. But as she was quickly learning, he wasn't the biggest talker.

"What else is in Hallowell?" Eve finally asked, breaking the silence.

"Hmm? Well, as I said, south you have the Misty Moors." He nodded forward. "Last night we rode north, through the trees and cemeteries of the Haunted Hollows, and—"

"Wait," Eve cut in. "If everyone here is undead, who's in the cemeteries?"

"Some of it existed before Hallowell was founded and is merely home to the dead of the living," he answered. "But there are some undead who have gone there to build underground homes away from the village. Others have gone to find their eternal rest."

Eve recalled her trip to the village, wondering which of those groups belonged to the tombstones she had seen.

"As I was saying," the Pumpkin King rumbled on, "beyond the Haunted Hollows you have Hallowell Station, home to many that have flocked there for fellowship. Castle Dracula isn't much farther, presided over currently by Baroness La'Ment." At her name, Eve saw the Pumpkin King grimace. "There's also the Grimm Pine Woods that the werewolves are camped in, and beyond them you have . . ." He trailed off.

"And beyond them you have . . . ," Eve pressed, trying to get him to finish his thought.

"The Cursed Caverns," he said with a frown. "They lie at the base of the mountains. A maze of caves and canyons, home to evil things far darker than I care to tell you about. You must never go there. Do you understand?" The light of his eyes fell on her, and Eve saw something almost worry-like on his face.

Eve was taken aback. Vampires, witches, and werewolves seemed dangerous enough; the notion there was more wasn't exactly comforting.

"Okay, I won't," she promised anyway, making the mental note: *Cursed Caverns equals off limits.*

Content, he nodded.

"And you're the king of all of it?" Eve asked.

"King? Yes, I guess you could say I'm its king."

"You guess? It's literally half of your name."

"Well—hrmph—true," he muttered. "Though I do not rule as the word implies. Not anymore, at least. I learned the hard lesson long ago that Hallowell works best when left to its own devices—despite some claims by others. So, while I may preside over Hallowell's Council, I *try* to not hold sway in telling the coven how to go about their nights, nor the vampires in their castle.

"But I am still the steward of this place, watching over it and speaking on its behalf as you one night will. Hallowell was established as a sanctuary for the undead and hidden in the very shadows of the mountains themselves. An impenetrable fog separates us from the living, and as steward I am one of the few able to leave. And although I no longer go as often as I once did, I still visit the outside world every All Hallows' Eve. That is when I seek out the lost souls of the undead, those persecuted by the living for being different, and I bring them here."

"That's how you found me?"

"In part, yes. I must have sensed your plight. The emotions you felt when running, when trying to find a new life, would have been hard to miss. But also, a not-insignificant part of our meeting was purely chance."

"And . . . it's okay that I'm here and . . . living?" Eve asked, putting words to a concern that had been growing since the village.

"Of course. It is I who decides," he growled. But he must have sensed Eve's concern, because he quickly added, "You are the Pumpkin Princess now. My daughter. Living or undead, that makes you one of us."

Does it? Eve fretted. She wasn't so sure. All the stares back in town appeared to tell a different story.

"Now, hrmph, I believe we have delayed long enough," he continued, pushing away from the fence. "As Pumpkin Princess, you have much to do tonight. Harvest Festival is approaching, the night all of Hallowell comes to our land to celebrate autumn.

Outside of All Hallows' Eve, it's one of the biggest nights of the year. It's also the night that I, and now you, are responsible for hosting the entire valley."

He made for his horse, yet Eve rushed after him.

"But, wait, I still have more questions!" she protested. Everything she had wanted to ask the previous night when leaving the village was now piling up and wanting out. One question in particular more than the others.

"Ask the scarecrows. They will introduce the farm to you in my stead," he said, hopping onto Gleysol. "I must travel while rising-night is still early."

"No, not about the farm," Eve countered. "About . . ." She didn't know how to ask the one question she really wanted to. Part of her was scared to.

He grumbled something, and before them the nearby field of grain suddenly parted in two. Down the middle, the ground churned and rolled in on itself, revealing a new path that had definitely not existed moments prior. He turned back to Eve. "About what, then?" he asked curiously.

Eve shook her attention from the trail still settling behind him.

About me, she thought, and her mind flashed back to all the inhabitants of the village. When he had adopted her, Eve assumed he didn't have many other options, that being a giant talking pumpkin meant maybe he hadn't ever met any other kids. For all she had known, she was literally his only option. But the trip into Hallowell Station shattered that theory like glass, leaving Eve with the question:

"Why me?" she blurted. "Why didn't you adopt someone who was . . . undead?"

Eve could tell as soon as the words came out of her mouth that she had caught him off guard. There was a moment of silence before he spoke.

"Does it matter?" he asked.

"It does to me."

"Hrmph, so be it," he grumbled. "It is because you attempted to correct me the night we met."

"Tried correcting—wait, you mean about being able to smell fear and what makes seasons?" Eve asked, now her turn to be caught off guard. "*That's* why you chose me?" Eve didn't know what answer to expect, but that definitely wasn't it.

The Pumpkin King tilted his head slightly. "No, not because of what you said, but because you said it at all. Eve, there are very few, even in Hallowell, who do not fear me if pressed. Yet, despite your predicament the night we met, you were not scared—only curious and collected," he explained, Eve listening to his every word. "So many wear their emotions on their faces and are too easily read, but hrmph, not you. You were fearless and formidable. Two things the Pumpkin Princess *should* be. Living or undead."

The field near them rustled, and out came a scarecrow. He

wore two different boots under a heavy raincoat and had green pins for eyes.

"Now, if that is all, I'm afraid I must be off this time," the Pumpkin King continued. "We will talk when I return. Until then, the scarecrows will take care of you."

He gave Gleysol a nudge, and together they shot down the path the Pumpkin King had summoned from nowhere, only for them to disappear into the night.

Eve watched after him, wondering if she were actually as fearless and formidable as he thought she was. What if he found out about her nightmares and how scared she used to be? Would he still view her the same? Worse, would he still want her as his daughter?

She found her brooding cut short when two green pins leaned awkwardly into her vision.

"Whatcha thinking abouts, Prin'sis?"

Eve snapped to, her eyes refocusing on the scarecrow's. "Sorry, nothing," she answered. "So, what now, then?"

The remainder of Eve's night was spent in an apple orchard, learning perhaps some of the most bizarre lessons that she could have ever imagined.

According to the scarecrows, which hand you picked the apples with mattered, and where the moon was when you did it mattered even more. Somehow even stranger was the pruning, where Eve was instructed to ask each tree if it was okay to cut a branch before actually cutting it. When the scarecrows told her this, her first response was, *Seriously, talking trees too?* But she was wrong and soon learned the tree would give a slight wobble if it didn't want the branch cut, as if shaking its trunk no.

They then attempted to teach her about the different kinds of apples, which, to Eve's surprise, encompassed far more than the typical red and green ones. There were purple (poisonous, supposedly), slightly less purple (healing, ironically), blue (magical, to be sold to witches), yellow (delicious, like, *really* delicious), black (only handled with gloves), white (something about absorbing curses—Eve was struggling to remember it all), and every color in between, each grown with some surreal property or intent.

It wasn't until Eve was settling back into her blanket-fort of a bedroom, carefully lighting the candles atop her dresser, that the Pumpkin King finally returned.

"Eve?" came a grunt and a knock at her door. "May I come in?"

Stepping around leftover blankets strewn about the floor, Eve went over and opened the door.

"Thank you," the Pumpkin King said, stooping almost doubled over under the blankets that hung from her ceiling. "It— hrmph, are you not cramped?"

"I like it," Eve answered truthfully, sitting back onto the edge of her bed. "It's cozy."

He looked around for a moment longer, then shrugged and pulled a small, parchment-wrapped parcel from within his heavy coat. "This is for you."

Eve reached out and curiously took it from him.

"What is it?"

"You have to open it."

"Oh," said Eve, taken aback. "Like a present?"

The Pumpkin King merely nodded, his large triangular eyes fixed on the gift in Eve's hand.

She unwrapped it slowly and within found a well-used book. Scrawled across the front in looping red letters was: *The Banshee's Burden* by bestselling author Cecilia Shroud.

Eve riffled through the yellowed pages. The text appeared somehow handwritten.

"It's a book. You mentioned you enjoy them," said the Pumpkin King proudly. "I picked it up in town. It's a late birthday present for you, since All Hallows' Eve has come and gone, and I did not get you anything."

Eve stared, unable to take her gaze from it. She began to feel tears well up in her eyes. She had never been given a birthday present before. Her hands trembled slightly, and she worried that she might somehow damage the book.

"Do you not like it?" the Pumpkin King asked, looking rather uncomfortable.

"I . . . I love it."

"That is good," he answered from behind a great growling sigh of relief. "It comes highly recommended. So, then . . . happy birthday. I shall let you read now. And, erhm, firstmeal will be served at sundown. I will make you oats."

Before Eve could say anything, he turned on his boot and hurried from her room. Down the loft, she heard his door close.

"Thank you," she whispered to the book.

The following night, Eve didn't quite make firstmeal at sundown. Not even close. Having stayed up way too late reading, Eve had to be woken by a scarecrow and practically carried to the table (book still in hand, of course). And soon . . . very soon . . . that became part of Eve's nightly routine in her new home.

She would wake (drooling in her book) to the excited knocking of a scarecrow, where she would then eat whatever an apron-toting Pumpkin King made her for firstmeal. After which, it was straight to horseback riding lessons, because "No daughter of the Pumpkin King is going to need to be wagoned everywhere." Eve had a failed word with him about referring to himself in the third person—he kept asking who the third person was.

After riding lessons, her "middling-night" was spent in increasingly fantastical teachings about plants, insects, water, weather, astronomy, geology, some surprisingly detailed chemistry, and every other subject that the scarecrows or the Pumpkin King could cook up.

At first, Eve had doubts about the logic behind some—well, most—of their teachings. So, she took it upon herself to see what would *really* happen if she didn't say thank you to a pear tree after plucking its fruit. . . .

Sporting a new and swelling bruise that proved them right and her wrong, Eve decided to take all their teachings to heart.

Like when they told her potatoes would weep if planted near onions, or that if you laughed near corn it wouldn't take you seriously and would then grow in bizarre shapes. Or, and Eve's favorite so far, that you had to swear at basil when planting it to encourage it to grow. (Eve learned *a lot* of new curse words that night.)

Strangely, there was a lot more taste-testing than she had anticipated. Which she enjoyed during berry picking but wasn't so fond of when it came to learning about soils. Eve brushed her teeth several times before going to bed after that lesson, spitting out mouthfuls of dirt.

To her delight, the scarecrows were becoming more and more personable and were an absolute joy to learn from. So, despite the Pumpkin King calling it pointless, Eve began naming them to help tell them apart. Scrags was her favorite—though she would never tell the others. He was the one that had first woken Eve (and continued to wake her), with blue and white buttons for eyes and a motherliness about him that Eve found endearing.

Come "falling-night," the Pumpkin King would always call

Eve in for thirdmeal. Sometimes he would be wearing massive reading glasses, holding rolls of parchment and appearing grumpier than usual. Other times, he would be covered in dirt after single-handedly plowing a field that Peaty had refused to, and he would be much less grumpy. But not not-grumpy. He was still the Pumpkin King, after all.

Eve would scarf down her food as quickly as possible, excited to rush upstairs to the bedroom that was her own and reread the book that had been given to her for her birthday. Two things she had never had till the Pumpkin King adopted her. And before she knew it, Scrags would once more be knocking on her door to wake her.

It was a routine that Eve had been loving, until one evening when she found herself tugging at a defiant pumpkin, attempting to coerce it from its vine. There was a trick to it, but after several nights of continuous lessons, she had found herself beyond tricks. She gave a hard yank instead, but it proved too stubborn and Eve fell backwards with a splash, soaking the last dry bit of her pants in the freshly watered soil.

Eve stifled back a sigh.

It was not that she wasn't enjoying another lesson on pumpkins, which the Pumpkin King took particular pride in, but more and more she felt her mind starting to wander back to the village (specifically to a certain bookstore that had been mentioned to her).

She stared out across the pumpkin patch they were in, to where the Pumpkin King was conversing with two burly, human-like werewolves who had mysteriously arrived moments earlier—a surprise to both Eve and the Pumpkin King, as Scrags had once confided in her that outside of the Harvest Festival, visitors were rare.

"What do you think they're talking about?" she asked, her curiosity piqued.

Scrags looked up. "Probably werewolfs stuff," he said with a shrug. "Theys been having issues in town."

"Theys *always* having issues," muttered the scarecrow Eve called Digsy, on account of his shovels for hands.

Eve frowned. One of the werewolves appeared to be raising his voice while the other tried to calm him down. Finally, after what looked like a heated exchange, the werewolves parted, leaving the Pumpkin King to stride back toward Eve and the scarecrows.

He seemed even grumpier than when he'd realized they had visitors in the first place.

"Who was that?" Eve asked, her curiosity hardly allowing him time to kneel back down.

"Harlock, head of the werewolf pack," the Pumpkin King grunted. "And, hrmph, his son, Fenrik. They claim werewolves are being charged higher prices at the markets in town and don't feel enough is being done about it."

"Are they?" Eve and Scrags asked at the same time. The two smiled at each other.

69

"I doubt it. But the werewolves feel they are, and it's causing unrest. I promised I would handle it. Now, enough about were-wolves. Where were we?"

"Actually, about the town . . . ," Eve started hesitantly. Since arriving, she had begun to get this foreign feeling in her gut, a strong urge to prove herself. So she stayed diligent in her chores and lessons, knowing how important the Harvest Festival was to him and the scarecrows. But still . . . she was a girl, *not* a scare-crow. "I was hoping we could go again? I could use a new book."

"Do you not like the one I got you?" he asked, the hurt in his face making Eve immediately regret asking.

"No, no! I love it. But I've read it like a hundred times. Besides, how am I supposed to make Hallowell my home if I'm here all the time?"

The Pumpkin King grumbled under his breath, and Eve was distinctly aware she caught the words "Harvest Festival" before he finally spoke.

"Yes, fair point," he conceded with a nod. "We shall go after tomorrow night's rising-night ride."

"Really?" Eve asked excitedly.

"Yes, really. Until then, can you tell me at what age we stop patting the pumpkins?"

Thrilled by the prospect of seeing Hallowell's bookstore, Eve returned to her lessons. "Trick question, it's different for every pumpkin," she answered, half paying attention, half contemplating what kind of book she might get. "It's when they can roll over on their own."

Her lessons that night continued as they had been (weird, challenging, and ultimately kind of fun), until eventually Eve found herself tucked back into her cozy bedroom, once more falling asleep in the pages of her birthday present. But when she woke several hours later to a fresh new moon, the routine she had come to so enjoy came to an abrupt and sudden halt.

Because it wasn't Scrags politely knocking at her door that woke her, nor the smell of the Pumpkin King's cooking.

It was something else altogether.

Voices. Angry and panicked.

CHAPTER FIVE

Banished

THE VOICES WERE COMING FROM DOWNSTAIRS. ONE SOUNDED like a frightened Scrags and the other like a very, very angry Pumpkin King.

"She's my daughter! They can't banish her from Hallowell!" he boomed, practically causing the bedroom door to vibrate.

Eve shot upright in her bed.

Her? Banished from Hallowell?

Eve flung off her covers and burst through the door and out onto the long and narrow loft. Had it not been for the banister, she probably would have propelled herself right over the edge.

Two heads turned to look up at her from the floor below: a

worried-looking Scrags and a furious Pumpkin King, the blaze of his face outshining even that of the fire in the hearth.

Eve's stomach sank.

She hadn't misheard. She was being banished. *But why? What had she done?* Since that first night in the village, Eve hadn't even left the homestead. Who could she have upset so much that they'd want her kicked out of Hallowell?

Before she could ask the questions piling up in her head, the Pumpkin King had turned and stormed toward the door. "Evelyn, I need you to stay with the scarecrows while I see to something," he growled.

See to something seemed like an understatement to Eve, who was already flying down the loft's steps at a reckless speed. "What do you mean I'm being banished?" she called.

"Hrmph! I will handle this," he grunted as he pulled on his massive overcoat, then turned his attention to Scrags and added, "You stay with Eve until I return. Allow no one near her." He threw open the door to the Hall, letting in a gust of wind that tossed back the ends of his coat and froze right through Eve's pajamas.

"*Ugh!*" she groaned, sprinting back upstairs with Scrags right on her tail. There, Eve tossed on whatever clothes and shoes were in reach before racing back downstairs and out into the chilling air of rising-night.

"We's were told to stay here," Scrags protested, chasing after

Eve as they both ran down the hill in the Pumpkin King's wake. Before them, twisting vines and rolling pumpkins quickly cleared a path, barely having closed behind the Pumpkin King himself.

"No, we were told to stay together," Eve corrected. "Where we stayed was not specified."

Rippled in the cold light of an early moon, the farm was just beginning to bustle to life as torches blazed and scarecrows started their nights—two of them practically had to dive out of the Pumpkin King's way as he stormed over to the barn and threw open its door. The reverberating shake caused a cloud of bats to billow out from the eaves, flying down and out into the night; Eve had to swat her way through them until she and Scrags finally reached the barn, coming in just as the Pumpkin King was saddling Gleysol.

"Hrmph!" he grumbled when he saw her. "I told you to stay in the Hall. And I told you to keep her there," he said to Scrags.

"Technically yous said to stay with her," Scrags corrected, repeating what Eve had told him moments ago. "Where we's stayed, yous did not specify."

The Pumpkin King's face warped from frustration to confusion and back, but Eve didn't give him a chance to respond (though she was quite proud of Scrags in that moment).

"What's going on?" she asked, standing in the doorway with her arms outstretched and hoping to block him from leaving. Part of her realized how pointless that must look to him, considering the door was easily wide enough for him to go around her, but the other part of her didn't care. She wanted answers. She *needed* answers.

Finally, his eyes met hers, and the anger in his gaze dampened—slightly.

"Everything will be okay," he said, his voice softening. "I will see to that. But I need you to move."

"Not till you tell me what's happening," Eve protested. "I deserve to know if I'm being sent away." She tried to sound braver than she was, but saying the words made a knot form in her stomach.

"No one is sending you away. It's just—hrmph—Baroness La'Ment," he grunted, as if that explained it all. "A broom courier arrived with an urgent letter from the mayor's office. The baroness has called an emergency meeting of the Council. She wants to . . . banish you."

"What? Why?" Eve asked desperately. "Did I do something wrong?"

"No. It is a problem with her, not you," the Pumpkin King explained angrily. "The baroness has long wanted more of Hallowell to herself. A fruitless notion, yet one she sees you, the Pumpkin Princess and my successor, as an obstacle to. So she's trying to have you banished for . . ." He trailed off.

"For what?" Eve pushed.

The Pumpkin King sighed. "For being . . . living."

The answer seemed to yank the air from Eve's lungs.

"She—she can do that?" Eve stammered.

"Not if I have anything to say about it," the Pumpkin King answered threateningly. "The Council has five seats, including my own. She'll need a majority vote, something that I will not allow to happen. Which is why I need you to move. Now."

"Fine." Eve obliged, moving from the barn door to unblock his exit. "But I'm going with you."

"No, you are—"

"—not, yeah, I know," Eve interrupted, throwing a saddle over a sleepy-looking Peaty. "I'm still going."

"Hrmph! Why must you be contrary?" he growled, so deeply that Peaty immediately snapped to, thinking it was he who was in trouble.

"Because—"

Eve struggled to think of a lie to tell him, something other than the real reason. It wasn't so much that she wanted to go, but that she couldn't convince herself to leave the Pumpkin King's side. Despite not knowing him all that long, Eve felt safe when she was with him. Hallowell was strange and unknown, but knowing he was there made it feel less so.

Why she felt comfortable enough around the Pumpkin King to trust him to protect her, but not enough to tell him this, Eve didn't quite know. She was feeling a series of emotions she had never felt, and in the rush was struggling to understand them.

"Because . . . just because, okay?" Eve finished weakly, unable to come up with a better reason and knowing her face showed it.

His pointed eyes bore into hers, and his mouth moved several times, cycling through a series of silent responses.

In the end, a nodded grunt was all she got, and she took it; for him, that was as good as any yes. She climbed up onto the back of Peaty and felt the knot in her stomach loosen ever so slightly.

"Yous don't let anyone take her," Scrags said pointedly to the Pumpkin King as the pair nudged their horses from the barn. "And yous come right back," he directed at Eve. "I's will have your favorite foods made up for when yous return."

"Don't worry, Scrags," Eve said, already hatching a backup plan. "If anyone tries to get rid of me, I'll dress like a scarecrow and hide with you."

"I's would like that very much," said Scrags from behind a worried smile, then waved them off and into the night.

Without a wagon towed behind them, the ride through the Haunted Hollows and into the village went far quicker than Eve had previously remembered. Not in small part because of the pace kept by the Pumpkin King and Gleysol. Eve felt like she was promising poor Peaty an apple a minute to encourage him to keep up.

Overhead, the moon tossed its shimmering light over the town, and a faint breeze rocked the many candle jars that hung from the rooftops. Once again, wandering eyes stared at Eve as she and the Pumpkin King slowed to navigate the creeping lanes of Hallowell Station. She did her best to ignore their looks, hoping none wanted her gone as badly as the baroness and waving meekly at those who stared too long. To Eve's surprise, some actually waved back. A group of elderly witches chatting near a bench even appeared happy to see her.

The lane they followed ended at a tall, official-looking manor surrounded by tilting and crooked columns. They had hardly arrived at the bottom steps when something resembling a human crossed with a spider burst through the doors, rushing down to them on eight legs.

"The rest of the Council—tk-tk-tk—just arrived," she said, taking the reins of both their horses with the arms of her human-like top half. "They're in the—tk-tk-tk—mayor's office."

"Hrmph," the Pumpkin King grunted, conquering the steps in three long strides.

Eve hurried after, following him through a pair of tarnished bronze doors and into a long entrance lobby. Torches alight with green flame hung from the walls and interior columns, casting their emerald hues across a wooden floor painted black. In the center of the room stood a tall obelisk that in fine silver scrawl read:

1st Floor–Welcoming, Nuisance
Management Dept., Critter Control

2nd Floor—Dwelling Dept., Oil Lamp
and Cobblestone Maintenance, Cemeteries
and Recreation

3rd Floor—Undead-Public Relations,
Mayor's Office

"All visitors must check in," drawled a large mummy who was signing in a line of undead at the front desk.

If the Pumpkin King heard the mummy, he didn't show it. Instead he strode steadfastly past, his dirty boots marring the otherwise clean floor.

"Um, excuse me!" the mummy called, snapping to and turning his attention away from a ghost at the front of the line. "I need to check you in!"

The Pumpkin King continued to ignore him, launching up the staircase at a speed that made it nearly impossible for Eve to keep up, and *definitely* impossible for the mummy who ambitiously tried to chase after them. (One of his wrappings had caught on the arm of his chair, dragging it behind him like an anchor.)

They passed the second level, where down a long hallway Eve saw an assortment of different undead occupying wooden desks and handing scrolls of paper back and forth. Arriving at the third floor, they came upon a foyer that split in two directions, divided by a golden-framed portrait of a small orange goblin that hung neatly in the middle.

Turning right, they found themselves in front of a pair of wide, mahogany doors marked with a placard that read: MAYOR BRUMPLE'S OFFICE. There, the Pumpkin King stopped.

"This time I need you to listen and stay put," he said, one gloved hand on the door handle.

"But—"

"Do you understand?"

Eve's shoulders drooped. "I understand," she said.

The Pumpkin King nodded and ducked inside the door. During the brief moment it was open, Eve heard the overtly snobbish voice of Baroness La'Ment: "SHE DOESN'T BELO—"

The door closed, and just as it did, the mummy chasing after them finally caught up. He arrived huffing and puffing, nearly doubled over as he gasped for air, a long strand of his wrapping trailing behind him and back down the stairs.

"Must—sign—you—in," he said between long breaths.

He held out a clipboard to Eve.

"Okay . . . have a pen?" Eve asked flatly.

The mummy's face fell. And with a look to the long flight of stairs behind him, mumbled, "I'll just put *guest*."

How long she waited on the wooden bench outside the mayor's office, Eve didn't know. She had tried to listen through the doors to get a sense of what was happening, but all she heard was unintelligible raised voices. So instead, Eve was left with something far worse than waiting; she was left with her own thoughts.

No matter how many times she repeated to herself that the Pumpkin King would make everything better, that he wouldn't let them banish her, she couldn't shake the worry that Hallowell might not agree with him. What if the Council members decided to side with Baroness La'Ment?

What if she *was* banished? What would they do with her? Surely, they wouldn't send her back to the orphanage . . . right?

The orphanage. The thought of having to go back made Eve sick to her stomach. She had tried so hard to get away from that place and the loneliness of it. And she had succeeded—or so she'd thought.

Panic started to set in. *How could this be happening?*

This was supposed to be her home now. She even had a family, and though it wasn't the one she'd ever expected, she couldn't just let the baroness take that away.

Desperately, Eve's mind scrambled for some kind of plan or solution that could save her, and the seedling of an idea took form, one she knew the Pumpkin King wouldn't like.

She'd give up the Pumpkin Princess title. With that gone, then hopefully Baroness La'Ment wouldn't see her as an obstacle to power and wouldn't push to have her banished. As far as Eve was concerned, the baroness could have the promise of Hallowell and being its queen; Eve didn't want any of that—she just wanted a home.

She raced to stand up. She had to barge in. She had to tell them she'd be okay with that before they decided for her and sent her away. The Pumpkin King would understand her decision . . . she hoped.

Eve made for the office, intent on doing whatever it took to stay, no matter the cost—but just as she did, the doors burst open.

Out stormed Baroness La'Ment, her pale face stained crimson in anger. In her rage, she walked right past Eve, when abruptly she stopped.

Slowly the baroness turned around, eyes black as a crow locking onto Eve's.

In three graceful strides, she loomed over, leaning down till her face was mere inches from Eve's own.

Eve stared back, hoping that the vampire's rage could only mean good news.

"Those fools might not see you for what you are," Baroness La'Ment seethed, "but I do. Pumpkin King or not, Hallowell will devour you. You mark my words. You might be its Pumpkin Princess for now, but no *living* will ever be its queen. That title belongs to—"

"HRMPH!"

An orange glow fell across Eve and the baroness, and both turned to face the source of the light.

The Pumpkin King stared down on them with a heated look Eve had not yet seen. Already taller than most and just as wide, he seemed even larger from where he now stood, framed on either side by an elderly witch in dark robes, a short orange goblin, and a wide-shouldered and weary-looking werewolf, gray streaks lining his pulled-back hair.

Baroness La'Ment turned her glare back on Eve. "You and I are far from through," she whispered in Eve's ear. Then, louder and with a pointed, evil smile: "Until next time." And with that, she stormed off and down the stairs.

Eve watched her go, hoping there would never actually be a next time.

"I dread her visits, I truly do," squeaked the orange goblin, and Eve realized he was the same goblin in the nearby portrait. He wore a striped shirt, knickerbockers held up by thin suspenders, and a bright, checkered tie that was far too long and tied in the worst knot Eve had ever seen. (Having never even tied a tie, Eve was confident she could do a better job.) "But I'm sure I don't have to tell you," he continued, speaking to the Pumpkin King. "She's had it out for you since before I was mayor."

The Pumpkin King merely growled in response, watching angrily as the werewolf also departed silently down the stairs.

"So, um, I take it I don't have to go?" Eve asked, looking to the Pumpkin King for answers. "I can stay?"

The three remaining Council members turned toward Eve, and the intensity of the Pumpkin King's glare seemed to lessen as he walked over and knelt before her.

"The baroness wasn't able to get the three votes she needed," he said, nodding.

Eve felt relief wash over her.

"But . . . ," he continued, and Eve's relief slid off her and melted into a puddle on the floor.

"But what?"

The Pumpkin King's face soured, his normal amber eyes turning an angry red.

"Nor was I. The vote was a tie."

A tie? "But you said there are five of you?" Eve pressed. Did a tie mean something different in Hallowell? *Wait—is math different here?*

"I, of course, voted nay. As did Mother Morrigan, who quickly came to your defense." He nodded toward the elderly witch behind him, who smiled kindly at Eve. "But the leader of the werewolves, Harlock, voted with the baroness. Mayor Brumple"—he shot the goblin a look that could curdle milk—"abstained from voting."

The mayor twirled his fingers nervously. "I—the—you know

how it is," he stammered. "I have to see how the village feels about her first. You understand, I'm sure, Princess?"

Mother Morrigan shook her head. "Darkness forbid you make a decision without worrying about how the town perceives you," shot the witch.

Eve barely even heard the two of them. Her hands were getting clammier by the second, and her mind was racing. Slowly she leaned closer to the Pumpkin King, trying to whisper as best she could. "But if you're king and speak for Hallowell, couldn't you just—"

"Overrule them?" he finished for her. "Yes, I could. And no doubt a younger me would have. But I am, hrmph, wiser than I once was. Me forcing you on Hallowell is not the way to get the undead to accept you as their Pumpkin Princess. We must earn that by the laws of this place. Which now means gaining the favor of the village, so that the mayor doesn't fear he'll be chased from office for voting for you. Once he decides, the Council shall hold another vote to formalize the matter."

"But . . . how do we get the village to accept me?" Eve asked, her worry growing. "And what if we can't?"

"We will," he answered, once more shooting Mayor Brumple a look that made the goblin wince. "And I am confident the mayor will come to his senses soon," he continued. "Hallowell is your home now. Its undead just need to get to know you. As I have." His brow furrowed, as if he were coming to a decision. "And we'll start tonight. I need to attend to a matter that just arose, but how would you like to still go to the bookstore?"

"I can't go with you?" Eve asked tepidly, not thrilled about being abandoned already (even if it was a chance to go to the bookstore).

"If you wish, you can come with me. Mayor Brumple has informed me some rare medicine has gone missing from the village doctor's office, so I'm going to investigate. *But* the bookstore would be a chance for the village to begin getting used to you." He eyed Eve knowingly. "You will be welcome and safe there, I assure you."

Eve paused; the notions of what she *wanted* to do and what she *should* do were dueling it out inside her head. "Okay," she said, more to herself than him. "I'll go to the bookstore." If there was a chance it would sway the mayor and help her remain in Hallowell, then Eve would do whatever it took. She refused to lose her new home. At least the bookstore would be somewhere she could see herself feeling comfortable, and probably the closest to being on her own turf as she could imagine.

One side of the Pumpkin King's jagged mouth curled into an approving smile, and he gave a curt nod.

Mother Morrigan snapped the two out of their conversation.

"I can take her," she offered. "It's my greater-granddaughter's bookstore after all."

The old witch hobbled forward. She had brittle white hair pulled tightly back, drooping cheeks under wise, violet eyes, and one of the few friendly smiles Eve had seen directed her way since arriving in Hallowell.

"Thank you for the offer, but I will see to it myself," the Pumpkin King said, standing. "Besides, I could use you at the doctor's. If magic was used—"

"Psh, I don't need to go there to investigate," interrupted Mother Morrigan with a bored wave of her hand. "I already know what happened."

"You do?" said a surprised Pumpkin King and Mayor Brumple at the same time.

"You've both met the doctor's assistant. She's hardly the most *competent*," Mother Morrigan said, rolling her eyes. "Annabelle either lost the Moon Thistle or misplaced it. End of story. Mystery solved."

The Pumpkin King frowned. "Hrmph, all the same. Moon Thistle is highly coveted, and the three of us should investigate. I will meet you two there after I take Eve to the bookstore."

Mother Morrigan gave a stubborn shake of her head, then begrudgingly followed Mayor Brumple down the stairs. As she did, she winked at Eve. "Enjoy the bookstore, dear, and best to put the vote from your mind."

Eve tried to force a friendly smile back, one she hoped masked the uncertainty she actually felt. But something about the banishment being unfinished felt that much worse to her, like a storm cloud had decided to follow her and only her, and she didn't know when the lightning would strike. Eve just hoped she could get rid of it before it did.

CHAPTER SIX

The Be-Spelled Bookcraft

EVE FOLLOWED THE PUMPKIN KING BACK OUT OF THE MAYOR'S office, her head hung low as she worried about her future chances of staying in Hallowell. She didn't quite share the Pumpkin King's confidence in her ability to convince the undead to like her. So far, other than the scarecrows, Eve hadn't had the most welcoming of welcomes.

Back outside, a clouded black sky matched her mood, and she hardly even felt the wind tossing about the ends of her hair.

Once down the front steps, the Pumpkin King grabbed the reins of both Peaty and Gleysol, then gave a frustrated grumble as he looked down either direction of the lane.

"The alleys have shifted. We'll need a Wayflame."

Eve looked up from her worrying. "A *what*?"

"A Wayflame." He leaned into the lane, waving down one of the balls of blue flame that floated about Hallowell Station's winding streets.

To Eve's surprise, it turned and floated back toward them, its gentle light illuminating the fog beneath it. "What's this for?" she asked, being sure to keep the burning ball at arm's length.

"They help guide undead around the village," the Pumpkin King stated simply. Then, speaking directly to the Wayflame, he said, "The Be-Spelled Bookcraft."

The Wayflame gave a slight bob, then began to float away from them and back down the zigzagging lane.

"You don't know where we're going?" Eve asked, confused.

"I know *where* we're going," he grunted. "But in the village, the *how* you get there can change. Some of the more haunted parts like to, hrmph, switch direction or even location. So the Wayflames act as guides. They were a gift from the candle-spirits after I brought them to Hallowell. Meant to help all the villagers who kept getting lost."

Before Eve could ask what a candle-spirit was, the Pumpkin King waved for her to come along. Then, together with the two horses, they followed in the wake of the Wayflame. It moved silently on, leading them dutifully under shadowy bridges and back up steep cobblestone paths.

As they went, the Pumpkin King nodded to the shop owners

of apothecaries, exchanged grunts with a goblin barkeep outside a tavern called the Tilted Spirit, introduced Eve to a troll blacksmith, and outside a woodshop waved to a pair of zombie carpenters, each with pale, sage-green skin that had decayed in several spots. (Eve wondered if their missing fingers were a zombie thing or a carpenter thing.) They then passed by a small post office and, turning down a candlelit lane, finally arrived at their destination.

Eve froze.

Whatever negative thoughts almost being banished had put into her head, the bookstore quickly helped to shuffle them away, each one chased off and replaced by the spine of a book now staring back at her.

The building before them was a tall and narrow shop, with a large bay window that gave a peek at the shelves inside.

Above the yellow door, a sign shaped like an open book read BE-SPELLED BOOKCRAFT in golden script. Then, to Eve's astonishment, a page of the book turned and the sign read OPEN, PLEASE COME IN.

"You are sure you're okay if I leave you here?" the Pumpkin King asked. When she didn't answer, he continued on. "A witch named Seline Creswick runs the shop. She is friendly and will watch over you. I will come find you as soon as I am done investigating the missing Moon Thistle with Mother Morrigan and the mayor."

Eve still didn't answer. In fact, she barely heard what he had said at all. She found herself too busy staring at all the covers through the bronze-framed window.

"Eve?" The Pumpkin King sighed. "Evelyn? Did you hear me?"

"What?" Eve asked. Then, seeing his dismay, she quickly added, "Yes, yes. Me, bookstore, witch, Seline, friendly. You, missing Moon Dizzle. Got it."

The triangle eyes of the Pumpkin King's face narrowed, and he barely had time to grumble, "It's Moon *Thistle*," before Eve whizzed around him and through the front door.

As soon as she entered, Eve knew she was where she was meant to be. Living or undead.

Back at the orphanage, there had been a small library, but it couldn't hold a candle to this place. Here, within the enchanted walls of Be-Spelled Bookcraft, books floated magically about the air and lined every surface that Eve could see. She watched in delight as an entire bookcase hovered off the wall at the nudge of a young zombie, revealing another bookcase behind it. A branching staircase led up to a second and third floor, where more undead bustled about the shop.

A woman who resembled a string marionette perused a shelf to Eve's right, her strings dangling loosely behind her. To her left, an old lady with a pointed hat surveyed books with hunky warlocks drawn on the front.

The door jingled shut behind Eve, and several of the faces turned.

There were audible gasps, then *all* the faces turned, and suddenly the whole shop seemed to freeze, all eyes pointed toward Eve.

"He—hello," Eve stammered to the room at large, hugging one of her arms as she did. For a brief second, she wanted to turn and run back out, but she knew why she was there. . . . "I'm, um, Evelyn," she finished with a wave as awkward as she felt.

Only silence answered. Directly above, a ghost's head stared from where it was poking through the level above.

"All right now, I'm sure you all have better manners than that," came a friendly voice from the side of the shop. A kindly woman with wavy brown hair stood there behind the sales counter, a smile on her face that looked as if it never left, and a witch's hat that hung loosely at her back by two strings tied about her neck. "Let the poor Pumpkin Princess browse in peace, or anyone caught staring will be charged a 'lingering eyes' tax at checkout."

The threat worked, and slowly (and reluctantly), everyone began to go back to their shopping. Eve mouthed a *thank you* to the lady she assumed was Seline.

The witch winked at her with soft purple eyes before returning to helping the goblin at the counter.

Immediately seeking out the nearest fiction section, Eve took the opportunity to navigate between the bookcases—muttering forced *hello*s and *how are you*s while she browsed—until eventually, she soon lost track not only of time but of her surroundings as well.

Sometime later, she was sitting in the thick cushions of a velvety blue chair, reading about goblins in an ancient and tattered book titled *To Be, or Not to Be: Defining the Undead*. According to the book, goblins had started out as mischievous house spirits, but over time took on physical forms. And that was it. The book was annoyingly brief. Not to mention incomplete; Eve had tried to read about witches or werewolves but couldn't find sections on either. Whether they had never been written or were one of the many missing old pages, Eve would never know.

Frustrated, she decided to switch back to something with at least a good story. Lowering the book to grab another, she suddenly found herself face to . . . wax face?

Three young children stood before her. Or at least what resembled children. They were made entirely of translucent bluish-green wax, which wasn't nearly as alarming as the fact that half their heads were melted, revealing green candle flames sputtering atop waxy hair.

"Are you the living bean?" asked one of the children, her voice sweet and innocent.

"I am," Eve answered, forcing a smile. Then her smile disappeared. "Wait, did you say bea—"

"Is it true living beans control lightning?" asked another, leaning in and sniffing her.

"What? No," Eve said, taken aback. And why did everyone in Hallowell want to sniff her? "Hold on, do you mean electricit—"

"Or that the sun makes them stronger?"

"Or that—"

And then, before Eve knew what was happening, she was being bombarded by increasingly ridiculous questions about what "living beans" could or couldn't do, until she somehow found herself saying—

"What? No, what doesn't kill me doesn't *actually* make me stronger—wait—why do you want to know that?"

"Hey! Shoo, shoo, you little sootlings," intervened a young witch about Eve's age, coming along and chasing away the strange candle-children. "Leave the Pumpkin Princess be."

Shorter than Eve, she wore a black skirt with white ruffles that stopped at her knees, and dark torn leggings that ended in pointy black shoes. Over her wavy brown hair, she had on a wide-rimmed black hat, bunched over and bent at the top and wrapped in a purple ribbon at the base.

"Thanks," breathed an overwhelmed Eve, watching the children scurry away. "They were . . . um . . . curious."

"Most candle-spirits are," the girl said with a shrug. "Figured you might want saving."

"You figured right," Eve said, thankful for the reprieve (and happy to figure out what a candle-spirit was). "I'm Evelyn, by the way."

"I know, heard you downstairs. And also the Pumpkin King rode around telling everyone about you."

Eve felt caught off guard. "He did *what*?"

"Oh, do living have bad hearing?" asked the girl, then began speaking much, much louder. "I SAID he rode all over town, and I think even up to the castle and beyond. Nights ago. Told everyone that you're his new daughter, and that makes you one of us. So you're off-limits, and no funny business."

"I didn't know he did that," Eve said, her cheeks reddening (whether because she was more embarrassed by the girl shouting at her or what the Pumpkin King had done, Eve wasn't entirely sure). But that must have been what he was doing that night at the homestead when he'd ridden off and hadn't said why.

"I hope he was polite about it," Eve continued. "I wouldn't want any hard feelings on my account." *Any more than there already are*, she thought, realizing the last thing she needed was more undead upset with her.

"There are definitely hard feelings on your account," the girl said earnestly. "I overheard a couple trolls saying you'd make a better pumpkin stew than a Pumpkin Princess."

She had a very straightforward way of speaking, as if she expressed her thoughts exactly as they were.

"Oh, wow. Is that all?" Eve asked sarcastically. As much as

she was nervous about being the Pumpkin Princess of Hallowell, she was quite sure she'd take that over being a stew any day.

"No, that's not all," the girl answered simply, not catching Eve's sarcasm. "I've heard the La'Ment family is super angry, but everyone knows the baroness doesn't approve of the Pumpkin King and would probably do anything to be steward herself."

You don't say, Eve thought, and before she could help herself, blurted, "Shame someone doesn't use the baroness and her daughters for a stew." Then, realizing the young witch might be friends with them, quickly tried to walk it back. "I didn't mean that. That was a bad joke."

"No, it was a good joke. They're awful. They always make fun of my outfit." The girl eyed Eve up and down. "They'd probably make fun of your outfit too."

"What's wrong with how I'm dressed?" Eve asked, but as soon as she glanced down, she knew the answer. In her haste to chase after the Pumpkin King earlier that night, Eve hadn't paid any mind to how she looked when she'd left the homestead. Had she looked in a mirror then or at any point since, she would have seen that her mismatched shoes did little to distract from the pants she had on backwards.

"I personally like how you're dressed," the young witch commented. "But my mom keeps some books about fashion somewhere in here if you're curious. I usually find them kind of boring."

"Seline is your mom?" Now that Eve thought about it, the

two had the same wavy brown hair, kind face, and light purple eyes.

"Yep! My name is Lyla. Lyla Creswick."

"Nice to meet you, Lyla," Eve said with a smile. "You can call me Eve."

"Shhhh!" came a harsh whisper from behind a nearby book-case. "Some of us are trying to read!"

"Sorry, Mrs. Belfry," Lyla said loudly. Then, leaning toward Eve, she whispered not-so-quietly behind her hand, "She's been grumpy ever since the doctor made her stop eating toads because of all the warts."

Eve stifled a giggle. She was beginning to like Lyla. Her matter-of-fact way of talking was refreshing; so was the fact that she didn't seem bothered by Eve being living. So far, the only other friendly person her own age was Vlad, the young and food-starved vampire.

"Lyla," Eve said, forming an idea, "since this is your mom's store, I imagine you know the books pretty well?"

"Most. I help her stack them. The floating ones are my doing. I told my mom I like the way they look when they float, but really I just got tired of putting them away."

"Smart," Eve said with a laugh. "Any chance there is a cook-book section? I'd like to buy one for Vlad Jr. the 12th Jr. Jr. I met him the other night, and he seemed really nice, and also kind of hungry."

"I know Vlad! We run into each other in the village some-times. Not often, though. I think they have familiars and staff do most of their shopping. But, hmm, there is a cooking section on the third floor. We can check there. Except, I'm not sure I've seen anything for vampires."

With that, Lyla led the two of them up to the third floor. Here, several ornate chandeliers hovered untethered from the ceiling, flickering with candlelight and casting sporadic shadows in their wake.

Lyla took Eve to a far wall packed tight with books. Some were huge and appeared to have words the size of Eve's hands, while others were so tiny that Eve thought she might need a mag-nifying glass to read them.

The two scoured the section until finally Lyla pulled one out, blowing decades' worth of dust from the top. Proudly, she handed Eve a crimson book with black lettering across the front: *Bloody Bites: A Vampire's Cookbook* curated by Vika Vila.

Eve flipped through its obviously long-neglected pages, spot-ting images of crimson-red carrots and potatoes the shade of spilled blood.

"You think he can use this?" she asked.

Lyla shrugged. "Not sure. But if he doesn't like it, you can just give him your blood. I'm sure a vampire would like that," she said with a quick glance down to Eve's neck.

"Pretty sure I like my blood where it is. I still kind of need it."

"For what?" Lyla asked, looking both surprised and curious.

"Huh?" Eve responded, unsure if she were more confused by the question itself or the fact Lyla had asked it in the first place. "What do you mean for what? Without it, I'll die."

"Oh. Interesting," Lyla answered casually. "I'm not technically alive, so I'm not sure I need my blood really. I think it's just there to keep me from deflating."

"That—that can't be true?"

"Okay, maybe I wouldn't deflate. But I'm definitely undead. The first witches gave up their lives long ago. Traded them for magic in a deal with the Darkness or something. All of us born since have magic instead of life. I've always wondered what it would have been like if I wasn't born a witch. Now I've met you, so I'll get to see what being living is like."

"I . . . was not aware of any of that," Eve admitted, reminded of how little she knew about Hallowell. "I might try and find a book about witches before I leave."

"Or I can teach you, and we can be friends," Lyla said, or asked—Eve couldn't quite tell if it was a question or a statement.

"I would like that!" Eve answered all the same. "How would you like to give this book to Vlad with me? You helped pick it out, after all."

"Sure! Honestly, I'll take any excuse to get out of the shop."

Though Eve found herself disagreeing on that last bit, she was excited to have made a friend. "Great! Maybe the Pumpkin King can take us tomorrow. I'll ask, and if he says yes, we can pick you up on the way!"

With that, Eve bid farewell to Lyla and headed back downstairs, ducking under several floating books drifting over the staircase.

Back by the front counter, Eve found Seline conversing with the hunched-over Mother Morrigan.

At the sight of Eve, Mother Morrigan's thin lips parted into a wide, happy smile. "Ah, you look to be in better spirits than when I last saw you," she said in a voice that sounded like creaking wood.

"I hope you won't let that banishment business ruin your opinion of all us undead," she continued. "I for one can't tell you how exciting it is to meet you. Hallowell can get oh-so-boring when you've been around as long as I have, and it's a delight to finally see a little *life* brought to our valley."

Eve mustered her friendliest face. Now that she was in a somewhat better mood, she realized she had never properly thanked Mother Morrigan for coming to her defense. Yet the words *thank you* didn't seem like enough. That Mother Morrigan had sided with Eve and protected her from being banished meant a lot to her, and she wasn't going to forget that anytime soon.

Just as she opened her mouth for some kind of thanks, Seline spoke instead.

"Evelyn, I don't believe we've been properly introduced. My

name is Seline Creswick, and I understand you already know Mother Morrigan? She is Mother of the witch's coven in the Misty Moors and a greater-grandmother of mine, not to mention greatest-grandmother to my daughter, Lyla. Who should also be somewhere around here."

"Oh, I've already met Lyla," Eve said happily. "She is very nice. Just like your bookshop."

"Well, one of those things is true," Mother Morrigan mumbled. "That daughter of yours needs to learn to filter her words from her thoughts. If you'd just leave her with me at the coven . . ."

Seline sighed. "I've tried, but you know her. She finds the coven boring."

"Boring!" gasped Mother Morrigan, appearing insulted. "Typical young person! In my night, young witches had no choice but to learn the old ways."

Seline gave a jovial shake of her head, turning her attention to Eve. "This is a frequent debate, if you can't tell. Anyway, did you find everything you were looking for?"

Mother Morrigan stepped aside and made room for Eve, though she still looked flustered.

Eve lifted her tote up onto the counter, and Seline began to shuffle through it.

"Let's see here," she murmured. "Ooh, big fan of fiction, I see, and quite a few from Cecilia Shroud, good choice—she has some murder mysteries you might like as well. Oh, and I see you

102

did grab a little nonfiction too: *Defining the Undead . . . Famous Ghosts and Ghouls . . .* and . . . a vampire cookbook? Interesting choice, but still, all great selections." Seline riffled through them one last time, quickly summing them up on her fingers. "Total will be fifteen shards. Or would you prefer to barter?"

Shards? Barter?

Eve's cheeks reddened.

She had never been asked to pay for something before. At the orphanage, what little she had was usually provided for her. Here, she had been too excited to even think about how she would pay for something.

"Actually . . . never mind," Eve said, feeling dejected. "I'll put them back."

For a moment, Seline's eyebrows rose in confusion, then she gave Eve a soft smile.

"Don't you worry. I'll send the Pumpkin King the bill," she said with a wink.

Eve instantly perked back up. "Thank you!" Excitedly she grabbed her bag of new books, but then realized she didn't quite know where to go next. *Speaking of the Pumpkin King.* "Mother Morrigan, Ms. Creswick, any chance you know where I can find . . . my . . . um . . . the—?"

"Your father?" Seline offered. She then leaned in and with a sly grin whispered, "He's over in the parenting section." She nodded toward the back of the store.

Parenting section? Eve blushed, leaving both Seline and Mother Morrigan with an embarrassed *thank you* and a wave.

The parenting section wasn't hard to find. For starters, the Pumpkin King took up most of the store and was fairly easy to spot once she knew where to look. The other giveaway was the *very* pregnant vampire wearing what appeared to be a black maternity corset and tossing baby book after baby book to her increasingly nervous husband. Both of whom eyed Eve suspiciously as she approached.

Eve waved awkwardly at them. Then her eyes landed on the book that the Pumpkin King was engrossed in. . . .

And she bit her cheek to keep from laughing.

"Whatcha reading?" Eve asked coyly.

The Pumpkin King's head shot up. "HRMPH—NOTHING—HRMPH," he stammered, rushing to re-shelve *Twill Creaksly's Guide to Single Parenting: Your New Monster and You*. "I—ehrm—was just browsing. Are you, hrmph, are you ready to leave?"

"Sure," Eve said, fighting with all her might not to let her smile show (too much). "I mean . . . unless you want to keep . . . *browsing*?" She couldn't help herself.

He grumbled and hurried awkwardly by her, and as soon as he passed, Eve finally let her smile out. Then she turned, practically dragging her tote along the floor after him.

"How did it go at the doctor's?" Eve asked, giving the

Pumpkin King the courtesy of a subject change. "Find whatever went missing?"

"No," he growled. "Unfortunate too. It's her entire supply of Moon Thistle that is gone. It's extremely potent. Not to mention rare."

"What do you think happened to it?"

"My first hunch was that it was stolen, but apparently the assistant had locked herself inside after closing up the day it went missing, so that can't be it."

"Locked *herself* in?" Eve asked, perplexed.

"Hrmph, yes. The doctor's assistant is unreliable at best, and forgetful even on a good night. Which is why I'm confident Mother Morrigan was right and it's either lost or misplaced. We're hoping it turns up on its own. Moon Thistle is not something that is easy to go buy more of."

The bell over the door let out a light jingle as the Pumpkin King held it open for Eve.

"Um, speaking of buying things," Eve started hesitantly, passing underneath his arm. "Seline said she'll send you a bill for the books. Is that okay? I can—I can return them if not."

"It is no bother," he grumbled.

Once again, Eve felt herself smile. "Oh, and also," she continued, feeling somewhat emboldened. "I was hoping you could take me and my new friend, Lyla, to go see Vlad tomorrow?"

There was a louder and far grumpier grumble.

"Vlad lives with the baroness," he said pointedly. "Do you really want to be going there?"

Eve didn't have to think long on this; in fact, judging from the way the twins and their mother had treated Vlad, it gave her even more reason to see him.

"If he lives with her, then he definitely needs something to cheer him up," she answered honestly. As little as Eve wanted to see the baroness, she knew what it was like to be surrounded by others and still feel alone. It gave her the sneaking suspicion that Vlad might want friends as badly as she did . . . even if that friend happened to be living. "Please?" she finished.

His head drooped forward, and a steaming sigh rolled down his chest. "Hrmph, fine."

Eve felt herself getting excited, and if she weren't anchored down by a tote that probably weighed as much as Peaty, she might have jumped for joy.

Wobbling back to the horses, Eve found that her mind wasn't on her new books at all, nor the vote she needed from Mayor Brumple—but rather on the fact that she had just made her first-ever friend (one that wasn't a scarecrow, that is) and might soon be making another. She was so distracted, she hardly even noticed the Pumpkin King's grumbling when he went to help lift her tote and finally saw how many books he had just paid for.

CHAPTER SEVEN

Friends and Fangs

THE NEXT NIGHT, JUST AFTER SECONDMEAL, THEIR WAGON groaned and dipped as the Pumpkin King lumbered up beside Eve.

"You're going to want this," he grumbled, handing her a waxy overcoat and a weathered black umbrella.

"What for?" asked Eve.

He pointed off toward the distant mountains and mumbled something that Eve couldn't understand.

Looking out to where he pointed, she saw black clouds swirling around the mountaintops, pouring down sheets of rain that lit up with every bolt of crackling lightning.

"Are you sure you still want to visit Vlad?" he asked, clearly digging for an excuse not to see the baroness himself. "That storm will be upon us soon."

"You want me to make Hallowell my home, right? Well, then, I should probably have some friends," Eve answered. "Vlad was nice when I met him, and it's not his fault he lives with the baroness."

He grumbled once more and flicked the reins of the horses, leading them out into the night.

It was eerily quiet as they went, with even the usual fluttering bats hiding from the impending storm.

They traveled silently, or somewhat silently, for the Pumpkin King kept grumbling to himself. Eve meanwhile busied herself in a book titled *Spirits of the Valley: A History of Hallowell's Most Famous Ghosts and Ghouls*, the faint gray lettering lit only by the swaying lamplight that hung overhead. She was browsing a chapter on the ghost Cecilia Shroud, the reclusive author of the book the Pumpkin King had given her.

In the building wind, it was Eve who finally spoke first. "What's a book-burrower?" she asked, coming across it in her reading.

"Hrmph?" he grunted, distracted. "Oh. Small, paperlike creatures. They hide in neglected books and eat at the parchment, but are otherwise harmless. Why?"

"Apparently Cecilia Shroud—the author of that book you got me—keeps one as a pet. This says she feeds it the chapters that she writes but doesn't like. Calls it Fred."

"Interesting," the Pumpkin King responded, but in such a tone that Eve doubted he had even heard her, let alone found it interesting.

Catching the hint, Eve closed her book and placed it on her lap.

"Something on your mind?" she asked, perhaps a little more sarcastically than she intended.

"I'm fine," he mumbled, quite obviously *not* fine.

"You're grumbling louder than you snore. And that's saying something."

"Hrmph."

"See, there it is again! If you don't want to see the baroness, you can drop me and Lyla off. We'll make it quick. I'll be safe, I promise. . . . Wait, I *will* be safe there, right?" Eve asked, realizing she was asking to be left alone in a castle full of vampires. In that moment, the tiniest sliver of Eve wondered if her lack of fear might actually be working against her best interests—but then the rest of her shut that notion down, refusing fear even the slightest of footholds back into her life.

"You'll be safe," the Pumpkin King grunted. "Not even the baroness is bold enough to lay a finger on the Pumpkin Princess. That's why she—"

"Is trying to have me banished instead?"

"Yes," he said angrily. "But it matters not. I have no choice, I have to speak with her anyway. She's responsible for supplying the Harvest Festival with blood wine."

"*Blood wine?*" Eve repeated.

"It's what the vampires drink since they don't have living to prey on. There is an ancient burial site beside their castle, and they found that by growing grapes in its soil, they could cultivate blood grapes. They use them to make blood wine. Half the time, the smell of alcohol on them is worse than the stench of blood."

"Wait. So vampires are drinking alcohol all the time?" Eve asked. "Even Vlad?"

"No, they use the burial grounds to make alcohol-free blood juice as well. Over the centuries, the vampires became so talented at growing and splicing grapevines that they took over all the wine for the valley. It might be the one thing someone can grow better than I can."

Ah, so that's part of it, Eve realized. Not only did he not like the baroness to begin with, but Eve couldn't see him much liking someone being better with plants either. And no wonder Vlad longed for something else to eat: drinking the same thing for years on end would get old quickly. Hopefully the cookbook she had wrapped and tucked in her jacket would be able to help.

There was a flash of scarlet lightning overhead, followed by a rumble of thunder rivaled only by the Pumpkin King's own grumbles. Rain began to patter down around them. Eve draped the coat he'd lent her over herself—with plenty of room to spare—and extended open his umbrella, doing her best to hold it against the strengthening wind.

Entering the village, they passed by a long-armed swamp crea-ture conversing with what appeared to be a sludge monster, neither of whom looked even remotely bothered by the storm. Which, by the time Eve and the Pumpkin King arrived at Seline's Be-Spelled Book-craft, had completely consumed the sky above. Heavy gray clouds now covered all of Hallowell, pelting it with rain and lightning.

Here, the lane was empty, everyone no doubt sheltering inside.

Everyone except three: Eve, the grouchy Pumpkin King sitting beside her, and the young witch holding her hat down against the wind and running in their direction.

"Good evening!" Eve shouted over the wind.

"It's not really!" Lyla shouted back as she hopped in the cart.

"That's not what I meant!" Eve tried to clarify, her voice swallowed by the storm.

"Huh?"

"THAT'S NOT WHAT—oh, never mind," Eve said, giv-ing up and making room for Lyla beside her.

The Pumpkin King waved a large hand at the figure of Seline in the window and then they were off.

The usual fog of Hallowell that covered the town's lanes was either washed or blown away, replaced instead by rivers of water rippling over cobblestone.

Eve wrapped the extra-large coat she was in over Lyla and did her best to cover the two of them with the umbrella, though at this point it felt like the rain was coming at them from all directions.

As they went, the buildings of Hallowell Station became fewer and more derelict, turning from storefronts and townhouses to huts and muddy lanes.

Eve attempted to ask where they were, but once more her voice was lost in the storm.

The path began to rise steadily, and gradually the huts started to disappear into the night. Around them, the many hills of the Hallowell Valley became steeper and more severe, and rolling knolls turned into sharp cliffs with drastic drops.

Ahead there was only sheer blackness until a brilliant bolt of lightning cut through the sky, lighting up the night and revealing a Gothic castle. It loomed over them like a gaping mouth about to devour their wagon. In that quick flash, Eve caught sight of steep gables and ornate railings; menacing stone gargoyles perched along crevices that were tucked into tall walls. Thunder followed, rumbling throughout the valley and shaking the black windows that stared eagerly down on them like hungry eyes.

There was a second flash of lightning, and Eve noticed that several of the gargoyle perches now stood empty. Instinctively, the logical part of Eve tried to tell herself that she'd imagined it, but the new and developing Hallowell side of her said otherwise.

The horses led them over a drawbridge that spanned a thin, dark moat, finally rolling to a stop outside two large iron-wrapped doors. They all hopped out, hurrying to the doors and some form of shelter from the downpour.

BOOM-BOOM-BOOM. The Pumpkin King's fist rang against the doors.

Nothing happened.

They stood underneath a small stone arch, getting what little protection they could from the rain.

BOOM-BOOM-BOOM. He knocked again.

Again, nothing.

Eve and Lyla both stared expectantly up at him.

"Maybe no one's home!" Lyla yelled.

"Hrmph," the Pumpkin King growled. And just as he lifted his fist once more, the door opened with an ominous creak.

It was Vlad.

"Hello, Mr. Pumpk—Eve? Lyla? What are you doing here?"

Eve couldn't help but notice the worry on his face when he saw her.

"Think you might let us in?" Lyla asked. "It's a bit wet out here."

"Sorry, sorry, come in," he said, stepping aside and making room for them through the doors.

They entered into a cavernous entrance hall, as dim as it was uninviting. The air was stale and musty, like a damp room long boarded up. Oil lamps emitted what little light there was, hung from walls peeling with old wallpaper. A grand staircase led up to two balconies that wrapped to either side, a velvety red carpet flowing down its steps like a river of blood. Furniture that might once have been regal sat covered in layers of undisturbed filth, and below a nearby chair, Eve was sure she saw something moving.

The Pumpkin King's glowing gaze seemed to take it all in, and Eve was confident she heard him mutter something about being ashamed. "They have you opening doors now, Vlad?" he asked. "Where are the staff and familiars?"

"Hiding from Corina and Elisabetta. The twins just let a pack of gargoyles loose out of boredom again," Vlad answered, equal parts casual and sad. "You're all soaked. Can I get you a towel?"

"Worry not! I can remedy this!" said Lyla in a strange voice, removing a wand from somewhere up her sleeve.

Before Eve could ask why Lyla was talking so oddly, Lyla gave a flick of her wand, and suddenly the Pumpkin King's coat that Eve was still wearing caught fire.

Quickly Eve shot out from under it, leaving it smoldering to a crisp on the floor.

"What was that?" Eve said, checking herself for flames as the Pumpkin King stamped out the coat. Thankfully, Vlad's gift was still safe within her own jacket.

"Oops, jinxes," Lyla stated plainly. "Not how I meant to dry you off."

"We'll take those towels," the Pumpkin King grumbled,

staring sadly at the remnants of his coat. "Then can you point me to the baroness?"

"She's in her tearoom," said Vlad, tossing them moldy towels that he grabbed from a nearby armoire. "Do you know the way?"

"I can manage," the Pumpkin King said with a sigh. "I'll come find you three when I'm done."

"Oh, you're not all here for the baroness?" asked Vlad.

"We're here to see you," Eve said, trying to regain her composure after nearly being set on fire.

At this, Vlad's pink cheeks lit up with a smile. "Wow! Well, we should get out of here before the twins find us. Follow me."

The Pumpkin King headed up the central stairs as Vlad led Eve and Lyla through a small door off the entrance hall. Circling up a coiling stairwell, they stepped out into a long and narrow hallway, flickering with lamplight. Along one wall, painted portraits of vampires were hung above dark wainscoting; along the other, large panes of glass looked out and into the storm. There was a flash of lightning outside, and without warning, the lamps of the hall fluttered out, leaving the three of them in complete darkness.

"Oh man," said Vlad, sounding suddenly worried. "I hate when they do this."

The lamps flared back on, and there, standing before them,

each with a doglike stone gargoyle on a leash, were the smug La'Ment twins. The gargoyles snapped and barked, their carved wings stretching restlessly from the backs of their grotesque bodies.

"Hello, Corina. Hello, Elisabetta," said Lyla, feigning a high posh accent and ignoring the growls. "Pleasantest of nights to you!"

"Tsk. Tsk. Tsk," said one of the twins, ignoring Lyla and staring Eve in the eyes.

"Mother will be so displeased, Vlad," said the other. "Bringing filth like *her* into the castle."

"Maybe she'll finally let us put you in the dungeons this time," one sneered.

Eve took a defiant step forward, putting herself between Vlad and the twins. If the two La'Ment daughters thought they could scare her, they were woefully mistaken.

"Vlad didn't do anything wrong," Eve said, trying to sound as bored as possible to show them how much they weren't getting to her. "If you want someone to pick on, maybe give me a go. See how the Pumpkin King likes that."

At his name, their faces twisted.

"Maybe we will. Not even he could find you hidden in the dungeons of *our* castle."

"Technically speaking," interrupted Lyla, "it's not *your* castle. It's shared by the royal vampire families and is under the care of the head family's leading member, which currently is your mother, Baroness La'Ment. Or did you not know all that?"

Eve bit down her smirk.

"It *is* our castle," the twin hissed, rounding on Lyla with a stare that could burn through wood. Slowly, her eyes drifted back to Eve, fixing her with a knowing look. "And *you* don't belong here."

"Well, here I am," Eve said plainly. "And if you don't mind, we'll be on our way now. I'd hate to keep you from picking on defenseless staff."

Vlad began to inch warily around the twins, the stone gargoyles snapping inches away from him as they pulled their leashes taut. Eve followed closely, locking eyes with the vampires. Lyla was right behind her, looking utterly oblivious to the tension in the air.

They had almost rounded the corner when one of the twins' voices echoed along the dim walls.

"You don't belong here!"

"You said that already," Eve called back, not bothering to turn around.

"She doesn't mean the castle," called the other sister. "No *living* can ever call Hallowell home. You might be his daughter, but you'll never truly be undead. You'll never fit in, no matter what you do!"

Eve faltered as the sisters struck a chord.

117

She stopped and turned, but the corridor was empty, and the twins nowhere to be seen.

Did they have a point?

Was she just fooling herself in thinking she could ever get the undead to truly accept her? How many others thought like the twins? And if Eve couldn't change their minds . . . then the mayor's vote on her banishment was practically already decided. Eve felt her hands go clammy.

As rain threw itself against the windows, she stood rooted to the spot. Vlad and Lyla didn't seem to mind that she was living, she told herself. There was also Ellie the skeleton and Mother Morrigan.

"Is everything dandy?" Lyla asked. "You look ever-so-sickly."

Eve broke from her brooding, then gave Lyla an odd look. "Are you talking different?"

"I know not what you mean," Lyla said, definitely speaking differently.

"Come on," Vlad urged. "My chambers are around the corner."

Regaining her composure, Eve followed after him and tried to force the worries from her mind. Still, she struggled to shake the notion that she had traded one temporary home for another.

He led them into what appeared to have once been a sprawling banquet room, with a gold-fringed red carpet down the center and a long, silver table pushed against one of the walls. Tucked into the corner was a coffin with its lid raised and quilted sheets pouring from its side. Littered over every inch of floor and table were odd contraptions made of wood and metals, gears and strings. Like strange toys invented by a mad scientist.

"Is this your room?" Eve asked, somewhat surprised.

"It is now. My old room wasn't big enough for all my inventions, so I moved into here."

"It is the finest of abodes," Lyla said, still in a voice quite unlike her own. "Really, just the finest!"

Vlad and Eve both gave her a bewildered look.

"What?" Lyla asked incredulously. "We're in a castle. You're supposed to talk fancy in a castle."

"You're really, really not," Vlad said, looking like he wasn't sure if Lyla was kidding.

Lyla looked surprisingly let down. "Really? Then what's the point of living in one?"

Eve shook her head and laughed, not knowing how to reply. Instead, she reached into her jacket and pulled out the book she had brought for Vlad.

"We got you something," she said, handing him the present. "It's from both of us."

"You got me a gift?" he asked, surprised. He reached out to take it, but his hand stopped just shy.

"This isn't some kind of trick, is it? Did the twins put you up to this?"

"What? No, definitely not," Eve said, somewhat insulted he would think she'd be with them. "It's more of a treat than a trick. And sorry if it's a little wet. I did my best to protect it from the rain." Several drops had soaked through the wrapping.

"I can fix that," said Lyla, breaking her attention from the weird rolling device she was nudging on the floor and pulling out her wand.

"Um, maybe don't?" Eve said, thinking back to how Lyla had "dried" the coat in the entrance hall.

Thankfully, Vlad didn't give her the chance to try a spell, quickly unwrapping his gift and revealing the book within.

Vlad's eyes widened as he read the title.

"Is this what I think it is?" he asked in awe.

"It seemed like something you might enjoy," Eve said. "Do you like—"

Vlad didn't answer; instead he rushed around her and toward the extravagant table pushed against the wall. He threw himself onto a seat at the table and, setting the book down before him, quickly sifted through the pages.

"I'll take that as a yes," Eve said, happy her gift was a hit.

She walked over to Vlad, careful not to step on any of the inventions scattered across the floor.

"There are so many things to try!" Vlad said excitedly. "I didn't know a book like this existed. I wish I'd found it sooner!"

Lyla jumped up beside him. "It was pretty buried. Took even me a while to find it."

Eve began to clear a spot for herself, moving the devices crowding the table. "Did you make all of this by yourself, Vlad?" she asked, inspecting a small contraption that looked like a wooden bat with paper wings.

Meanwhile, Vlad was busy staring at the food drawn across the pages of his new book.

"Blood carrots and blood potatoes and—OH! Careful with that!"

It was too late.

The device Eve was playing with sputtered to life and its wings began to flap, but before Eve could catch it, the wooden bat flew up into the room, sweeping wide circles over their heads.

"It works!" said a surprised Vlad. "I can't believe it—"

But before he could finish his sentence, the wooden bat slammed into a lit candle chandelier overhead and caught fire. The device burned brightly and then burst apart, spewing flaming pieces in every direction.

"Watch out!" yelled Vlad as he dove under the table.

Lyla shielded herself with her witch's hat, and Eve quickly

grabbed a nearby seat cushion, narrowly blocking the flaming parts that rained down.

The last of the smoldering pieces landed among the other inventions on the floor, and Eve tossed a now-smoking pillow onto the ground before stamping it out.

"Is everyone okay?" she asked.

"Yeah," Vlad said, crawling out from under the table. "Could have been worse."

There was a snap, and the chandelier dropped from the ceiling, crashing loudly onto the floor below.

"Okay, that's worse," Vlad said with a nod.

Eve stared at the disaster she had caused. "I. Am. So. Sorry."

"Honestly, it's fine," Vlad assured her, dusting his vest of the dirt it had collected from under the table. "I'll have one of the staff help me hang it back up later."

"No need," Lyla said proudly. "I think I can do it!"

Once again, she pulled out her wand, and with a whispered word and a wave, pointed it at the chandelier.

For a moment, nothing happened, and both Eve and Vlad turned to look at Lyla expectantly. Then, in a hot flash, all the candles of the chandelier erupted in a flame that blazed from the floor all the way up to the ceiling before quickly burning themselves entirely out of wax in a fraction of a second.

Scorch marks now marred the ceiling where the chandelier once hung.

"Oops. Jinxes."

"You burned my ceiling," Vlad stated, staring at the blackened rings overhead. "You know a lot of this castle is wood, right?"

"Did you mean to do that?" Eve asked, gaping at her friend.

"Not exactly. I wanted the chandelier to touch the ceiling, but the spell must have thought I meant the flames," Lyla said, inspecting the smoldering chandelier.

"Is, um . . . magic . . . always so unpredictable?" asked Eve.

"Well, not exactly. Mine can be," Lyla said. "Still kind of a witch-in-training and all, so my magic can have a mind of its own."

"It's okay," said Vlad. "Not the worst thing one of my inventions has done."

"Sorry we broke your things," Eve added.

"Don't worry about it," Vlad said, waving a hand. "They break all the time. Usually because I made them wrong, but sometimes because my cousins come in and mess things up, or one of the gargoyles gets to them. At least I got to see that one work before it broke." Vlad hopped back up on his chair and returned to his new cookbook. "I never thought about blood peppers!"

"Think you can eat them?" Eve asked, taking a seat beside him and looking around at some of the art hanging from the walls.

"Maybe. If I can manage to grow them. I've never actually grown anything before," Vlad answered, still absorbed in his book.

Nearby, a painting that looked newer than most was hung haphazardly, angled hard to the right. In it was a small pudgy baby, held by a pretty woman with shining black hair, and a wide-shouldered man with an equally wide smile, revealing two pointed fangs.

"Is that you?" Eve asked, nodding toward it.

"What?" Vlad asked, finally looking up from his book. "Oh, yes . . . and my parents."

"Where are they now?" Eve asked.

"Dead, I'm told," Vlad said with a shrug.

"Definitely dead," Lyla said absently, looking up from studying her wand.

"Lyla!" Eve blurted.

"It's all right, I've met Lyla before," Vlad said knowingly. "She didn't mean any harm. At least, I don't think."

"What?" Lyla asked, confused. "They haven't been seen in years. There was a funeral and everything."

"I'm so sorry, Vlad," Eve apologized, wishing she hadn't brought it up at all. She knew all too well the pain of missing your parents. "I didn't know. . . ."

"That vampires could die?" he finished for her. "It's possible.

124

Same with all the undead. And it's okay. I don't remember them very well."

Eve sat silently for a moment, staring at Vlad's parents in the painting. They looked so happy together. She wondered if somewhere there existed a photo of her and her birth parents, one where they looked as joyful as Vlad's family; the thought caused a twinge of sadness that constricted her chest.

"I . . . I don't remember my parents either," she said finally. "I was all alone when the Pumpkin King found—adopted me. I was actually running away when I met him, before I came here."

Vlad's eyes lowered, and when he spoke, he spoke quietly and to the table rather than to her.

"I've thought about running away," he muttered. "Baroness La'Ment and my cousins are family, but they're really mean. The staff think so too, but they would never say it. We all miss my parents."

"The staff miss your parents?" Eve asked, confused.

"Yeah," Vlad said sullenly. "House Dracula, my family, used to look over the castle and all the vampires. But when my parents disappeared, my mom's sister, Lady La'Ment, took over and became the baroness. I was too young, they said. Now I'm mostly on my own."

"There aren't other vampires you could be with?" asked Lyla.

"They're all scared of the baroness and my cousins, so they

steer clear of me. I pretty much stay in here alone all night and make things." He prodded another small invention covered in triangular gears.

A memory stirred in Eve, and before her flashed a girl alone, sitting on a bench reading while other orphans ran and played.

Eve sat quietly; she could feel her hands begin to shake. Quickly, she balled them up into fists in hopes of stopping the tremble. She had more than a semblance of what it was like to be in Vlad's position. Eve wouldn't wish that feeling on anyone.

She scooted closer, pulling Vlad's book toward her.

"So, blood corn, huh?" she said, forcing her thoughts to something less painful. "I've learned a thing or two about growing vegetables if you want my help?"

"I can help too!" offered Lyla.

"That would be grand!" Vlad said, and a smile returned to his face. "But . . . you two probably shouldn't eat anything we make."

"Probably a good idea. Also . . . we may want to do it soon," Eve added, feeling her mood darkening once again. "I might be getting banished from Hallowell." (*So much for less painful subjects*, she thought dryly).

"WHAT?" shouted Vlad and Lyla in unison.

Before Eve knew what she was doing, she found herself confiding in the two of them all that had happened with the Council. She hadn't planned to tell them; it was her problem, not theirs.

But something about being with Vlad and Lyla made her let her guard down, like she could be herself.

"Ugh, my aunt is the worst," Vlad finally said once Eve was done recounting everything that had happened.

"But you can't go. You just got here," Lyla stated, as if it were a simple fact. "We'll just have to convince Mayor Brumple he's worried over nothing."

"And how do we do that?" Eve pressed. "Seriously, how?"

Vlad's face lit up. "The Harvest Festival!" he said excitedly. "It's only a few weeks away, and everyone in the village loves the feast! Show them you can help the Pumpkin King throw a good one, and that will *have* to change the mayor's mind!"

"You think so?" Eve asked, her hopes rising. "But that's not that far away, and there is still a lot to do. . . ." She faltered, a wishful idea taking hold. "You two . . . wouldn't want to come help, would you? The Pumpkin King usually doesn't like visitors, but I'm sure I can convince him to let you both come over."

She was scared of their response. What if they said no?

Thankfully, she didn't have to wait long.

"Anything if it helps you stay in Hallowell," Lyla said enthusiastically. "And to be honest, I'd love for somewhere else to practice magic for once. How about tomorrow?"

"You mean it?" added Vlad. "You're inviting us to the Pumpkin King's farm?"

"Yes," Eve said. "If you'd like to, that is?"

"Definitely!" Vlad exclaimed. "Not sure how helpful I'll be, but I'll try and learn if it means you don't get banished."

"Will the baroness even let you?" Eve asked, realizing Vlad's aunt probably wouldn't approve of him helping her stay.

"Half the time, they don't care where I am," he said, sounding happier than he probably should have. "But I may need a way there."

"I can take you on my broom," Lyla chimed in. Then, seeing the question form on Vlad's face, said, "I'm much better on a broom than with a wand, I promise."

Vlad laughed. "All right, good enough for me, I guess."

With a plan for dealing with the banishment, and two friends who wanted to help, Eve felt her spirits lifted in a way she hadn't thought possible.

For some time the three sat talking, and Eve, her mood now much improved, watched as Vlad's eyes lit up over each and every new recipe in his book. Eventually, a knock at the door ended their evening, and the Pumpkin King arrived to take Eve and Lyla home.

It wasn't until they had dropped Lyla off that Eve noticed the broken glass stuck in the Pumpkin King's collar, or the red wine staining the lapel of his coat.

"I take it things with the baroness didn't go well?" she asked, attempting to feel out his mood before asking if her friends could come visit.

"Hrmph. No worse than any other year," he answered grumpily. Then, when he saw the look Eve was giving him, quietly mumbled, "All right, a little worse."

His extra-grumbly demeanor told Eve that her question could wait, and instead her mind wandered to the two new friends she now had (which, frankly, was two more than she'd ever had). That Eve had spent *years* at the orphanage without someone she felt close to, and yet here had already found a family and two others like her, gave her hope that she could make this work: that despite the baroness trying to banish her, Eve could make Hallowell a home for herself after all.

CHAPTER EIGHT

The Harvest Festival

EVE WOKE WITH A START.

Quickly, she pulled on her pants, grabbed a shirt and jacket, and threw open her bedroom door.

"Good evening, Scrags," Eve said to a surprised scarecrow on the other side of the door. (It was one of the first times Eve had gotten up without the "assistance" of Scrags—usually on account of her staying up too late reading.) This evening was different, though. Tonight, her friends were coming.

But first she had to ask—well, at this point, tell—the Pumpkin King. Eve hoped it wouldn't be an issue.

"Good evening, Prin'sis," Scrags said. "You'res up early?"

"Or maybe you're up late?" Eve teased, dancing around Scrags and down to firstmeal.

"I's never late," she heard him mutter to himself.

Downstairs, the Pumpkin King was lighting a fire in the hearth when Eve came up behind him, handing him the kettle to hang over it.

"Here you go," she said.

"Thank—Eve?" he said, startled. "What are you doing up? And dressed? And not carrying a book? Is everything okay?" Behind him, logs crackled to life and the fireplace began to wake.

"Everything is good," Eve said, struggling to contain her giddiness. She had never felt this way before; she was so used to being a loner. The thought of having friends who wanted to hang out with her, and that she actually wanted to hang out with as well, was foreign, as foreign as Hallowell had been when she first arrived.

"Hrmph," he growled, still eyeballing her as if something were amiss. "All right then, if you say so."

He headed into the kitchens, and Eve sat down at the great table that spanned the Hall.

"Just oatmeal for me, please," she called.

All she heard back was some grumbling, followed by several pots and pans clattering noisily to the ground, followed by even louder grumbling.

He came out with two bowls of oatmeal topped with cinnamon and fresh berries, and after filling hers with steaming water from the kettle and his with warm ale, set them down on the table. His bowl was big enough that Eve could have washed her face in it.

"So, about tonight," Eve began before either of them had even taken a bite.

"Ah, here it is."

"Here what is?" Eve retorted.

"What you want," he said plainly from behind a bite of oatmeal.

"What makes you think I want something?" She found herself oddly perturbed by being caught. She didn't like thinking that someone could know her that well already.

"Because, since you arrived, it has taken a poor scarecrow—"

"Scrags," Eve interjected.

"I'm not naming them," he fought.

"You're not," Eve concurred. "I am. He's called Scrags. Go on."

"Hrmph," he growled. "Every evening poor *Scrags* has to drag you from your bed to this table. Where you usually fall asleep once more while reading. Meanwhile, the food I prepared gets cold beside you."

"So?"

"So, tonight you come down fully dressed, ready to eat, and practically bouncing on your toes."

132

"I am not bouncing on my toes," she argued, consciously stopping her feet from wiggling under the table.

"Okay then," the Pumpkin King said, returning to his first-meal. "So you don't want anything?"

"Well . . . actually . . ."

The Pumpkin King's bowl of oats turned brilliantly orange as his eyes blazed. It was a look that would have frightened most, but not Eve; she just saw the vindication in his face. Before he could say anything, she cut in.

"I kind of told Vlad and Lyla that they could come help prepare for the Harvest Festival," Eve rushed. "Is that okay?"

His mouth fell open. "You what?" he said. "Vlad and Lyla? Outsiders to the farm, helping *me*, the Pumpkin King, with the Harvest Festival?"

"What did we say about referring to yourself in the third pers—oh, never mind," Eve said, realizing there were more important things at the moment. "Well, don't think about it like them helping you. Think about it like them helping me."

He frowned, and though it was rare that he ever directly told her no, Eve saw the word forming on his jack-o'-lantern-like face.

"Please, I've never had friends before," she added hastily, letting a little of her vulnerability through. "Friends that weren't you or the scarecrows, I mean."

He stopped what he was about to say, opening and closing his mouth several times.

"Hrmph, fine," he grumbled at last. "But if they slow anything down, or interfere with the quality of our harvest, they go. And you are responsible for getting them up to speed."

"Thank you!" Eve beamed. "You won't regret this!"

A little after rising-night, Eve was diligently cleaning out the barn, though often taking breaks to peek outside and into the moonlit sky.

What if Vlad and Lyla didn't show up? What if they changed their minds?

But then, on what had to be her fiftieth time checking, Eve saw something.

It started as a small speck before the gray moon, and Eve wondered if it was just a big bat. But as it neared, two figures began to form, and soon Eve was able to make out a broom beneath them.

"Hello, Eve," Vlad called, attempting an awkward bow on the back of the descending broom.

Meanwhile, Lyla guided them down, where she hovered with her feet dangling inches from the ground.

"How was the flight?" Eve asked, helping Vlad from the broom.

"It was much better than expected," Vlad said honestly.

"I told you, I'm good at flying," Lyla remarked, hopping from her broom and leaning it beside the barn. "We would have been

134

here sooner, but my mom wanted me to practice a little bit of my magic first."

"It's okay! I'm just glad you're here," Eve said. "Are you ready to get started?"

"Yep! I even brought working gloves that I borrowed from one of the gardeners," Vlad said.

"I did not," commented Lyla. "I don't have a gardener. But I do have a wand. Will that work?"

"Um, probably not," answered Eve, remembering the chandelier Lyla had momentarily turned into a volcano. But not wanting to hurt her friend's feelings, she quickly added, "The Pumpkin King is pretty particular about how we do things. But don't worry, I'll show you both what to do. Come on!"

Thankfully, it didn't take long to get Vlad and Lyla up to speed with what needed to be done that night. To Eve's relief, and the relief of many a scarecrow, they proved to be quick learners with some of the more straightforward tasks on the farm. They stayed together for the most part, Lyla and Vlad helping Eve with whatever was needed of her.

Despite Lyla's and Eve's protests, Vlad insisted on taste testing everything he could, knowing full well it would make him feel queasy. Peaty, on the other hand, loved it, and took to following Vlad around and eating the remnants of whatever Vlad sampled. Soon the two were inseparable.

At first, the scarecrows kept their distance from the young

vampire and witch, watching carefully as the three splashed around in a cranberry bog and only intervening when one of them was about to do something wrong—like when Lyla picked a berry clockwise instead of counterclockwise. Scrags was the first to accept them, offering a soaking-wet Vlad help with a wheelbarrow full of cranberries. Shortly after, the other scarecrows started to follow suit.

"Thank you," Eve said to Scrags, giving him a warm smile. She appreciated him making the effort.

"I's do it for yous, Prin'sis," he said.

The Pumpkin King showed up around middling-night, when the moon was at its peak and surrounded by the dark of a starless sky. He watched intently while the three worked alongside two scarecrows, cleaning the cranberries they had plucked. They were to be used for sauce at the festival and required a special type of bathing. Yet, despite his best efforts, even the Pumpkin King couldn't find much wrong with the way they were working.

Silently, he walked over to them.

Everyone stared up expectantly at him, and Eve could tell the two scarecrows were a little concerned that maybe they shouldn't be helping the outsiders.

To everyone's surprise, the Pumpkin King grabbed a nearby apron the size of a bedsheet, wrapping it around his broad torso.

"Scooch over," he rumbled to Vlad, taking his place beside the group and beginning to help wash.

Eve looked up at him as he hunched over the wash barrel with all of them, and a warm feeling spread through her chest.

The remainder of the night whistled by like wind in a storm, and to Eve's immense pleasure, the Pumpkin King invited both Vlad and Lyla back the next night. And the night after that. And the night after that. Until invitations were no longer necessary, and the sighting of Vlad and Lyla floating down on a broom was becoming a typical part of the evening routine.

The three were closer than ever, and often inseparable on the farm. If they weren't busy preparing for the Harvest Festival, they could usually be found huddled together in a field or lying across the side of a hill. Eve would read quietly by torchlight, looking up every so often to see Vlad fidgeting with some invention he had brought while Lyla practiced her magic on things about the farm. The scarecrows had learned to tie down a lot of the equipment after a few instances of Lyla causing things to float off and then having to chase them down on her broom.

No one loved their visits more than the Pumpkin King's horse, Peaty, who would follow Vlad around hoping for food. Of course, by now, Vlad had already tried most of what the farm had to offer, but that didn't stop him from sneaking food to Peaty at every opportunity.

Yet, as much as Eve loved their company, it was never quite enough to fully distract her from the fact she still needed to win over the rest of the village and sway Mayor Brumple to her side. Which is why, even long after Vlad and Lyla had left each night, Eve pressed on. She'd scarf down her thirdmeal and rush right back outside, tirelessly preparing for Hallowell's beloved Harvest Festival, determined to prove that *living* or not, she could make it as great as it had ever been before. Maybe then her friends would be right, and the undead of the village might finally start to see her as the Pumpkin Princess and accept her as one of their own.

As the week leading up to Harvest Festival ticked by, the farm became a scene of nonstop activity.

Carts began to arrive almost hourly, each somehow more full than the last. Decorations and supplies were sent from the village, enchantments and entertainment from the witches, meats and game from werewolves in their forest. All seemed eager to contribute, even the emissaries from Castle Dracula, who brought dozens of barrels of wine and grapes (though they also came with a nasty letter from Baroness La'Ment that the Pumpkin King refused to read aloud).

He in turn had remained so busy that it felt like Eve only ever saw him at meals. Meanwhile, she, Vlad, and Lyla helped Scrags in whatever way they could.

Until finally, the night of the Harvest Festival had arrived, and whether in ornate black carriages, wagons pulled by trolls, or by walking, crawling, or flying, denizens from all across the Hallowell Valley began arriving at the Pumpkin King's farm.

Eve quickly realized why it was everyone's favorite night of the year.

The farm was positively bursting at the seams with everything fall, like one big send-off for what remained of autumn. Golden fields had been harvested, and the farm was stacked with freshly baled hay for everyone to sit on. Candles bewitched by Lyla (then double-checked by her mother) floated freely over trails and gathering areas. Clusters of glowing jack-o'-lanterns lined the various walkways and paths, leading everyone to the field that had been cleared out in front of the barn—Eve, Vlad, and Lyla had done most of the pumpkin carving. When she asked if it was weird, decorating the Pumpkin King's farm with other, smaller versions of himself, Vlad explained that it was an old tradition originally started in the Pumpkin King's honor, and one that carried on from the early years of Hallowell.

And, if all the amazing decorations weren't enough, there were also the smells wafting from the kitchens: the savory scents of soups and stews, potatoes and stuffing, sauces and casseroles, all intermingled with the sweet smell of puddings, candies, pies, and cakes—Eve could practically taste the air. As far as she was concerned, the scarecrows had completely outdone themselves with their cooking. They paraded it around the farm, serving it proudly from trays—even when guests didn't necessarily want any. Poor

Peaty on the other hand looked like he was going to faint from temptation.

Overhead, the moon was full and round and shining a silvery orange, as if it too were dressed for the Harvest Festival. Eve stood beside the Pumpkin King at the main entrance, a tall arch formed from stalks of corn and wheat, covered in the warm light of nearby torches. Here he greeted each and every individual as they arrived, a mug of ale in one hand while the other rested proudly on Eve's shoulder. He wasted no time introducing her to the many that she had yet to meet, his voice booming loudly every time he said the words "My new daughter" or "Pumpkin Princess." By now most of the valley had heard of the *living girl* in their midst and, while many seemed curious to meet her, there were still some who appeared less than pleased by her mere existence.

Eve couldn't help but feel overwhelmed. Not only did years of being on her own make her a bit awkward in front of so many new faces, but combined with the exhaustion of prepping for the festival and the nerves about what was at stake, Eve was fairly certain she might implode on the spot. But something about having the Pumpkin King beside her made Eve feel emboldened, and whether it was his confidence building her own, or that it was something else entirely, Eve slowly began to feel more at ease.

She curtsied to witches, waved politely to ghosts, was lifted by the Pumpkin King to shake the hands of trolls, struggled with which eye to look into on giant spiders, and said hello to every other undead who called Hallowell home. Thankfully, it was only a few who looked at her the same way Peaty hungrily looked at apples—those undead the Pumpkin King hurried along and told her to watch out for. She was wiping spiderwebs off her hands when she heard a familiar witch's voice.

"Hi, Eve!"

Eve broke into a large smile when she saw Lyla standing before her.

She was wearing her typical black skirt and scrunched-up witch's hat. Her mother, Seline, stood happily beside her, shaking hands with the Pumpkin King.

"The festival looks as inviting as ever," Seline was telling him.

"How's it going up here?" Lyla asked Eve as the other two conversed.

"I've never said so many hellos in all my life," Eve whispered back. "My cheeks are killing me from all this smiling."

"Can you get away? I think Vlad is already here, and we need to stop him before he eats something that makes him sick."

"He's here," Eve said. "Came through a little bit ago with the La'Ments. But I . . ." Eve faltered. As much as she wanted to run off with Lyla and find Vlad, she knew how important it was for her to meet as many undead as she could and make a good impression. "I should probably stay up here and greet the guests," Eve muttered, her shoulders drooping slightly. She knew Lyla would understand, but still, Eve was a little let down she wouldn't get to enjoy the festival with her and Vlad.

There was a loud grunt from Eve's right.

"Hrmph, no," interrupted the Pumpkin King. "This is your first Harvest Festival, and you have worked hard at it. You should be with your friends."

Eve hesitated. "Are you sure? What about the . . . well, you know?"

"I am sure. There is no reason you can't make a good impression while also enjoying the festival. Go."

Eve smiled up at him, and before Seline could even finish saying, "Run along, you two," Lyla had grabbed Eve's arm and pulled her toward the festival.

The two dodged in and out of talking and laughing crowds, making their way to all the food set out before the barn. To neither of their surprise, that's where they found Vlad, staring longingly at a plate of bread rolls slathered in butter.

"You know he got something specifically for you, right?" Eve asked.

Vlad looked up from behind his round spectacles. "Come again?"

"The Pumpkin King. He ordered some really fancy blood sausage made with extra blood from the butcher's shop," Eve answered. "He didn't want everyone to eat them all before you could try them, though, so he hid some."

"What? He did? For me? Where?"

Eve and Lyla both laughed.

"Come on, I'll show you," Eve said. She led them off to the side of one of the fields where there sat a few tables covered in large barrels dripping with crimson fluid. At the end were several dishes that looked a little too raw and unappetizing for Eve, but she saw that several vampires and werewolves disagreed and were happily partaking.

"The good stuff he hid for you below the table," Eve said, pointing under the checkered tablecloth.

She had barely finished the sentence when Vlad dove under, returning with a platter of ready-to-burst blood sausage.

"I didn't realize vampires and werewolves ate all the same food?" Eve asked curiously, watching the two different groups enjoying the feast together.

"Kin' ohm—" Vlad took a massive swallow before repeating himself. "Kind of, but also not exactly. Werewolves will eat the whole thing, meat and all. Vampires *typically* just drain the blood from the meat or whatever and get the flavor that way. That was always too much work for me, though. I prefer the werewolf method, even if it makes me a little ill."

"That's like me when my mom bakes sunflower seeds," Lyla

143

commented. "Taking off the shell is too much work. I just eat the whole thing."

"Yeah . . . ," Eve began slowly. "You're definitely not supposed to eat the shell, Lyla."

"Still here," said Lyla with a shrug.

The three continued to talk (well, Vlad ate; meanwhile Eve and Lyla kept daring one another to sample a ghost pepper—something the Pumpkin King grew that was so spicy, even ghosts could taste them. In the end, neither was willing to risk it). Around them, undead feasted and socialized, enjoying the Harvest Festival.

Eve felt a sense of pride swelling in her, watching as all her hard work paid off before her. It was something she had never felt before, providing for others in a way she never could have at the orphanage. In that moment, Eve felt somehow closer to the Pumpkin King, as if she suddenly understood him that much better.

"Can we go watch the pie-eating contest?" Vlad eventually asked. "I want to see if Gribmor the troll can beat his record."

"Sure," Eve said, now equally excited to go see a troll eat a lot of pies. "I think Scrags is the judge. Let's go find him."

As they made their way through the festival, Eve became distracted by a particularly noisy group of zombies and accidentally walked straight into someone.

The figure spun, and a familiar skeleton's face erupted into a smile.

"Evelyn!" Ellie cried. "Oh my, you—*hiccup*—look ador'ble! My clothing suits you well," she added, eyeing Eve's outfit up and down between her slurred words.

"Thanks, Ellie," Eve said politely, happy to see a face she recognized among the undead.

Ellie took a deep swig from a smoking chalice she was holding. Beside her stood her husband, Franklin, asking a mummy about vintage fabrics while Digsy proudly shoveled mashed potatoes onto dishes nearby.

"Although, I do say—*hiccup*—" Ellie mumbled, reaching for a needle and string from her purse and grabbing a handful of Eve's sleeve. "Your shirt could use some adjusting, right about—"

Suddenly, it was as if the earth had been pulled right out from under Ellie's feet. In the blink of an eye, her bony legs shot backwards out of her dress and she stumbled skull first into Eve. Eve felt a pinch in her arm and the two fell heavily to the ground together, colliding with the table on the way and sending mashed potatoes flying everywhere, covering several nearby bystanders.

"My's potatoes!" came Digsy's concerned voice.

"I do say, Ellie dear," said an abashed Franklin.

Then another familiar voice worried over. "Oh my, is everyone all right?"

Eve looked up and saw a concerned Mother Morrigan leaning over them.

"I'm okay," Eve answered as Vlad and Lyla helped her to her feet. "Are you okay, Ellie?"

"I—I don't know what's gotten in'na me," Ellie said, looking embarrassed. "I've barely drunk a drop."

"Come now, Ellie," Mother Morrigan consoled. "Let me get you up—no, dearie, hand me the sewing kit first before you poke anyone—all right, there you go." She helped the confused-looking skeleton up. Then, with a flick of her wand, the mashed potatoes covering both Eve and Ellie disappeared.

"Wow, thanks," Eve said, surprised.

Mother Morrigan gave her a quick wink.

"Hey!" fretted Digsy. "What did yous do with my potatoes?"

But Eve felt herself distracted by something other than vanishing potatoes; every nearby undead was watching the scene unfold, feverishly whispering and murmuring into one another's ears. And there she was, the Pumpkin Princess, causing a scene at the Harvest Festival. Her cheeks flushed with embarrassment, acutely aware of every eye on her. Several undead were openly pointing now, and Eve hoped that the Pumpkin King hadn't seen. Or worse, the mayor . . .

In that moment, more than anything, Eve wanted to disappear and find a quiet place to be alone with Vlad and Lyla, the two people she felt most comfortable with, and the only two she knew weren't judging her right now.

A soft hand found her shoulder, and Eve turned to see Mother Morrigan looking gently back at her.

"Why don't you three go ahead and run along," Mother Morrigan said with a knowing smile. "I think I'll stay and tend to Ellie here. I'm sure I have something in my bag to clear that skull right up."

"Yeah, I—thanks," Eve muttered, once more feeling saved by Mother Morrigan. "It was, um, nice seeing you, Ellie. Your dress is gorgeous, by the way."

Ellie beamed at the compliment before turning to a potion Mother Morrigan offered her. Eve then took the opportunity to escape alongside Vlad and Lyla.

To Eve's relief, they were able to break from the commotion and find a bench on the outskirts of the farm, lit only by the flickering yet quiet eyes of jack-o'-lanterns. It sat on a rising hill, allowing them a good view of the lights of the festival before them. Behind them, a tall cornfield dressed in its own shadows stretched out and into the night.

Vlad plopped himself down on the hill, resting his back against the bench and pulling several blood sausages from his pocket. Meanwhile, Lyla began telling Eve about a new mystery series the bookstore had received. Eve listened intently, already set on asking the Pumpkin King for it.

Eventually, Eve felt her attention drift back to the Harvest Festival going on down below them. She desperately hoped that the incident with Ellie hadn't caused as big of a scene as Eve felt it had. Not just because she had worked so hard to make a good impression with the festival, but because she knew that the scare-crows and Pumpkin King all had too. They wanted Hallowell to accept her just as badly as she did (Scrags maybe even more), each knowing what was at stake in getting the undead to accept Eve: to let her stay in her new home.

Her home. Even the idea still felt somewhat foreign to her.

Just as new to her was the notion that somewhere below, in the midst of the Harvest Festival, was the Pumpkin King, her—

"You're bleeding," Lyla said suddenly, pointing to Eve's arm.

Eve looked down and saw red seeping through her white sleeve.

"Hmm. Ellie must have accidentally stabbed me with her nee-dle when she was trying to adjust my shirt." Eve frowned, eyeing the red stain.

"She did seem . . . a bit wobbly," Vlad commented. "Could have been what she was drinking."

"I didn't even know skeletons *could* drink," Eve said, some-what surprised. "I mean, where does the liquid go?"

"Straight to their skulls," Vlad answered simply. "It's a bewitched steam that floats up and sometimes literally fogs their head. Probably why she tripped into—"

Something large rustled behind them.

Vlad looked up from his snack. Lyla spun around. Eve stood.

"Did you hear that?" Vlad asked.

"I did," Lyla whispered. "What do you think it was?"

Eve stared suspiciously into the tall field of corn. She could see nothing but dark leaves and consuming shadows.

"Let's find out," she said with a nonchalant shrug. Without waiting for a response, she walked into the field, allowing herself to be swallowed up.

There was a moment's delay as Vlad and Lyla hesitated behind, but then Eve heard the shaking of leaves as they entered after her, nervous looks on both their faces.

The corn was taller than they were, veiling them instantly from the moon and lights of the Harvest Festival. Jagged leaves reached out and snagged at their clothes, as if the field were pulling them deeper in.

"Eve, be careful," Vlad cautioned, finally catching up with her. "We don't know who or what it could be."

"That's what we're going to find out," Eve said casually. Yet, sensing the concern in his voice, she stopped and turned.

In the darkness, Eve could just make out the faces of her two friends and was surprised to see that they looked afraid.

They were from Hallowell. What did they have to be scared of?

"There's nothing to worry about," Eve said, her own fear long since bottled up. "This is the Pumpkin King's farm. It's probably just a scarecrow getting a head start on chores—"

The sounds of hushed arguing cut Eve off.

Lyla and Vlad squatted down, and Eve turned openly toward the sound.

Vlad reached forward and pulled her down. "Careful," he whispered.

"You never know in Hallowell," Lyla said. "Could be something evil. Maybe something got out of the Cursed Caverns."

"And you're . . . well . . . ," Vlad started, and Eve could tell he was trying to not say something.

"Living?" Eve asked, feeling herself getting annoyed. "So what?"

"We're just saying, we don't know," whispered Lyla. "It's okay to be a little scared. Better safe than sorry, Pumpkin King's land or not."

"I'm not scared," Eve argued. "And at the very least I'm going to check it out."

She shrugged off Vlad's hand and began to sneak toward the voices, careful not to rustle too much of the corn.

Hesitantly, Vlad and Lyla followed behind. As they snuck closer, Eve began to make out the words of two gruff voices.

"I'm tired of waiting," one growled, his voice coarse, like rocks in a grinder.

"Be patient," said another in a calmer tone. "It will be soon. But not tonight."

"He's parading around down there like he owns Hallowell! It's time we—"

"Lower your voice," the calmer one hissed. "If others hear that we are trying to move against him, it will show our hand—"

Eve peeked through the corn, and in the dark she spotted two werewolves veiled in shadows. It wasn't their burly human frames or muscular arms that gave them away, but their unmistakable eyes. Eyes that shone with all the sharpness and instinct of the wolf in their blood.

"—we will act, but only when the moon is right," the voice continued. "We just—what's that? Do you smell something?"

Eve froze, holding her breath. Ahead of her, she heard the two werewolves sniffing.

"I smell meat. And warm blood," said the more agitated one. "It's coming from over there."

Something behind Eve pulled on her jacket.

She turned and saw Vlad's terrified eyes from behind his glasses. He was pointing to the blood on Eve's sleeve.

From nearby, the sounds of rustling cornstalks grew louder as the werewolves crept toward them.

It reminded her of the night she'd escaped from the orphanage, with the guard dogs Watcher and Curfew hot on her scent.

The orphanage escape . . .

She had an idea.

Eve, her mind clear from fear, reached into Vlad's vest pocket and found where he had undoubtedly hidden another extrabloody blood sausage. Then, with as much strength as she could, she threw it over the approaching werewolves and far in the opposite direction.

As quick as they were dangerous, Eve heard the two werewolves whip around and rush after the smell.

Eve turned to Vlad and Lyla. "Run," she whispered.

And run they did.

Rough leaves ripped at their clothes and arms as they tore back through the cornfield and out the way they had come.

They emerged panting back into the moonlight. Down below them stretched the glow and bustle of the Harvest Festival.

"What do you—think that—was about?" gasped Vlad, doubled over and looking like he might vomit. No doubt he was regretting the amount of blood sausage he had eaten.

"Do you think they were talking about the Pumpkin King?" Lyla asked.

"I don't know," answered Eve. "But I'm going to find out."

CHAPTER NINE

Haunted Holidays

To her dismay, Eve's recount of the werewolves' argument on the night of the Harvest Festival fell on uninterested ears.

She and the Pumpkin King were sitting over evening first-meal, Eve busy ignoring hers while the Pumpkin King was too tired to pay his food any mind. In fact, it might have been the first time she was more alert than he was this early in the night. To be fair, Eve had no idea when he had eventually gone to sleep; she had tried to wait up for him to tell him about the werewolves, but had fallen asleep by the fire long before he ever came in.

"How come this isn't bothering you?" Eve asked, irritated. "It sounded like they wanted to overthrow you as king!"

"Evelyn," the Pumpkin King grumbled slowly, rubbing at his

eyes. "As I told you, werewolves arguing is not an uncommon occurrence. It is far more likely they were arguing over some internal strife."

"They were talking about owning Hallowell," Eve protested.

"The werewolves have never shown signs of being unhappy with their forests in the north. Trust me."

"But—"

"*But,* now that Harvest Festival is over, we have to start on your winter lessons, as well as prepare for the cold."

Eve sighed. She could tell from his tone that he was done arguing. She wasn't ready to give up on the subject, however, and decided to keep an eye out for anything suspicious. She didn't care what he said—whatever the two werewolves were arguing about sounded bigger than some "internal strife."

"And speaking of Harvest Festival," he continued. "You should know I had words with Mayor Brumple last night."

Eve snapped to. For the briefest of moments, the werewolves scheming had made her forget about the banishment. "And?" she asked, literally on the edge of her seat. "Did he decide?"

"He had only good things to say—"

"So I'm not banished?" Eve interrupted excitedly.

The Pumpkin King frowned. "The mayor is not yet ready to make up his mind, but I believe he is very close to coming around to our side. The Harvest Festival was as great as any year before, and many undead were pleased to meet the new Pumpkin Princess."

"Oh . . . ," Eve mumbled, struggling to hide how let down she felt. She was glad the Harvest Festival was a success, but deep down had let herself believe it would have been enough to change the mayor's vote on the spot. That it hadn't was far from what she wanted to hear.

"I know you had high hopes for the festival, but you must understand," the Pumpkin King began, in a tone that suggested he sensed her disappointment, "the baroness employs many from the village as castle staff, and she holds much sway over them. Yet take this as good news. Soon, what she thinks won't matter, as others form their own opinions."

"Okay," said Eve, trying to take his words to heart as best she could. If she could trust anyone in Hallowell, it was him. "I *am* glad everyone had a good time, though," she added truthfully. "It was fun seeing them enjoy everything we set up."

He nodded. "Agreed. You did well. And, hrmph, so you know, I am proud of you."

The words took Eve by surprise, causing the color to rise in her cheeks. No one had ever told her they were proud of her before. And despite the banishment still looming, Eve somehow found herself smiling from ear to ear.

Outside, the silvery orange that the moon had worn the night before had dulled to a warm rust color, and the crisp smell of recently harvested fields lingered in the air.

Eve busied herself in the pear orchard, but found she was far too distracted to get any meaningful work done. She kept glancing up at the moonlit sky, hoping to see Lyla and Vlad floating down. (The tiniest sliver of her worried that without the excuse of preparing for the Harvest Festival, the two would stop coming.)

What she was *supposed* to be doing was thanking the pear trees by placing some kind of smelly oil at the base of each tree. According to Scrags, pears were fickle and wanted gratitude for their contribution to the Harvest Festival, otherwise they wouldn't be as generous with their fruit the following year. It was one of those lessons that Eve struggled to find any scientific logic in, but learned to take to heart nonetheless. The Pumpkin King's green thumb was unrivaled for a reason, and Scrags knew many of his tricks as if they were his own.

Finally, to her excitement, Eve caught sight of Lyla and Vlad outlined by the tranquil light of the moon.

"Hello!" Vlad called as they drifted nearer. He was holding a heavy-looking red pail.

Eve put down the jug of scented oil at the base of a nearby pear tree and ran over to the two of them. Out of the corner of her eye, she saw a branch move in the breezeless night and knock the jug down all over its own base. The tree seemed to sigh, and all the branches drooped in total relaxation.

"Uh, is that much okay for it to have?" Vlad asked.

"Oh, shoot, now the rest are going to want the same," Eve answered distractedly. She made a mental note to go get more later. A lot more. "I'm glad you both came! I was worried you wouldn't anymore now that the Harvest Festival is over."

"Of course we came," Vlad said. "The Pumpkin King told me to sneak some dirt from the Castle's cemeteries that we grow our blood grapes in, and that he would help me try and grow some blood carrots in it here." He lifted the pail he was holding, showing Eve the crimson-hued dirt within.

"But more important than blood carrots," Lyla said, giving Vlad a look, "did you tell the Pumpkin King about the werewolves last night?"

Judging by Vlad's face, he didn't quite think it was more important than blood carrots.

Nonetheless, Eve repeated to them the conversation she and the Pumpkin King had over firstmeal.

To her relief, they were as annoyed by his dismissal as she was.

"Well, at least the mayor is coming around, though," Vlad said once Eve was done. "That's good news!"

"My mom says it takes him forever to make any decision," Lyla offered. "But every time we see him in town, she tells him how wonderful you are. It's a little annoying actually."

"Oh, gee, thanks," Eve said with a laugh. "Sorry my future existence is a burden on you."

"You're forgiven," said Lyla.

157

"Yeah . . . the baroness kind of does the opposite when she sees him," Vlad chimed in. "Anyway, think we can go find the Pumpkin King so he can show me what to do with all this dirt? It's getting really heavy."

Eve smiled and Lyla shook her head.

"All right, let's go see if a scarecrow knows where he is," said Eve, leading the two out of the orchard.

Thanks to Digsy, they found the Pumpkin King in the western fields, where he seemed to have shaken off his lack of sleep and appeared glad to see both Lyla and Vlad, even dropping his chores on the spot to help.

"I thought we couldn't plant this close to winter?" Eve asked, following the Pumpkin King down meandering dirt trails.

"Never underestimate my skill," he growled. "And, hrmph, that is what the greenhouse is for."

The path came to a sweeping bend that curved rightward along rows of recently plucked green bean plants, at which the Pumpkin King gave a wave of his hand. The ground churned before them, turning the entire path left instead.

It was down this new trail, buried deep in an orange grove, that they found the greenhouse. Resembling a giant, fancy lantern, its walls were made of crystal-clear glass, each pane wrapped in a dark metal frame. The top arched inward, forming a domed ceiling that shimmered in the moonlight.

The Pumpkin King led them in, and unlike the crisp evening chill, inside was warm and damp, like a sauna for plants. Raised planters wrapped the walls and formed rows up and down the long stretch of tiled floor. Picking one, the Pumpkin King set to helping them mix in Vlad's soil. Once that was done (and after an impromptu lecture about which seeds need to be planted under a waxing moon and which under a waning moon), the Pumpkin King took his leave and went back to his nightly chores. Eve and her friends remained behind, Vlad staring impatiently at his freshly planted carrot seeds while Eve and Lyla inspected the different plants in the greenhouse.

Some Eve recognized from her lessons with Scrags, such as the withershade plant and its void-black petals, or the dread leaf lettuce and its scarlet-veined leaves, but others she didn't know, like the large potted vine moving and twisting in the corner, or the bush with jaw-like flowers that seemed to lean toward them every time they passed by it.

"Well, I should probably be going," Lyla said after some time. "My mom and I are making fig stew tonight. It's a winter tradition we do every year after Harvest Festival."

"Fig stew?" Vlad asked, finally lifting his gaze from the seeds they had planted.

"I'll bring you some, but we both know it will make you sick," Lyla said simply. "Just don't vomit on my broom again. It

159

took forever to clean the bristles that night you tried the Pumpkin King's dried apples."

"But they smelled so good," Vlad protested.

Lyla merely shook her head. "What about you, Eve?" she asked. "Do the living have any winter traditions?"

"Mainly just Christmas," Eve said absently.

Both stared at her with empty expressions.

"What?" Eve said. "You don't have Christmas here?"

"Never heard of it," Vlad said.

"Come on, sure you have," Eve pressed. "Christmas trees, lights, stories of Santa, presents? No? Nothing?"

They each shook their heads.

Eve was surprised.

The orphanage had always done its best to try and make Christmas special for the children come the holidays. They would bring in a tree and all the children would help decorate it together and sing carols. Then Eve would often watch from the outside, feeling left out as everyone made one another gifts, wrapping them in gift paper that the orphanage provided.

"Hrmph," Eve mumbled. "Never mind then."

Both Vlad and Lyla laughed.

"What?" Eve asked.

"You just grumbled like Mr. Pumpkin King," Vlad said with a smirk. "You're starting to take after him."

"I did not!"

"Whatever you say, Pumpkin Princess," Lyla mocked.

Eve rolled her eyes and stuck her tongue out at them.

Later on at the dining table, Eve stared at her thirdmeal (diced potatoes and chopped vegetables), her mind elsewhere.

Meanwhile, the Pumpkin King was going on about the soil that Vlad had brought and how he should have tasted it before telling Vlad how deep to plant the seeds.

"It's not soil I've worked with. The only way to—"

"We should do Christmas," Eve interrupted, finally figuring out what was bothering her. For years, she had experienced Christmases at the orphanage with no family to share them with. Now that she had a family, it didn't seem right that there was no Christmas to share.

"We should do What-mas?"

"Christmas," Eve repeated, then set to explaining the holiday to him.

He listened to her, frowning curiously at her as she went through all the different Christmas traditions she knew about.

He struggled the most with the idea of Santa.

"So . . . a man in a red suit breaks into children's homes during the night, eats their food, leaves suspicious boxes, and, hrmph, all are okay with it?" he said. "Yet a witch brews potions alone in the forest, and I have to go save them all from being hunted and tied to a stake?"

Eve didn't quite know how to answer that one, but eventually the Pumpkin King seemed to grasp it all, understanding at least the core concept.

"This exchanging of the gifts, this is something you want to do?" he asked.

"Yes, I believe so," Eve answered. "Christmas is about giving. And—" Eve didn't say what she wanted to. That she finally had someone she cared about to give to. Instead she said, "And Lyla and her mom have winter traditions. I thought we should too."

At this his face warmed up, and a gleam formed in his previously perplexed eyes.

"Hrmph! Then gifts we shall exchange!" he growled proudly. "It will be our first tradition together. We can celebrate the night of the Winter Solstice, under the midwinter moon."

"Actually, it's usually on—never mind," Eve said, catching herself. "I would like that." She couldn't explain it, but something about the act of picking the date together made it that much more special to her. It was equal parts her and him. Christmas from the living, and tidings of the moon from Hallowell. She loved it.

Eve hid her smile behind a bite of her thirdmeal, not wanting him to see how happy she was to finally have a Christmas to be excited about.

Back at the orphanage, Eve had always wondered why the other orphans all got so excited about Christmas, spending the days leading up to it in increasingly annoying states of glee. But now, watching each passing moon bring the Winter Solstice closer, Eve started to understand. Not wanting their first Christmas together to be a dud, Eve's mind had become entirely preoccupied with trying to think of a gift to get the Pumpkin King. At first she had welcomed the reprieve from fretting about banishments and werewolves, but as the solstice grew closer, Eve started to panic. She had nothing.

At last, after weeks of trying and failing to come up with something, she finally landed on an idea that she was content with, but it required a trip into the village. So the following evening, Eve asked if she could borrow Peaty to ride into town. The Pumpkin King was hesitant at first, but after Scrags agreed to go with her, he finally gave in.

Across Hallowell, the remnants of autumn were drifting away like leaves from a tree, and a chill was beginning to settle across the valley. Scrags and Eve rode together on Peaty as they made their way through the now frost-covered Haunted Hollows that lay between them and the village. Shimmering, mirror-like black ice had formed throughout its shadowed pockets, covering the once-mossy tombstones and forming dangerous icicles that hung precariously from the branches of dark and twisting trees. Each time they passed under one, Scrags would dramatically shield Eve with his arms as if she were about to be impaled at any moment.

By the time they arrived at the village—impalement free—a

163

faint snow was beginning to fall, each flake glimmering in the light of lampposts and the town's colorful candles.

Once there, Scrags insisted on waving down a Wayflame for help finding a shop called Plumfeld's Café & Creamery, where he then bought Eve a peppermint fizz and something called a sapsicle—a sugary and minty shard of frozen sap that Eve found quite delicious. When they were finished (and after Scrags was done spoiling Eve with a second and third sapsicle), the two made their way back to where she had wanted to go, the Looming Loom.

While Scrags waited patiently outside with Peaty, Eve headed in, finding Ellie conversing with someone near the front counter.

"Be right with—oh, Evelyn!" Ellie said excitedly, standing on her toes to stare over the shoulder of the tall brunette before her.

"Hi, Ellie!" Eve waved, wading through a rack of corsets usually preferred by vampires. "Are you busy? I can come back?"

"Not at all, hun, I'm just finishing up with a customer," Ellie explained. "This here is Annabelle. She's the assistant over at the village doctor's office."

Annabelle turned, and judging from her purple robes and lack of sharp, werewolf eyes or sharper, vampire teeth, Eve could only assume the woman was a witch (mummy, zombie, ghost, and goblin were all pretty easy to rule out too). She had a round, friendly face, though with a bit of a blissfully vacant look to her.

"Hello, Princess," Annabelle said brightly and with a small

curtsy. "I wondered when I might meet the only *living* girl in Hallowell."

"Hi, nice to meet you too," Eve said awkwardly back, the curtsy throwing her slightly. "I'm surprised we didn't meet at the Harvest Festival?" It felt to Eve as though she had met every other undead in the entire valley that night.

"Well . . . you see, I tried to go," explained Annabelle, who was surprisingly cheerful about it, "but I forgot how to get there and got lost along the way. The doctor had to come find me a couple nights later. Good thing she did too! I was wandering around aimlessly in the completely wrong part of Hallowell. Would you believe it?"

"Oh, wow—sorry to hear that," Eve said, wondering how someone could get lost trying to find the Pumpkin King's endless farmland. Though she seemed to recall the Pumpkin King mentioning a forgetful assistant, and then she remembered why: "Did you ever find that Moon Thistle that went missing?" she asked, wondering if it had ever turned up as the Pumpkin King thought it would.

"Unfortunately not," Annabelle said, her smile faltering somewhat. "Shame too, it's a really rare plant and only grows in certain parts of the valley. The doctor isn't happy it's still missing. She uses it for healing certain magical burns, but in the wrong hands it can be used for all kinds of powerful spells or dangerous moon rituals."

"I'm sure it'll pop up somewhere," Ellie offered, patting her on the shoulder. "No need to beat yourself up. You probably just misplaced it, that's all." Then, turning to Eve, she added, "Annabelle here can be a bit forgetful at times, you see. But that's just one of the things we love about her, of course."

Annabelle beamed absently. "Aw, that's so nice of you to say. But I could have sworn I locked the Moon Thistle up before it went missing. My memory isn't *that* bad."

"Hun, this is the seventh time this year you've come to me for a new witch's hat because you keep losing yours."

"Well, true. But in my defense, my remembering has been extra spotty lately." Annabelle frowned. "And hats are just so easy to lose, you know?"

"You're kind of proving my point, sweetie," Ellie said with a sigh. "Anyway, I'll get started right away on this new one, and maybe this time I'll add some strings so you can keep it tied about your neck when you don't have it on your head."

"No need, I seem to have recently forgotten how to tie a knot as well," Annabelle said, giving a careless shrug. "But thanks for everything, Ellie! And nice to meet you, Princess. You're much prettier than everyone says." With that, the witch spun on one of her black slippers and strode happily out and into the night.

"Um, thanks, nice to meet you too," Eve said, frowning to the air behind her. *Who forgets how to tie knots?* She turned back to Ellie. "She works at a doctor's office?"

"Makes you hope to never end up there, doesn't it?" the skeleton said with a fretful look. "Now, what can I do for you, hun?"

Eve set to explaining her and the Pumpkin King's upcoming Christmas, and though Ellie also had never heard of the holiday, she seemed thrilled to be a part of their new tradition.

"Oh, darling! That's such a good idea, I love it!" she said. "I'll have Franklin finish Annabelle's hat, and I'll get started on your gift right away!"

Back at their homestead, Eve used the nights Ellie spent knitting to begin decorating the Hall for Christmas. She gathered pine needles and fallen branches, making wreaths that she hung along the walls. Candles flickered in multicolored jars that now dangled from the banisters and around the doorframes. Even the scarecrows were beginning to get in the spirit, helping to chop down a tree and drag it inside the Hall. She recruited another group to assist in making ornaments, which they then used to decorate the tree; meanwhile, the Pumpkin King labored on the farm wondering where all his helpers had gone. Stealing some of his massive socks, Eve hung them over the fire that now blazed around the clock, keeping the biting grasp of deepening winter from reaching the inside. (She washed the socks first, of course. Multiple times, in fact.)

Several nights later, Eve once more asked for permission to borrow Peaty and excitedly headed into town with Scrags.

She felt a tad guilty putting the Pumpkin King's own gift on his personal tab at the Looming Loom, but seeing as she had no other way to pay for it, hoped he would understand.

That same night, she returned home to their festively decorated Hall atop the hill, where she quickly set about wrapping the gift with parchment paper.

The Pumpkin King had yet to return from his work, so Eve placed the present neatly under the tree and began touching up the decorations. Several of the scarecrows hadn't quite grasped that ornaments went on the tree and had hung them anywhere they could, so Eve went around plucking them off tables and chairs and relocating them to branches draped in cranberry garland. She found the tree topper Scrags had made for her (a star crafted out of dried straw), then pulled over a chair to try and place it at the top. Even then she struggled, leaning precariously forward as she reached up high.

The chair teetered, and then its legs slipped on the wooden floor, sending Eve falling into the tree.

But she never collided with it.

Eve pried her eyes open, relaxing her scrunched-up face.

The tree was inches from her, her feet dangling loosely over the ground.

Deep-green vines had tangled themselves around her, protruding from two cracks in the floorboards below and holding her suspended in air.

"Hrmph," came a grumble from the door. "You should be more careful."

The Pumpkin King growled, and slowly the vines lowered Eve down before then retreating back through the floor.

"Yeah, sorry. Thanks," said Eve, staring at where the vines had gone. "Do you think you can put this on top for me?"

The Pumpkin King crossed the room and, taking the star from her, easily placed it at the tip of the tree. He studied it, appearing unsure, then he looked up and down at his Hall and all its decorations.

Eve hoped he liked it. "What do you think?" she asked, eager for his thoughts.

"This is part of the Christmas?" he asked, a slight crease forming above his eyes.

Eve felt herself worry slightly. She knew he wasn't the biggest fan of change, and wondered if maybe she had pushed it too far.

"It is," she said nervously. "I—I can take them down if you don't like it."

He continued to survey the decorations, and for a moment said nothing. Then the glow of his gaze finally fell onto Eve.

"No, leave them. It is part of our tradition now. I like it."

Eve smiled. In fact, her whole body felt like it smiled.

"Your present!" She quickly reached under the tree, handing him his gift.

From the parchment, he unwrapped a large holiday sweater,

169

decorated with orange pumpkins and green vines sewn into the knitted fabric.

Ellie had done it perfectly. In a fashion book from Seline's, Eve had found something that resembled a sweater, then added her own decorations to mimic the Christmas sweaters she had seen staff wear at the orphanage.

"It's a Christmas sweater. Do you like it?" Eve asked hopefully.

The Pumpkin King held it out in front of him, studying it with quizzical eyes.

"Try it on," Eve pressed. "I had Ellie make the collar extra stretchy."

Without saying anything, the Pumpkin King pulled it over his wide head, and Eve was relieved when the collar stretched enough to fit, popping back around the neck. It fit snugly over him. The pumpkins and vines danced through the argyle pattern of its thickly knitted yarn.

"How do I look?" he asked.

Ridiculous, Eve thought.

"I love it," she answered all the same. And it was the truth.

"As do I." The Pumpkin King beamed, the corners of his mouth curling. "I will wear it always."

Eve laughed, explaining it was only for Christmas time. "Think of it as part of the tradition," she said.

"Fair enough. Now, it is your turn," he said. "Come with me."

Eve looked up at him, confused, as he turned and headed out of the Hall. She struggled to keep up with his long strides but finally caught up with him walking down the pumpkin-strewn hill (though now with notably fewer pumpkins after the Harvest Festival).

Arriving at the barn, the Pumpkin King threw open the wide door. Inside, Gleysol was sleeping in his stall while Peaty snacked on an apple that Eve had snuck him earlier. Except now Peaty had parchment paper and a bow hanging haphazardly across his back.

"Sorry I did not wrap yours," the Pumpkin King apologized. "I tried, but he struggled too much."

"He?" Eve asked, not catching on.

"Peaty," the Pumpkin King stated. "He is your gift. Truth is, I think he likes you more anyway."

"You—you're giving me your horse?" Eve said, astonished.

"Only if you promise to take care of him. You'll have to clean him and feed him. Not to mention exercise him. Though, I must warn you, he's not fond of that."

Eve was speechless. She just assumed he would get her another book.

She loved Peaty, but he had always been the Pumpkin King's horse.

"Do you not want him?" the Pumpkin King asked into the silence. "I am new to the Christmas. I can try again."

171

Eve looked up at him. She loved words, but right now they betrayed her. She couldn't think of a single one to say.

Instead, she stepped toward him, and for the first time ever, went to wrap her arms around him. His sheer width made it difficult, and while neither of her hands even got close to reaching the other, Eve didn't care.

"What—hrmph—what are you—?" he mumbled, his arms frozen by his side.

"Hugging you. It's part of the tradition," she lied.

He smelled of soil and fall, and his new sweater itched against Eve's cheek.

Slowly, he lifted his arms and wrapped them around Eve, hugging her back.

Neither spoke, Eve not wanting the moment to end and him never one for needlessly filling the silence. Together, they were finding their home in one another's quiet.

And Eve wouldn't have had their first Christmas together any other way.

They finished their night beside the tree, drinking hot chocolate that Eve had prepared. She sat silently reading as usual, only glancing up when she saw the Pumpkin King pulling at the chest of his sweater to try and get a better look at it.

Eve smiled.

"Ellie did a good job, huh?" she said, feeling particular pride over her gift.

"She did."

"I ran into the doctor's assistant," Eve added, remembering her visit to the Looming Loom. "She seems even more . . . forgetful . . . than you said she was."

"Yes. She has always been a bit, erhm, absentminded."

Absentminded? Absentminded people didn't forget how to tie knots, or lose several witch hats throughout the year. "Should a doctor's assistant be that forgetful?" Eve pressed, her curiosity morphing into suspicion. A thought occurred to her then. "What if she had something to do with the Moon Thistle? What if she is just playing dumb?"

"Hrmph!" the Pumpkin King grunted, bordering on a chuckle. "Annabelle is far too innocent and well-intentioned for that. It's those traits the doctor sees in her, not her flaws."

"But what if the doctor is wrong?" Eve suggested, frowning. The more she thought about it, the more sense it made. "No one seems to suspect her, and even Annabelle says that she was the only one there the night it went missing."

"No one suspects her because we all know her," the Pumpkin King growled. "She doesn't have an evil bone in her body. It will turn up. I am confident of that."

Eve leaned back into her chair and sighed. "All right, if you say so." She knew a hopeless argument with the Pumpkin King when she saw one, and wasn't about to ruin a perfectly good Christmas. Especially their first one together.

But even then, she couldn't help but wonder if her not already knowing Annabelle allowed her to see something he didn't.

CHAPTER TEN

A Sleepless Sleepover

IN THE WEEKS FOLLOWING CHRISTMAS, A COLD AND STORMY winter settled across the Hallowell Valley, bringing with it gales of brisk wind, swirling billows of snow, and ground so frigid that Eve began to wear three pairs of socks within her shoes.

When the Pumpkin King realized her jacket and shoes weren't cutting it, he had disappeared for a night only to return with bags of thick gloves, heavy coats, cozy scarfs, what resembled tight long johns, and countless other layers for Eve to stack on top of herself—not to mention a brand-new pair of snow boots that went halfway up her legs.

From that point forward, Eve felt somewhat invincible out on the homestead. She even started to enjoy the winter, relishing in building snowmen with Scrags and basking in the glimmer of a snowy twilight.

Unsurprisingly, the Pumpkin King still managed to keep her and the scarecrows busy despite the winter pressing down on them. They tended the plants protected by the warmth of the greenhouse, repaired fences, practiced horseback riding, kept up with her lessons, prepared for next year's crop, and even covered some of the more "sensitive" plants with warm blankets so they didn't shiver.

Often Vlad and Lyla would show up, Vlad to check on his blood carrots in the greenhouse and Lyla so she could practice her magic freely about the farm. (Turns out, a spell going awry in a wheat field is a bit less destructive than what happens in a bookstore packed with books and shoppers.) And when they weren't at the farm, to Lyla's dismay and Eve's enjoyment, they would find themselves sheltering from the winter in Seline's bookstore. Vlad would tinker with some new invention of his in the corner; meanwhile, Lyla would chip away at the lessons her mom had for her or pretend to stack books; and Eve would read—or help and *actually* stack books.

But as time went by, Eve found the comfort that Christmas had brought slowly start to fade, replaced instead by the worry of whatever the werewolves had been planning the night of the Harvest Festival. She tried her best to be a good Pumpkin Princess, to follow the Pumpkin King's advice and stay out of what he called "werewolf business." But despite her best efforts, the worry only grew, until it was almost all Eve could think about.

So, after several nights of hounding him about it, the Pumpkin King finally broke.

"Fine!" he grunted, sitting in his chair by the fire. He wasn't in the best of moods as he attempted to mend a new hole in Scrags's already heavily patched jacket, poking himself with the needle several times in the process. "I will go see Harlock tomorrow night. If anything is going on in his pack, he'll know about it."

Eve, thrilled to finally gain some ground on the subject, pushed his hands away from the jacket and started sewing it herself. Sewing was one of the things taught at the orphanage, and though she hated it, she was *far better* than the Pumpkin King.

"Good. Thank you," she said, relieved. "I'll go with you."

"No, you won't," he growled, handing her another patch to sew on. "The werewolves aren't fond of—"

"Humans? The *living*?" Eve said defensively.

"Exactly."

"Well, all the more reason they might be planning something. Still, I'm going with you," Eve said fearlessly. "I might recognize the voices from—"

"You aren't going," he said, but he must have sensed that she was about to argue, because he quickly added, "How about I drop you off in the village on my way?"

"But . . . well, all right, fine," Eve said, giving in. If he wasn't

177

going to budge on her visiting the werewolves with him, the least she could do was get a peppermint fizz and sapsicle (or two or three) out of it.

"Tha' goo'," Lyla said behind a mouthful of sweet and icy sap.

Eve shook her head. "You're going to give yourself a—"

Lyla's palms shot up to her temples.

"—brain freeze," Eve finished. "Told you to eat it slow."

She had found her friend on the second level of the bookstore, not long after the Pumpkin King had taken her for sapsicles before then departing himself. Eve was eager to tell Lyla that she had finally convinced him to look into whatever the werewolves had been scheming the night of the Harvest Festival.

Lyla winced, then finally swallowed down the rest of the sapsicle Eve had brought her. "Good," she said. "Now we'll know if the werewolves were actually up to something that night."

"Maybe . . . ," Eve said slowly, "or maybe their leader is in on it too."

"I doubt it. My mom says Harlock is an honorable werewolf."

"Well, he did vote to banish me," Eve commented, still not convinced. "But I guess we can hope. So, no Vlad tonight?"

"Nope. I flew over to pick him up a little after dusk, but apparently the baroness is hosting some special wine-tasting thing and wants Vlad there for it. He said it will probably take all night."

"Poor Vlad," Eve said, feeling sorry. "I hope the twins don't pick on him too much."

"They will," Lyla said very matter-of-factly. "But I'm sure he'll be fine. Knowing him, he'll probably just go hide out in the kitchen with the castle staff anyway," she pointed out. "And speaking of things taking all night, my mom and I are making jam later. Do you want to come help? You can sleep over too, if Scrags won't die of separation anxiety, that is."

"Oh, um. . . ." Eve hesitated. She had never slept over at a friend's before. "I'm not sure, I didn't bring anything to sleep in. And I'd have to ask my—Pumpkin King."

"Ask *your* Pumpkin King?" Lyla repeated, confused. "That's a weird thing to say. Well, I'm sure he won't mind. And you can wear some of my pajamas!" She eyed Eve's lanky frame up and down. "They might be a few inches short, though."

"All right, then," Eve decided, her initial hesitation turning to excitement. "Sure! I'd love to."

"Great!" Lyla beamed. "I already know what apron you can use! And till then, any chance you want to help stack?"

Eve rolled her eyes, but nonetheless grabbed a nearby pile and set to work.

She was making good progress too, at least until she came to the mummy section—then she had to keep pestering Lyla to help her decipher the hieroglyphics on the covers.

Her progress hit even more of a snag back down on the first floor. There she stumbled across Cecilia Shroud's latest mystery novel, *Only Ghouls Rush In*, and soon after, the tower of books she was supposed to be stacking became a backrest as Eve blazed through its opening chapters. She had become so engrossed that she hardly heard the *tap tap tap* coming from the bay window until a nearby vampire spoke beside her.

"I think he's trying to get your attention," said the vampire, a fashionable woman in a tight corset.

Eve followed to where she pointed and saw the Pumpkin King waving back at her.

"Oh, I didn't hear him, thanks," Eve said, placing her almost-half-read book back on the shelf.

The vampire's gaze fell momentarily to Eve's neck, but then quickly flashed up, appearing embarrassed.

"Sorry—sorry," she stammered. "I didn't mean to—"

"Don't worry about it," Eve interjected, putting on a smile. By now she was used to the occasional looks she got in the bookstore, though truth be told, they were happening far less often now than when she'd first arrived in Hallowell.

The vampire smiled back, and Eve saw her look at the book she had just placed on the shelf. "That's her latest, isn't it? Any good?"

"So far, very," Eve said happily. It wasn't often strangers struck up a conversation with her, especially the vampires. "Have you read *Banshee's Burden*? It's my favorite. It's about—"

TAP TAP TAP.

Eve spun back around and mouthed, "Sorry," to an increasingly impatient Pumpkin King. Then to the vampire she said, "Um, sorry, I need to go. Have fun reading!"

Eve hurried outside, where through the window she saw the vampire grab a copy of *Banshee's Burden* and take it to the front counter.

"Well?" she asked, turning her attention to the Pumpkin King. "How did it go with the werewolves?"

"I told Harlock about what you heard during the Harvest Festival," he answered, the wind playing with the ends of his black traveling cloak.

"And?" she asked impatiently, hugging her own jacket closer to ward off the chill in the night air.

"I think it caught him by surprise because he was troubled by it. But he assured me he would handle it personally and that I worry not."

"And you believed him? What if he's part of whatever is happening?"

"Harlock? Hrmph, no, he is an old friend. We can trust him. As I told you before, it sounds like internal politics, and I am no longer the type of king that forces himself into all matters. We shall wait and see what he finds."

"But—"

"*But* we have more pressing concerns than the werewolves.

I see that you were talking with Latia just now. Hrmph, that is good. Soon the mayor will see that the village has accepted you, and this blasted banishment vote can be over."

Eve sighed. She knew he was changing the subject on purpose, but at the same time he very much had a point. As much as she would love to know what the werewolves were planning, she'd definitely like to know her fate as well. She had done her best at the Harvest Festival, and since then, winter had made it difficult to get out as much, but she tried to be as friendly as possible to every undead she met.

"Are you ready to go home?" the Pumpkin King asked. "I'd like to return and squeeze in some work on the homestead."

"About that," Eve said tentatively. "I was actually kind of hoping I could stay the day at Lyla's house? She invited me to make jam and sleep over?"

"But . . . I was going to make your favorite tomato basil soup and grilled cheese for thirdmeal."

"Tomorrow night maybe?" Eve asked hopefully.

"Fine," he said with a sigh, and for a brief moment she thought she saw sadness, but quickly he perked up. "You have a good time at Lyla and Seline's. I'm glad you have friends. And do not forget to remove your shoes before crossing their threshold."

Eve tilted her head. "Is that like a witch thing?"

"Hrmph? No. It's just proper manners." He gave Eve's shoulder a squeeze, bidding her farewell before taking the horses back home.

Eve smiled after him, then ran back into the bookstore to tell her friend the good news.

Later that night and after Seline had closed the bookstore, Eve found herself in a crooked lane surrounded by two, three, and four-level homes, each tilting this way and that.

The Creswicks' residence was one of the smaller houses, two levels and squeezed narrowly between homes on either side. Three small steps with a black iron railing were all that separated it from the narrow street.

The second floor protruded forward slightly, from which two glowing eyes peered down from a round window draped in lace. Eve stared back curiously until the eyes turned and a bushy tail jumped down and disappeared into the house.

Seline pulled a key from her pocket, and with a twist of the lock, the door swung open.

They entered into a quaint living space (but only after Eve took off her shoes), where a thick quilt was spread over an orange loveseat against the wall. Across from it was a small fireplace, its mantel adorned with pots springing with vines and leaves. Pictures lined a narrow staircase that led from the entryway and up into the second level.

"Welcome to our little cottage, Eve," Seline said, closing the door behind them.

"It's a really nice home," Eve complimented her. And it was.

It felt lived-in and cozy, with almost every surface covered by some type of plant or heavy blanket.

Lyla pulled her excitedly through a small door between the family room and staircase, and they entered a snug kitchen. Wooden countertops were lined with glass jars full of every herb imaginable, each labeled in fine gold handwriting. Glass cabinets stuffed full of dishware framed either side of a window that looked from the kitchen into a tiny fenced yard. On a green island in the center sat three cauldrons, all empty.

Seline entered behind them and, pulling some berries from a basket, set to cleaning them in a tarnished copper sink.

"You can wear one of my aprons," Lyla said. "It's a bit messy, but it does the job."

She handed Eve what might have once been a sky-blue apron but was now so covered in stains, burns, blotches, and patches that it made it hard to tell.

Lyla grabbed another that hadn't fared much better.

As Eve tied the apron loosely around herself, a slender black cat leaped onto the counter beside her, nuzzling her arm.

"Don't mind her," Lyla said. "That's just Kedabra. Her sister Abra is in the backyard, probably chasing rats."

Eve scratched Kedabra between the ears. The cat gave a rumbling purr and stretched her spine into a tall arch before brushing up closer against Eve.

"How can I help?" Eve asked eagerly.

"Here, you two can start by mashing the berries," Seline said, handing them a bowl of freshly washed fruit.

Lyla and Eve set to work cutting and mashing, and it wasn't long before Seline turned and laughed at the two faces covered in so much fruit sauce that they looked like raspberries themselves.

With a wink and a twirl of her wand, Seline made the messes on their faces disappear, then tasked them with washing jars in preparation for the jam as she began heating the cauldrons.

"Can't I use magic to wash them?" Lyla complained.

"Probably best if you didn't," Seline said knowingly. "Remember last time you used magic in the kitchen? We practically had to use a Forgetfulness Hex on poor Kedabra just so she'd start coming in here again."

"All the pumpkin sauce came out of her fur! Well . . . eventually it did," Lyla protested. Then under her breath she added, "I really am getting better, though."

Eventually the cauldrons began to bubble and froth, and they each took a cauldron to stir.

As they stirred, Eve began to realize just how much jam they were actually making. "This isn't all for just you two, is it?" The thought gave Eve a stomachache.

"Oh, Darkness, no," Seline said with a faint laugh. "It's for Lyla to take over to the next coven gathering."

"What!" Lyla immediately shouted. "But Mommmm!"

"Come on, it's not that bad," Seline consoled. "Besides, you

185

know how much it means to Mother Morrigan. She hates how little of the old ways witches outside the coven remember."

"That's because the old ways are boring! And annoying. And depressing," Lyla countered. "And did I mention boring?"

"Are they that bad?" Eve asked.

"You have no idea," answered Lyla. "It's all weird chants and reading from creepy old books. None of the magic is even fun—"

"Lyla Gertrude Creswick," Seline cut in firmly, punctuating each syllable with a spoon that sent raspberry sauce splattering across the table. "You are going whether you like it or not. It's been ages since you last went."

Eve tried to make eye contact with her friend, mouthing the word *Gertrude?* in amused surprise.

Lyla rolled her eyes in an abundantly dramatic fashion. "Fii-innne," she drawled. "When are we going?"

"Oh, I'm not going," Seline said incredulously. "I already served my time."

"MOM!"

While Lyla pouted, Seline began to tell them about the jam they were making and how it was a family recipe passed down from generation to generation. Eve could tell Seline treasured it and thought she would too if she ever had something passed down for generations. The thing about growing up without a family is that you don't get many family recipes, or moms and daughters bickering. Which might be why Eve also found herself enjoying Lyla and Seline's squabbling.

A clatter came from outside, followed by the sounds of several pots falling.

"Oh, jinxes," Seline said, looking up from the cauldron she was stirring. "Lyla, can you go check on Abra and clean up whatever mess she's made?"

Lyla sighed a loud sigh but ran out the back door anyway.

"Do you think she needs help?" Eve offered.

"No, it's okay. It's just Abra chasing rats again," Seline said, returning to her jam. "So, Evelyn. How are you liking Hallowell now that you've been here a few months?"

"I like it," Eve answered truthfully. "The villagers don't look at me like food anymore . . . not as much anyway. And even the ones that do don't bother me, at least not as much as the Pumpkin King's snoring."

Seline set to washing a few of the dishes, but Eve noticed her expression change slightly at something she had said. "If you don't mind me asking," Seline went on, her tone somehow different, softer. "I've noticed you still call him the Pumpkin King?"

"What do you mean?"

"Well, you don't call him your dad. Do you want to talk about it?"

The question threw Eve off.

Suddenly she found herself unable to look up at Seline, instead feigning interest in the jam she was stirring.

"I . . . um . . . I hadn't noticed," Eve lied. But the truth was she had; she just wasn't aware that others had picked up on it as well. It was not that she didn't want to call him that, especially with how freely he called her his daughter, but she struggled to ever say it back. The words made her feel something she couldn't let herself feel—scared.

So her body instinctively did what it did best: buried the notion deep down just like it did with the nightmares and fear that had once ruled her life. Because she knew that once she called him *Dad*, it made it real. And once it was real, it was something that could be lost or taken away. She had parents once, two people she was sure she'd thought of as *mom and dad*, but that hadn't stopped Eve from losing them.

Her mind flashed back to the orphanage. To being alone and scared on a bench, entirely unwanted.

"Eve, are you okay?" Seline said. "You've gone pale."

"What? Oh, yes, I'm fine."

"Okay," Seline said hesitantly. "I hope you know I'm not trying to pry. But I'm here if you ever need to talk. You know, to someone who isn't the Pumpkin King or a scarecrow."

"It's okay. There's nothing to worry about," Eve said, hoping Lyla would come back in and they could change the subject.

"You know the Pumpkin King loves you, right?"

"I do," Eve answered awkwardly. She could feel the color rising in her cheeks.

The back door opened, and Eve breathed a sigh of relief as Lyla came in and interrupted their conversation. "What's going on?" she asked. "You two look serious."

"We are," Seline answered, and Eve felt her breath catch. The last thing she wanted was to have this chat in front of her friend. "I was just telling Evelyn about the *very serious* time that you tried to magic your hair a different color and ended up blasting it all off."

Eve's tension melted away, replaced by a laugh at the thought of a hairless Lyla.

Once the jams were canned and cooling on the wooden counters, and after a shepherd's pie for thirdmeal, Eve found herself in Lyla's bedroom for the first time.

A circular shag rug, the color of a blue moon, spread across light wood flooring. A metal bed frame rested against one wall, with another bed made of pillows and blankets created next to it for Eve. Lyla's broom was tilted in the corner; hanging from it was her crumpled witch's hat.

Lyla lit an oil lamp and several candles before jumping onto her mattress, causing its frame to squeak in protest.

"Want me to light this one?" Eve asked, pointing to a black candle sitting atop a dresser.

"Huh? Oh, no, that's for communicating with other witches," Lyla said, hanging her head upside down off the bed. "You write a note, cast a charm, then burn it and the Black Candle does the rest. They're really rare. Mother Morrigan just gave me that one. She's the only one that ever writes, though. She's always asking me to come visit or to check in on you and see how you're doing."

Eve plopped down onto the pillows spread across the floor, where she immediately had to fend off Kedabra for one of her blankets. "Can I ask a question?" Eve said, still wrestling with the cat.

"Is it why am I so bad at magic?" Lyla said unexpectedly.

"Um, no, but . . . Now that you mention it . . ." Truth is, Eve had begun to wonder if all young witches struggled so much with magic, or if it was just her friend. But she never quite knew how to ask without sounding mean. (She *had* planned to ask why Lyla's hat always looked like a troll stomped on it.)

"I'm not that far behind for my age, really," said Lyla. "And I'm great at potions and brewing. At least there I have a recipe to follow. Other magic is tough, though. It kind of has a mind of its own. Mom says I just need to follow her lesson planning more closely and learn to control my emotions, whatever that means." Lyla gave an over-the-top shrug. "I think it might be a little easier if I took classes like others and wasn't homeschooled, but Mom says she didn't go through all the trouble of conjuring me up just to let someone else watch me all night. She's always really liked her time with me."

"That makes—wait, *conjuring* you up?"

"Yeah. I'm a cauldron baby," Lyla answered casually. "Mom picked the ingredients and brewed them herself. Then drank them and, boom, pregnant."

Eve frowned. That sounded *way* too much like a line one of the orphanage staffers had fed her when she became too inquisitive after reading a biology textbook.

"You couldn't learn from Mother Morrigan?" Eve asked. At least then Lyla would still be with family, Eve thought.

"No way!" Lyla said incredulously. "The coven's magic is super old and outdated. It's the main reason witches started leaving the coven a long time ago and moving to the village. Too held up on 'the old ways.' "

"I hate going there. They're always talking about how things were before I was born and performing spells that take entire nights to cast. Last time"—Lyla leaned in really close—"we spent five hours stewing a potion. *Five hours.* And it *still* wasn't even done. Never even found out what they did with it. Probably used it to remove some boils or something. Mom can do that with a flick of her wand."

Ew, Eve thought, wondering what grossed her out more, the thought of removing boils or the idea of stirring the same pot for that long. She couldn't even see Scrags enjoying that chore. Still,

Eve liked Mother Morrigan. She was one of the first to accept Eve, voting against having her banished, and had started to feel like what Eve imagined having a grandmother felt like.

Lyla flipped around on her mattress and began shooting sparks out of her wand for Abra to chase.

Eve got cozy herself, despite the fact that Kedabra was laid smack-dab in the middle of her own makeshift bed.

The hours dwindled as the two continued chatting. They stayed up talking about anything and everything, and about nothing all the same.

Maybe, had they not been so distracted by each other's company, they would have noticed through the window the faint chains crawling around the moon, or that when morning came, the sun never rose.

CHAPTER ELEVEN

The Clock Tower

IT FELT AS IF EVE HAD BARELY FALLEN ASLEEP WHEN SUDDENLY she was being shaken awake.

"Eve, Eve, wake up," came the Pumpkin King's voice.

Then Seline's. "You too, Lyla. Get up." She sounded panicked.

Eve opened her eyes. Before her knelt the Pumpkin King, taking up most of Lyla's bedroom. Eve struggled to discern the look on his face. Was it fear? Was it worry?

"Rise and get dressed," the Pumpkin King said firmly, standing and hunching over so that his head didn't hit the ceiling. "We must go. *Now.*"

"What's going on?" Eve asked, reaching for her clothes and

pulling them on over the too-short pajamas she had borrowed from Lyla.

Rather than answer her question, he turned to Seline. "I've summoned the Council. We're meeting at the clock tower outside of the town square. That way I can address everyone outside as soon as we're through. Can you instruct the Wayflames to guide everyone there? On the Pumpkin King's orders."

"I will," Seline said dutifully.

The Pumpkin King led Eve downstairs and out onto the fog-riddled streets, to where they found Gleysol tossing his head impatiently.

Down the lane, Eve could see a skeleton rushing from lamp-post to lamppost, lighting them with a long torch.

"What's the matter? Did something happen?" Eve pressed.

"The sun never rose," he growled. "Nor has the moon moved."

"It—wait, *what*?" Eve said, freezing in her tracks. "Is that even possible?"

She looked up and into the night, where a silver moon floated dressed in hues of blue. Yet something seemed . . . off.

It took Eve a moment of squinting before she realized what it was: translucent green chains—hardly visible to the naked eye—were wrapped around the moon, fading in and out of focus and stretching across the black sky.

"What are—"

"I do not know, hrmph, but I intend to find out."

The Pumpkin King lifted Eve from where she stood and placed her easily onto the back of Gleysol before then hopping up behind her. He cracked the reins and squeezed in his heels, and they launched forward like an owl swooping into the night.

The inhabitants of Hallowell Station shouted up at them as they passed, many trying to ask the Pumpkin King what had happened and if the sun would return. He told them to head to the town square if they had questions and to head there even faster if they had answers.

Gleysol tore down the lane and deeper into the village, his hooves clacking against the cobblestones with each stride. Meanwhile, Eve kept trying to look up toward the moon, attempting to catch a glimpse of the chains wrapped around it.

Before them, the lane opened up, becoming the village town square. It was a place many of Hallowell Station's twisting streets and alleys eventually led, like a lake fed by numerous meandering creeks. At its center, rising from the mist atop a wide pedestal, was a stone vessel in the shape of a large basin. Hovering within the bowl was what appeared to be a giant Wayflame, and Eve watched as normal-sized Wayflames leaped from it and out into the night, casting their blue light across the confused faces that were gathering.

Gleysol rushed around the crowd, carrying her and the Pumpkin King to a black clock tower that sat on the edge of the square. Toward its top, wrought from golden metal and azure glass, were several complicated clocks all stacked on top of one another, each made of delicate dials and rings. Seeing it from up close, Eve recognized roman numerals around the outermost ring, and within it was another with more golden-laced numbers. Then a smaller dial, where the moon and sun chased each other around signs from the zodiac. Finally, the four different seasons were displayed, each marked with a unique gem. Currently, one of the golden hands was halfway between a winter-blue crystal and a spring emerald.

Coming up under the clock tower, the Pumpkin King hopped from his horse, lifting Eve to the ground and tossing the reins over a rail in hurried motions. With a key he pulled from one of the deep pockets of his overcoat, he unlatched a rusted lock, and the door groaned as he forced it open.

Inside was complete darkness and air that was long stagnant. The Pumpkin King grabbed a torch from a wall, and with an exhale of his breath, it lit aflame. In its small light, Eve saw a series of cobweb-covered beams and posts supporting a stair-case that wrapped higher and higher into the tower. It all seemed to sway slightly, and Eve wondered if a strong wind would not knock it completely over.

"You think the rest of the Council will know something about what's happening?" she asked, still trying to figure out what was going on.

"The Council is meant to represent much of the valley. They

have unique ties to Hallowell's regions and the undead that call those places home. So yes, it is my hope one of them already knows the cause of this."

"Has the sun ever not risen before?" Eve asked.

Before she got her answer, the door opened, and in walked two werewolves in their gruff human form.

Eve recognized the first as the gray-haired werewolf from the mayor's office, the one who had voted to banish her. "You remember Harlock, I am sure," the Pumpkin King whispered to her, before then nodding to the younger-looking one. "That is Fenrik, his son." Fenrik was well-muscled like his father and shared the same wide, square jaw. But his shaggy black hair lacked the gray of his father's, and his eyes had none of the softness. Eve also couldn't help but catch the threatening look Fenrik gave her as he entered.

They were followed shortly after by the small Mayor Brumple in his brightly checkered tie, and then a frazzled-looking Mother Morrigan.

To Eve's dismay, Baroness La'Ment arrived as well, though she too seemed to have just woken, squinting with bagged eyes away from the torch the Pumpkin King was holding.

"Good, we can finally begin," the Pumpkin King grunted. "As I'm sure you are all aware, the sun did not rise this morning. Instead, it looks like something is affecting the moon. I have called upon you to see if anyone might know something?"

There was no response. Only quiet faces looking back at him.

"No? Hrmph, that bodes unwell," he continued. "We must find out who is responsible and put a stop to it. And fast. I cannot express the seriousness of this."

"Serious for whom?" said Baroness La'Ment, rubbing at her temples and sounding annoyed at being summoned at all. "Your little plants?"

"Those plants feed this entire valley," the Pumpkin King rumbled. "Without them, most here would starve."

The younger of the two werewolves spoke, the black-haired Fenrik. "The meat we hunt in the forest does not need sunlight to grow," he growled in a voice that would have rivaled the Pumpkin King's grumpiness.

Eve's eyes doubled in size.

She had heard that voice before. On the night of the Harvest Festival, shrouded in the shadows of a corn field and plotting to overthrow the Pumpkin King. As coarse and angry now as it was then.

"Us werewolves are stronger in the moonlight," Fenrik continued. "If anything, this makes our lives easier. Not all of us get to live privileged lives—"

"Son, quiet," cut in his father, Harlock. "You know well that without the sun, the forest we call home would soon die. Taking with it the animals we hunt."

"There are always . . . *other* snacks," offered Baroness La'Ment, her gaze falling dangerously onto Eve.

The Pumpkin King stiffened, and his eyes blazed with a fire that made the torch in the room seem faint.

Eve saw his melting glare reflected brightly in the baroness's black eyes. She took a step back, and for the first time, Eve saw fear strike her smug face.

It was Mother Morrigan who broke the tense exchange. "I believe the baroness merely misspoke," she said warningly. "Surely, she is smart enough to not call down the wrath of the Pumpkin King *and* my coven just for a snack. She would know we would never let any harm befall someone as important as Hallowell's Pumpkin Princess."

Mother Morrigan gave Eve a grandmotherly smile, and once again Eve felt grateful for Lyla's greatest-grandmother taking her side against the baroness.

Baroness La'Ment shot Mother Morrigan an inscrutable look before finally stepping aside.

"Hrmph," the Pumpkin King growled, wrenching his gaze from the baroness and turning his attention to Mother Morrigan. "It looks to be some kind of spell, but I do not recognize—"

"It could also be a ritual," Mother Morrigan interrupted. She stepped forward, looking far more worried than Eve had ever seen her.

The Pumpkin King's eyes narrowed to a harsh frown. "Are you sure?" he stressed, and Eve could tell he didn't find that to be good news.

Mother Morrigan pursed her lips. "It's . . . too weak to tell. The difference can be subtle sometimes. I don't think we can rule it out."

Eve awkwardly raised her hand. "Um, what *is* the difference?"

She received glares from both Baroness La'Ment and Fenrik, but stood her ground all the same (even shooting the baroness a nasty look back).

"The difference is that any undead who knows what they're doing can perform a ritual," the Pumpkin King explained. "A spell must be done by someone who can perform magic."

Mother Morrigan turned a softer eye to Eve. "Unfortunately, it means that anyone could have done this."

"Which makes finding who's behind it that much harder," added the Pumpkin King.

"Will—will—will it go away on its own?" stammered a fretful Mayor Brumple.

"I believe so." Mother Morrigan nodded. "We may not have to do anything at all. The chains look weak, which is why no one saw where they came from. It's possible someone was fooling around and didn't mean to do it in the first place. It wouldn't be the first time something like that has happened in Hallowell. I'm sure you all remember that troll, Tarlog, and his little rain ritual that caused a yearlong storm."

"Yeah, and it almost cost *that* mayor his post!" Mayor Brumple yelped, tugging nervously at his tie. "And if no one knows what's happening now, then what am I supposed to tell the village? They are going to want answers. Answers we don't have."

"I will address them with you," the Pumpkin King said. "This problem extends beyond Hallowell Station to all of the valley."

"And in the meantime?" asked Harlock. "What can we do to help?"

"If this truly is a ritual, then use your positions to seek out whatever clues we can find," the Pumpkin King answered. "We must discover who or what is behind this."

"Let's just hope the sun simply rises tomorrow and we can put this whole mess behind us," stated the mayor.

"I will still want answers," growled the Pumpkin King. "We cannot risk them trying to attempt it again."

Fenrik made to open the door, but the Pumpkin King reached out a hand and slammed it shut. "We're not done," he growled.

There was a look in the Pumpkin King's eyes that Eve didn't recognize, but whatever it was, it sent a ripple of palpable fear across the rest of the room, through everyone *but* Eve; Fenrik faltered, his father drew him back, Baroness La'Ment and Mother Morrigan each flinched, and Mayor Brumple quivered.

"This nonsense of banishing the Pumpkin Princess has gone on far too long. Can we finally bring it to its end?" he rumbled, addressing the mayor.

Eve snapped to, everything else knocked from her head as she anxiously looked around the room. *Could this be it? Could it finally be over?* she hoped. Beside the Pumpkin King, Eve saw Fenrik shoot his father a dangerous look.

"I—erhm—yes, I believe I have changed my—" the mayor began to stammer, and Eve felt her heart jump.

"Forgotten how many of my staff live in the village, have you?" hissed Baroness La'Ment. "And how they'll do whatever, *or vote for whichever mayor*, they can to please me."

"HRMPH!" the Pumpkin King fumed, steam pouring from his mouth. "Openly threatening—"

"Okay, okay, everyone calm down," soothed Mother Morrigan. "We have more important things, and now is obviously not the time for this. And especially not with the poor girl forced to watch. Can we all agree here and now that we'll put this banishment on hold, and only reconvene for the vote once this business with the moon and sun is addressed, and not a minute sooner?"

There were agitated and resentful nods all around, but nods nonetheless.

So close . . . Eve sighed, her hopes dashed and shoulders drooping. Dejected, she watched as the Pumpkin King allowed the werewolves to finally leave. She wondered if what happened to the sun had anything to do with what Fenrik was planning the night of the Harvest Festival. Was it possible that he could make the sun disappear? He definitely seemed to think the werewolves would be better off that way.

As she stared after him, Baroness La'Ment made for the door and disappeared into the night.

"Don't you worry about her," Mother Morrigan said, snapping back Eve's attention. She must have thought the baroness was who Eve was staring after. "In fact, I think I might have a little chat with our vampiric friend. It's time someone gets her to drop her banishment scheme for good."

"See to it that you do," the Pumpkin King ordered, in a tone unfamiliar to Eve. "I am beginning to lose my patience."

Mother Morrigan gave a firm nod, then hurried after the baroness, a determined look on her face.

"Now, Mayor Brumple," continued the Pumpkin King, some of his anger subsiding. "You and I should address the town."

The Pumpkin King made for the door, but suddenly one of his legs gave way and he stumbled, falling to one knee.

"Hrmph," he grumbled, starting to lift himself back up.

He swayed, and Eve watched helplessly as he crumpled and fell heavily to the ground.

The gust created by his impact sent dust billowing in all directions. The glow of his face dimmed, fading to a faint orange before going out completely.

Mayor Brumple looked on, horrified, and Eve stood frozen in shock. Deep inside her, Eve felt something cold and dark take root, spreading like ice through her veins and tightening around her chest. Something Eve hadn't felt in a long time, something she thought she had buried deep down for good—

Fear.

CHAPTER TWELVE

The Wailing Water Wheel

EVE SAT HUDDLED IN THE CORNER OF HER ROOM, AND DESPITE being surrounded by blankets, she felt cold. Cold and alone.

Two doors down, the Pumpkin King lay in his bed, tended to by the village doctor. He still hadn't moved since his fall at the clock tower, and it was filling Eve with dread.

The door to her bedroom opened slowly, and in walked a witch she had yet to meet. She had strange symbols tattooed on her hands and wrapping up her forearms, not to mention dark brushstrokes of paint under her shadowy and mysterious eyes.

"'Ello, Evelyn," she said quietly, the faintest trace of a French accent in her voice. "We 'ave not been properly introduced. My name is Cleo On'Jure. I am the village doctor."

Eve hardly even registered the introduction. "Is he going to be okay?" she asked, unable to take her eyes from her own hands.

Dr. On'Jure knelt down before Eve and rested a friendly hand on her forearm.

"I believe he will be," she said soothingly, despite the very obvious *but* that Eve could tell was coming. "But when, I cannot say. Would you like to see him?"

Eve thought to the image of the Pumpkin King collapsing, and the light of his face fading. Not to mention the fear she had felt when it happened, fear she hadn't felt in years . . . not since the nightmares.

"No," Eve answered flatly. She couldn't see him again like that, not him. He was the Pumpkin King. He was supposed to be invincible.

"No?" Dr. On'Jure asked, and Eve could hear the note of surprise in her voice. "Are you certain?"

Eve said nothing, brooding instead in the emotions that were twisting her insides like vines. Not wanting to see him made her as embarrassed as it did angry at herself. She knew she should, that Dr. On'Jure even expected her to. That others would expect her to. But she couldn't bring herself to do it. She felt weak and pathetic.

"I . . . can't be scared," she finally murmured, more to herself than to the doctor.

"I see. Then you don't 'ave to," Dr. On'Jure said knowingly. "And just so you know, he'll be all right. In large part, thanks to you."

"What do you mean?" Eve asked, finally looking up from her own hands.

"It was you that 'ad him brought back here, was it not? Doing so appears to be returning some of his strength."

"It's what he would have wanted," Eve said with a nod. "Do you know what's wrong with him? Does it have to do with the sun?"

"I believe so. The timing is too suspect to be coincidence," she answered. "Unfortunately, the Pumpkin King 'as always been one of a kind, which, as you can imagine, makes him difficult to understand from a medical point of view. He's older than 'allowell itself and even more mysterious. In fact, some have suggested he's more force of nature than undead. Yet, that being said, I believe I am starting to figure him out."

"What do you mean?"

"Well, when the sun didn't rise, the fields, his plants, his pumpkins—all of them missed the nourishment they needed from its light. So, it is my belief that they leeched the nourishment they needed from him instead."

"They can do that?" Eve asked, confused. Once again, it seemed there was something about the farm she didn't understand. "How?"

"For ages, his power 'as seemed to grow, the magic around him swirling. I 'ad my assumptions, but this appears to confirm them. His power comes from *here*. From the nature itself and the life on his lands. As 'allowell grew, his fields grew to support it, and his power always seemed to follow. I now believe that connection to go both ways."

"But . . . now it's killing him?"

"Killing him? No, it would take more than one missed sun to bring down the Pumpkin King. It was a heavy bout of exhaustion that took him, that is all. Assuming the sun returns at dawn, he'll be fine."

Eve looked out her bedroom window to a still-dark evening sky.

She knew better than to ask the final question on her mind. The one with the answer she knew she wouldn't be able to bear.

What if the sun doesn't return?

Instead, she was saved by the door opening. Eve felt a weak smile on her face when she saw who it was.

In rushed Mother Morrigan, even more frazzled looking than she had been at the clock tower.

"Evelyn, are you okay? I came as soon as I heard," she said, worry in her voice as she ran over to check Eve's forehead. She turned her attention to the doctor. "What's his condition? Is he responding to blackroot mixed with chanterelle? What about—"

"Mother Morrigan," Dr. On'Jure interjected, "I know you mean well, but medicine 'as come a long way since your nights. I promise, though, I am giving him the utmost care. We all worry for the Pumpkin King. His stewardship feeds and protects us all."

Eve could tell Mother Morrigan didn't care for that answer. Her pursed lips had turned a bleached white.

"On that note," continued Dr. On'Jure, "I think I shall go and check on my patient and leave you two be."

The door had hardly closed when Mother Morrigan scoffed, "Little Miss Know It All, isn't she? Witches these nights forget where they came from."

Eve barely heard her. Instead, she was too busy worrying about the Pumpkin King.

"Mother Morrigan, why would someone do this to him?" she asked, bordering on pleading. The Pumpkin King had taken her in when no one else would. He was everything to Eve, and him being sick, or whatever this was, was forcing her to realize it.

Mother Morrigan bit her lip, frowning down at Eve. "Honestly . . . ," she began hesitantly, as if she were searching for the answer herself. "I don't think whoever *was* behind this could have predicted this outcome. The Pumpkin King has never shown any sign of weakness before tonight. It's what makes him such an imposing steward, and it helped keep everyone in line ages ago when all the undead were first starting to mix."

Eve hugged herself tighter, trying to not let too much of her own fear show. "You . . . you don't think they'll try again, do you?"

Mother Morrigan paused, worry creasing her brow. But before she could answer, a knock at the bedroom door cut her off. It cracked ever so slightly, and there was Seline, looking in with loving and worried eyes.

"You have a couple more visitors," she said, opening the door enough to reveal both Lyla and Vlad.

As Eve's friends came in, Mother Morrigan left with Seline, but not before giving Eve a concerned look and telling her once more not to worry.

"How's he doing?" Vlad asked once the three of them were alone.

"And what happened?" asked Lyla. "No one will tell us anything."

Eve filled them in on everything that had happened since leaving Lyla's.

The meeting at the clock tower; the disgruntled werewolf, Fenrik, and the angry baroness; the Pumpkin King collapsing out of nowhere; and what Dr. On'Jure had said about his connection to the land and his need for the sun.

"What if it doesn't come back?" asked Lyla, putting words to Eve's worry.

She could only shake her head in response.

"Lyla, you're a witch," started Vlad. "Is there anything that can make the sun come back?"

Eve's head shot up, hopeful.

"Not that I know of?" Lyla answered slowly. "But I've never heard of anything like this happening before."

"What about others?" Eve asked, looking back and forth

between Vlad and Lyla. "Someone in the valley has to know if something like this has happened before. And what to do if it has."

"Well, I think the Pumpkin King has been around the longest," Lyla answered. "He's super old."

"I can't exactly ask him right now, can I? Who else?"

"Maybe the wise old crone that lives down at the water wheel," Lyla offered. "She's got to be as old as him. She's been around forever."

"At the *Wailing* Water Wheel?" Vlad shuddered, some of the color leaving his cheeks. "No way. They say she left ages ago. Now the place is abandoned and, like, big-time haunted. Everyone knows to stay clear of it."

"The coven witches still whisper about her," argued Lyla.

The two began bickering, but Eve paid them no mind. She was already grabbing her jacket for the ride.

"Wait—" said Vlad, finally drawing himself from his dispute with Lyla. "Eve, where are you going?"

"To this Wailing Water Wheel," she answered, half out the door. "Are you two coming or not?"

They told Seline that Lyla and Vlad were going to stay and keep Eve company, and that Lyla would fly the two of them back before sunrise (assuming there was a sunrise at all).

Once Seline had departed, the three of them snuck quietly out of the Hall and down to the stables, where Peaty would no doubt be trying to sneak a middling-night nap.

"How far is this water wheel?" asked Eve.

"No more than a short flight," Lyla answered absently. She had found a pitchfork in a pile of hay and was seeing if she could make it fly.

"Can your broom carry all of us?"

"I don't know. I've already ridden it a lot tonight. It might be a bit tired."

"Um, okay. Then how long by horse?" Eve asked, beginning to saddle up a confused and put-out-looking Peaty.

"A normal horse? Or him?" Lyla asked, lifting an eyebrow at Peaty.

"Lyla . . ."

"Less than an hour," Lyla answered. "But add a little time if Peaty spots an apple tree."

Peaty gave an indignant neigh, and Eve hoisted herself up, grabbing Vlad's hand to help him do the same.

Lyla went and grabbed her broom from where it was leaning beside the barn, and soon the three were off.

They headed south, down paths that wove through acres of farmland, over hills covered in orchards, and between rows of small shrubs and berries.

Eventually, they came to the southernmost border of the Pumpkin King's lands. Here, the purple mists that formed the edge of the Misty Moors lapped at the grass like waves on a beach, shrouding the rolling knolls in the distance with violet haze.

"Well, no time to waste," Eve said, giving Peaty a gentle nudge with her heels and following Lyla into the moors.

Now that she had a semblance of a plan, Eve found herself resolute. The fear she had felt when the Pumpkin King fell was buried deeply and safely down inside her, where it couldn't bother her anymore. She had replaced it with a purpose, and as long as she kept moving forward, she knew it couldn't catch her. Right now, all that mattered was making sure what happened to the moon didn't happen again and that by morning the sun would rise as it always had, and her life would go back to normal—well, as close to normal as Eve had ever had, and deep down, ever wanted.

They pressed on, through mist so thick that it wasn't long before Eve's hair was hanging wetly down her back. Scrunched up behind her, holding Eve tightly around the waist and apparently nonplussed about the wet hair in his face, was Vlad, no doubt fretting about what they might find at the Wailing Water Wheel. Lyla rode ahead, leading them around hill after hill, humming a little tune from where she sat sideways atop her broom.

Finally, Eve's curiosity started to get the better of her.

"How come the fog here is purple?" she asked Vlad, hoping to maybe pull him out of his worrying. "Is it different somehow?"

"Huh?" he said, distracted. "Oh, no, pretty sure it's the same as the rest of the valley. It rolls in from the fog that surrounds Hallowell. But the mist here gets its color from the glowflies. There are thousands of them in the moors."

"Glowflies?" Eve repeated. "Like fireflies? I thought their light was supposed to be yellow?"

"We have those too. I think the Pumpkin King's farm gets yellowlight glowflies in the summer, but it's been a long time since I've had the chance to see any. There are all kinds of colors in Hallowell, though," Vlad explained, sounding more himself. "The purplelights here like eating a flower that's only in the Misty Moors, and I've heard there are palelights somewhere in the mountains that look like little stars, but I've never seen them myself."

They came upon a narrow valley between two steep hills, and Lyla drifted back, hovering next to them. "We're almost there," she said. "It's right around—"

A rolling billow of stale wind snaked through the hills, blowing away the fog. It was cold and warm at the same time, and Eve couldn't explain it, but it felt full of malice. Ahead, Eve could hear rushing water, accompanied by the sound of faint moaning.

Peaty neighed and reared back, refusing to go any farther.

"Whoa, whoa," Eve consoled him. "It's okay. I won't let anything hurt you."

But Peaty was having none of it, pulling at the reins and backpedaling away from the moaning.

"I think he might be onto something," Vlad whispered. "Maybe we should go back. To somewhere safe. And warm. And with doors. Where whatever is out there can't get us."

Eve hopped down from the saddle. "I'm going on ahead. But the two of you are welcome to stay here if you wish. Alone. In the dark. By. Your. Selves."

Peaty and Vlad stared at her, eyes as wide as saucers. Lyla hid a smile behind her arm.

"Didn't think so," Eve said. She grabbed Peaty's reins and led him on by foot, pressing confidently forward.

They rounded the base of a mossy hill, and an uneasiness settled over them. Even as steadfast as Eve felt in that moment, it still managed to chill her to her core.

That's when she saw it.

Rising from the bend of a river that was as black as the night above loomed a wooden water wheel and an adjoining shack. The tiny home looked more like the shadow of a house than an actual one, with derelict shutters that flapped in the wind, slamming against the mold-eaten wooden boards that held the rest of it together. A black roof riddled with holes and missing shingles pitched sharply above, and below, it was slowly being swallowed by the riverbed, sinking noticeably on one side. No light or movement showed from inside, only the emptiness and void of years of neglect and abandonment.

And yet, there was no doubt in Eve's mind that someone—or something—was watching them unseen from one of the windows.

"E-Eve," Vlad started to stutter. "I think we should turn ba—"

The door of the shack swung open, and for a split second, red eyes in a ghostly green face looked at them, mouth open in a silent scream.

Then, as suddenly as it had appeared, it was gone.

"All right, so . . ." Lyla frowned. "Even I have to admit that's a little concerning."

"You saw it too?" Eve asked. "What was it?"

"Poltergeist? Banshee maybe?" Lyla answered. "Either way, not what I was expecting to find. And definitely not good news. They usually only set in after a place has long been abandoned. Which means—"

"No wise old crone," Vlad cut in. "Told you. Can we go now? Please?"

"Not yet," Eve answered. "I came all this way for answers. Maybe whatever it is can tell us where this *crone* went."

She pulled on Peaty's reins, but he had planted himself firmly where he stood. Determined to get answers, Eve pushed on by herself. Vlad and Lyla exchanged a quick look before rushing after her.

"Eve, poltergeists are no joke," Vlad pressed. "And a banshee is even worse, especially for . . . well, you."

"Banshees lure the living to their deaths," Lyla explained. "Which, for you, could be happening right now."

"Guess we'll find out then, won't we?" Eve knocked firmly on the side of the open door, causing Vlad and Lyla to shudder with every knock. Inside, only darkness answered.

"Hello?" she called. "Mr. or Mrs. Poltergeist or Banshee! Is anyone home?"

Nothing.

Despite Vlad pulling at her jacket, Eve leaned in and peered around. The entryway was damp and dark with only two rooms leading off to either side. At its end was a rickety staircase, with rotted boards that gave way at several steps.

"Okay, I'm coming in!" Eve called.

Behind her, Vlad let out a slight groan.

Lyla, however, didn't seem quite as troubled. "Eve, if you die, do you think you'll come back as a ghost and we can still be friends?"

Eve cast her a look, then cautiously stepped inside, followed closely by Vlad and Lyla.

Behind them, the door slammed shut.

The shutters followed.

With a thud and a clap, the shack was completely shut off from the outside world.

Vlad huddled behind her and whimpered, and Lyla chuckled uncomfortably.

217

Then an ominous green light began to pulsate from the room to Eve's left, wrapping the tilted doorframe in verdant shadows.

Eve peered inside. It appeared to be a small parlor room, with two weathered sofas covered in what might have once been floral print. Beside them was a round end table, set with an oil lamp with green glass, the source of the light.

Another light fell across the doorframe behind her, and Eve turned to see the room opposite now lit as well.

It was a kitchen, littered with dust-covered saucers and mugs. Against one wall stood a three-legged table, atop of which a blue candle flickered.

Suddenly, two sconces in the entry hall blazed to life.

"What is going—" Vlad began to say, but before he could finish, the green light in the living room went out.

Followed by the blue candle in the kitchen.

Then the torches in the hallway.

Blackness swallowed them, and they couldn't see a thing in the resounding dark.

For a moment, nothing happened, and it felt to Eve as if the whole world were on edge.

And then, in a blinding burst, the lights came back to life. And when they did, so did the entire house.

The sofa lifted from the floor and flew at them, only to slam against the doorframe.

Plates flew from the kitchen, hurtling toward them.

The table lifted and jumped upside down onto the ceiling.

The shutters flew open and shut, swinging wildly back and forth. The door followed suit, banging against its hinges.

"You are not welcome here!" a shrill voice echoed throughout the shack. "Leave now! Or be prepared to stay for eternity!"

Lyla was ducking and covering her head from flying plates. Vlad cowered down behind Eve, hiding his eyes with both his hands.

Eve, however, was not scared. Not when she had a mission to accomplish, and surely not of something as trivial as a mere haunted house.

"Okay!" she shouted back, casually catching a cup inches from Vlad's face. "But first, I have some questions!"

Red eyes appeared at the top of the stairs.

"I said, leave!" the face shouted, with a voice so sharp it could cut glass.

"First tell me where the old crone that used to live here went," Eve responded, staring defiantly up the stairs.

The ghastly green face with glowing red eyes flew down the stairs and stopped inches from Eve. It smelled of rotten fish and burnt hair, and before Eve had a chance to mutter a single word, the banshee opened its mouth wide and—

Wailed.

The sound was like a thousand windows shattering at once and felt like it lasted forever.

Eve fought back tears from the sheer force of it, but continued to meet the banshee's angry gaze.

As far as Eve was concerned, its glare was barely as intense as the Pumpkin King's the time he hammered his own finger while mending the fence.

Finally, after Eve was pretty sure she had suffered some form of permanent damage to her ears, the wailing stopped.

And the face frowned.

"I'm not scaring you, am I?" it asked, rather plainly.

"Nope," Eve answered. "Sorry."

The lights all stopped flickering and the face before her disappeared.

The plates and cups floated back to their places, as did the table and the sofa.

Eve lifted Vlad from where he was cowering behind her.

Then, at the top of the stairs, the soft glow of a ghost appeared.

It was a normal ghost, like many Eve had seen in town. This one was that of an elderly lady.

Despite floating ever so slightly, she still hobbled down the stairs. She took one slow step at a time before finally stopping in front of them.

She was short and gray, with a small cane that was as translucent as she was, a knitted shawl pulled over her shoulders, and square glasses that hung from rather large ears.

"You're the old crone?" Lyla asked, sounding disappointed.

"Old crone!" the ghost snapped. "Who are you calling old crone?"

"You," Lyla answered. "Was that not clear?"

Eve fought back a smile.

"You come into my house, disturb my nap, and call me a crone! Used to be, children had the decency to keep to themselves."

She strode past them, making her way into the parlor room where she collapsed tiredly into a sofa, floating just above its cushions.

"But you *are* the wise old crone?" Eve pressed, following her in.

"Enough of this crone nonsense, but you can keep the wise bit. I do like that. Now, come. Sit, sit," the ghost said, indicating the sofa opposite her. "If you're going to bother me, at least be polite about it."

The three exchanged confused looks, but with their curiosity piqued, went and sat across from her.

She studied them each individually, staring through glasses thick as car doors.

It was then that Eve recognized the spine of a book propping up a short sofa leg.

"*Banshee's Burden*, that's one of my favorites," Eve said politely. Poor Vlad was still shaking beside her, and Lyla had become distracted trying to figure out what had made the sofa fly.

The ghost stared down at it as if she'd forgotten it was there.

"That old thing? That's one of my firsts. I'll sign your copy if that's what you're here for. Especially if it will get you to leave. I have writing to get to."

"No, we're here for—wait. Are you Cecilia Shroud? *The* Cecilia Shroud?"

"In the flesh. Well, in a manner of speaking."

Eve's eyes went wide and her hands went clammy.

"Ms. Shroud, I. Have. Read. All. Of your books," Eve gasped, momentarily forgetting the reason for their visit. "Is it true you have a pet book-burrower named Fred? Can I see him?"

"Sure. But your vampire friend is sitting on him," Ms. Shroud said with a shrug.

Eve had never seen Vlad move so quickly—Ms. Shroud barely finished her sentence before he launched into the air as if he had just sat on a burning stove.

Beneath where he had been sitting seconds earlier, and coiled into a small circle the size of a coaster, was something that resembled a two-armed serpent mixed with a sheet of parchment, words written on it and all.

"I just thought it was a scrap of paper!" fretted Vlad.

Lyla sighed. "Way to go. You killed her pet."

"Oh, Fred is fine." Ms. Shroud waved, unbothered. "They're used to living within the pages of closed books. It's near impossible to smash one.

"Anyway, I'm pleased to meet an apparent fan," she continued.

"Especially one determined enough to make it past all my haunt-ings. I must be losing my touch."

Vlad looked up from where he was now trying to squeeze between Eve and Lyla, away from the still-sleeping Fred. "I'd dis-dis-disagree," he stammered.

This made the elderly ghost smile, wrinkling her translucent cheeks.

"We actually didn't know who you were. We came here for something else," Eve said truthfully.

She then set to telling Ms. Shroud all about who she was, how she had arrived in Hallowell, how she, Lyla, and Vlad had become friends. She told her far more than she'd intended to, not in small part because she was still starstruck. Eventually, Eve arrived at the sun that never rose and how it had affected the Pumpkin King.

To Eve's relief, Ms. Shroud wasn't like the werewolves or vampires and was genuinely concerned about the sun not rising. Being a heavy sleeper, she'd apparently slept through it entirely. She also worried about the Pumpkin King, which made Eve hopeful she might be able to help.

"Well, that's quite the story," Ms. Shroud said once Eve had finished. "One that would rival some of my own, I daresay. But, alas, I'm not sure what you've come here hoping to accomplish?"

"We were hoping you would know if this has happened before? And how to fix it if it had," Eve answered.

"They say you've been around *forever*," Lyla added.

"Hah!" Ms. Shroud laughed. "I don't know about forever, but surely longer than most."

"Longer than Mr. Pumpkin King?" Vlad asked hopefully.

"Oh no, he's been here longer than me. But trust me when I say I have the better stories."

"That's not hard. All of his are about farming," Lyla quipped.

"Lyla . . . ," Eve moaned. "So, Ms. Shroud, you can't help us?"

"I didn't necessarily say that," the author answered. "I've haunted Hallowell for ages. I've been a ghost, a banshee, a poltergeist, even a phantom. And in that time, I've learned a few things.

"I've learned to never haunt a zombie—it's not as fun as it sounds. I've learned ghosts that haunt trolls are just lazy. I've learned that you're taken more seriously as a poltergeist, but you have more fun as a banshee," she added with a wink. "And I've learned that if you're looking for someone that hates the sun, you might want to start with those that love the moon."

"Fenrik," Eve murmured, recalling what he had said at the clock tower about werewolves being stronger under the moon. Not to mention what she'd overheard him saying the night of the Harvest Festival.

"Yes, I guess it could be the werewolves," Ms. Shroud agreed, "but they're not the only ones. The witches of the coven still practice an old magic that relies on the moon, and the baroness and her vampires would love to see the sun gone as well. No offense, Vlad."

"None taken," Vlad said, shrugging his shoulders. "But the baroness was uncorking a new vintage of wine and hosted a big party last night. I was with her the whole time. So were most of the vampires from the village. If she was up to something like making the sun disappear, it would have been hard to miss."

"And my greatest-grandmother is Mother of the coven," Lyla added. "Mother Morrigan would never let them do anything like this. She's always said that without the Pumpkin King's crops, a lot of Hallowell wouldn't be able to fend for themselves. Besides, it's the werewolves that are moon obsessed."

"Moon obsessed?" Eve repeated. "What do you mean?"

"Well, they get most of their transforming abilities from the moon," Lyla explained. "It used to be they couldn't control when they would shape-shift. But when they came to Hallowell, witches taught them some moon rituals to help bottle up the light of the full moon and put it into amulets. They wear them like necklaces to control their transformations. Since then, they've been moon fanatics."

Something triggered in Eve's memory.

She had heard someone mention moon rituals before, but where?

Then it occurred to her—the doctor's forgetful assistant, Annabelle. She had said the plant that had gone missing not only healed but could be used for dangerous moon rituals.

The question burst from her lips at the same time her mind developed the theory.

"Lyla, if the werewolves got their hands on some Moon Thistle, could they use it in a ritual to make the sun not rise?"

"Moon Thistle? I mean . . . maybe. Well, actually, probably," Lyla answered slowly. "It's supposed to be pretty powerful. But also really rare. I don't know how they would have gotten any."

Eve rushed to explain all about the supply of it that had gone missing. For her, it was one coincidence too many.

"—somehow they must have stolen it, or maybe Annabelle sold it to them, I don't know. Either way it doesn't matter. It has to be the werewolves," she finished confidently. "But how do we stop them?"

"Hmmm." Ms. Shroud frowned, scratching at her translucent chin. "It does sound suspect. Yet I'm not sure three children can stop a pack of werewolves by themselves. Best leave it to the adults."

"We can't just wait around for something to happen," Eve protested, both unwilling and unable to merely sit idle and hope for the best. "We need to do something before it's too late."

"Well, if it were one of my books, I'd say first you would need to find proof—evidence of what they are doing. That would be enough to stir the Pumpkin King and the Council into action."

Lyla and Vlad both looked at Eve, and she could see the question on their faces.

"Then it's time to find some evidence," Eve said.

Vlad sighed, and Lyla shrugged, and Ms. Shroud gave Eve an encouraging wink.

CHAPTER THIRTEEN

The Grimm Pine Woods

There, in the privacy of the blankets that swallowed Eve's room, they planned late into the night. With the vote on her banishment currently paused, Eve was dedicating all of her attention to figuring out what had happened to the sun.

Despite Vlad's protests and Lyla pointing out every way it could go wrong and they could get eaten, Eve was convinced the next step was to infiltrate the werewolves' encampment and catch them in the act.

Vlad had a general idea of where their camp was, but that was about where his and Lyla's knowledge stopped, as neither had ever been. So, instead, they planned how they would sneak out so no one knew they were going. Lyla knew her mother wouldn't let her go otherwise, and Eve doubted the Pumpkin King would say differently—that's if he were in any state to protest at all.

Eventually, the last hours of falling-night drifted away, and Vlad and Lyla said their goodbyes. Even then, Eve found herself unable to lie down to rest.

She waited, holding back the drapes of her window and staring at the horizon. The faded chains had finally disappeared from the moon, and as the hours of morning came and went, Eve watched nervously with bated breath. Eventually, long after it should have, a weak sun began to drag itself over the mountains, casting a cold and tired light across the valley, like a candle about to go out.

She'd take it, she thought. *Any* sun was better than none.

Finally, Eve mustered the courage to go and check on the Pumpkin King. Inching his door open just enough to see a plaid comforter spread over an oak bed frame the size of a boat, Eve peered in.

He lay slumbering, his chest rising and falling slowly.

He would be okay, she told herself. At least . . . for now . . .

Eve couldn't see how the werewolves wouldn't try again. Especially now that they knew how to stop the sun from rising, for whatever their moon-obsessed reasons might be. And if they tried again, that meant the Pumpkin King was still in danger, not to mention herself. Without him, Eve wondered how long her own safety would last.

Grabbing the heavy wooden chair that sat behind the Pumpkin King's desk, Eve dragged it over to the edge of his bed. She sat for what felt like years, each second scraping by with as much effort as the Pumpkin King's labored breathing. The fear Eve had felt when seeing him fall came back, forcing a quaking tremor in the pit of her stomach and causing her hands to shake. She finally pulled her eyes from him, looking out the window instead and shoving away a tear with her wrist.

This wasn't how her new life was supposed to go. Even as strange as Hallowell was, she had let herself believe this was finally her home. That she had found what she'd always wanted. *But this . . .* Was she destined to be alone forever? Left on her own again and again?

No, she told herself. She'd make sure it didn't happen again, and everything would go back to the way it was. To the way she had always wanted. To how she had felt at Christmas when the Pumpkin King hugged her for the first time.

Eve shook herself out of it, resolute on what she needed to do.

That next night, Eve knew that if she wanted to meet up with Vlad and Lyla to go seeking the werewolves, she no doubt had to keep Scrags from stopping her. (She couldn't really imagine him being okay with their plan.) So, being *somewhat* experienced in the art of getting out of places, Eve had pulled a page from one of her first escape attempts from the orphanage.

Then, when Scrags came knocking on her door for firstmeal, Eve explained how very, very ill she was feeling, and how what she really needed was a night of rest in bed. Unsurprisingly, this sent Scrags into a bit of a tizzy, and he checked Eve's forehead about a dozen times before promising to whip up some home-made chicken noodle soup, which Eve agreed to eat for thirdmeal *after* she rested. Once he was gone, Eve crammed some pillows into her bed to make it look as if she were sleeping, then snuck from the Hall and out to get Peaty.

And just like that, she was off, thinking how easy escaping the orphanage would have been if the hounds Curfew and Watcher hadn't been there. Yet, the farther she got, the worse and worse she felt about lying to Scrags. Had it not been for Eve repeat-edly telling herself it was for the greater good of the Pumpkin King, she probably would have run back and apologized. Still, she made the mental note of finding a way to make it up to him. Maybe he'd like some new gloves, Eve hoped.

As planned, Vlad, Lyla, and Eve met on the outskirts of one of Castle Dracula's blood vineyards.

Lyla floated down from atop her broom just as the night was turning from gray to blue. Vlad appeared shortly after the sun had gone down, making his way out of the castle and meeting them at the edge of a vine bursting with crimson-red grapes.

"Everyone ready?" Eve asked.

231

"No," Vlad said dejectedly.

"Not yet," Lyla said, pulling a vial out from a pocket of her black skirt. "First you should drink this, Eve."

"What is it?" Eve asked, staring at the blue bubbling concoction.

"What's it taste like?" asked Vlad.

Lyla rolled her eyes at him.

"It's to hide Eve's scent," she said. "Vlad and I are undead, but the werewolves will smell something living coming from a mile away. If we want to sneak in undetected, we can't have Eve smelling like a buffet. It's an old recipe of Mother Morrigan's. I brewed it myself."

"*You* brewed it?" Eve asked, hesitating to take it.

Lyla rolled back her head and her mouth opened in a large sigh.

"My wand-work might not be the best, but I'm really quite good at brewing cauldron spells," she said, shaking her head. "It's safe, I promise."

Eve studied the vial, its contents fizzing and crackling as Lyla pulled the stopper and offered it out to her.

Deciding she didn't really have a choice, Eve shrugged her shoulders and swallowed down the potion in three quick gulps.

Her fingers and toes went cold—then it spread to her arms and legs.

It felt like all the blood in her was rushing inward.

"Whoa," Vlad said, leaning forward and sniffing Eve. "I don't know about a werewolf, but it would fool me. I can't smell the living on you at all."

"Can you normally?" asked Eve.

"Oh, always."

"He's not the only one," Lyla said. "You're like a living-scented candle."

"Gee, thanks," Eve murmured.

"You're welcome," Lyla said happily. "And I told you my cauldron-craft is good. Now we can go."

Vlad and Eve both hopped atop Peaty while Lyla mounted her broom, and together they set out.

The spires of Castle Dracula faded behind them as they made their way north, through vineyards of blood-red grapes that slowly turned to barren fields of grass and dirt. Ahead, rising and falling with the foothills of the mountains, a line of towering pines grew ever closer, like the imposing wall of some great fortress.

"This is the Grimm Pine Woods?" Eve asked once they'd reached the forest's edge.

"Yep." Vlad gulped from behind her. "The werewolf encampment is somewhere deeper in. Hopefully not too deep, though."

"What do you mean?" Eve asked.

"The Cursed Caverns are on the other side," Vlad answered. "We definitely don't want to go there."

Lyla nodded her head in agreement. "Last year, a kid went in on a dare and got lost for like two nights. He was found eventually, but hasn't said a word since," she explained. "Oh, and unless you want Peaty to become werewolf food, we should go into the forest on foot."

Eve nodded and hopped down, followed by a nervous Vlad, though nowhere near as nervous-looking as Peaty. The horse bit and pulled at Eve's sleeve, trying to get her away from the tree line.

"It's okay," she assured him. "I'll be back before you know it. Just don't go anywhere without me, promise?"

He gave an uneasy neigh, then began to pace back and forth.

Lyla strapped her broom to the side of his saddle, and then she and Eve crossed into the forest. Then both reached back out and grabbed Vlad, pulling him after them.

Giant evergreens loomed over them, growing closer and closer until all they could see in every direction was forest. Overhead, trace moonlight cut swaths through the branches, gleaming off pine needles glittering with frost. Yet something about the forest seemed to sap the chill from what remained of winter.

It was strangely warm, like being near the side of a campfire. Sheltered from the wind by the trees, the air felt heavy, thick with the smell of damp bark and pine. It was no wonder no snow had stuck, instead leaving the ground spotted with mirror-like puddles that shone with the evergreens and stars above.

The three walked in silence, all too on edge to mutter a word. The only sound was that of ravens cawing at them from overhead.

They made their way deeper in, over a forest floor that rose and fell with the hills; meanwhile, the surrounding air continued to get warmer and warmer. With each step Eve felt less and less like she was in the woods at all, but rather in the belly of some strange creature, surrounded by a rib cage of pine trees that seemed to pulse with every hot breath.

Finally, they descended down the side of a steep knoll and came to a wide and deep hollow.

There was a clearing ahead, its edges lined with trees chopped to their stumps and grass trodden until it became dirt.

They could just make out the backs of makeshift cabins clustered together.

"That's one of the werewolf encampments ahead," Lyla whispered.

A violent light burned from somewhere in the middle of the huts, casting shadows out toward them. Eve could hear gruff voices and shouts.

"Something is going on," Eve said, straining her ears. "We need to get closer. Follow me."

She sprinted across muddy grass and over broken tree stumps, reaching the back wall of the outermost cabin with Lyla and Vlad close behind.

Carefully, she snuck to the edge and peered around.

At the center of the encampment, surrounded by werewolves in their human form, was a blazing fire that shed its rippling light into the night and across the huts. Even from where Eve was, she could feel the heat of it radiating off her cheek.

The werewolves seemed to be congregating, all facing and shouting toward the pyre. Save for two, who were arguing with one another and addressing the riotous crowd in turn.

"It's time! Time to rise up against this complacency!" shouted one of the werewolves at the center.

Eve recognized his voice immediately. It was Fenrik.

The werewolf next to him Eve recognized as well. His father, Harlock.

She saw him say something, addressing both his son and the crowd, but his voice was guarded and quiet, and did not carry as far as his son's.

Eve began to edge slowly around the side of the cabin. Ahead, about halfway between them and the mob, was an unattended cart full of chopped lumber. A perfect spot to hide and listen in.

Eve scooted forward, and with a quick glance for prying eyes, darted out and slipped underneath it.

A nonplussed Lyla followed suit, as did an extremely reluctant Vlad.

Scrunched together, the three lay low in the cold mud under the cart.

"—I urge you all, patience," Harlock was saying. "I understand your concerns. I have lived through them myself. But rushing this will not play out as you hope, I assure you."

"You're out of time, old man!" Fenrik shouted. "We're tired of hiding! It's our turn to shine in the moonlight. I demand we perform the ritual tonight!"

Several in the crowd cheered and roared in support.

"The ritual?" Vlad whispered fearfully.

"Shhh!" Eve hushed, trying to decipher what she was seeing. She inched slightly forward, listening intently as Harlock began to respond.

"Fine, if you can no longer be reasoned with, then we will bring it to a vote, as is custom," said Harlock sternly, and Eve could see the trepidation on his face. "But, Fenrik, son, understand I can't undo this when it's done."

The crowd began to cluster closer together, and finally after several minutes began to break apart, turning and once again making room at its center for Fenrik and Harlock.

It was then that Eve saw two yellow eyes staring their way, boring holes into where they lay beneath the cart.

"Don't. Move. A. Muscle," Eve breathed.

The three held their breath, all catching sight of the werewolf.

He stared for a moment longer, and, to Eve's relief, seemingly lost interest and disappeared back into the crowd.

"It's time to reveal the count," Fenrik roared into the night.

An aged and hardened woman stepped forward, her long braid of thick hair even grayer than Harlock's.

"Fenrik, Harlock," she announced gravely. "In the light of the moon, do you both agree to accept the outcome and its repercussions?"

"What is going on?" Lyla asked.

"I think they're voting on stopping the sun again," Eve whispered, trying to get a better sense of what was happening.

She inched forward, squinting into the night and trying to see through the throng.

It looked as if the elder was about to speak, when suddenly something flashed before Eve, and she found herself staring directly into the same yellow eyes she had seen moments ago, now mere inches from her face.

"Run!" shouted Vlad, before Eve could get out a word.

She heard him and Lyla scurry out from under the cart, and tried to crawl back herself, but two strong hands reached under and yanked her forward.

The werewolf lifted her up with arms like oak branches, his unlaced shirt struggling to contain his broad chest.

"Intruders!" he roared, and over one of his shoulders Eve saw countless heads turn. "We have—"

Eve took her opening, kicking forward with all her might.

She got lucky and caught him off guard, and he dropped her heavily to the ground.

Without looking back, Eve turned and ran as fast as she could around the cart and after her friends.

Howls erupted into the night behind her. Even the moon above seemed to blaze with anger.

For not the first time in her life, Eve found herself racing through a forest that was closing in around her, followed closely by voices shouting and the sounds of howling. Except this time she wasn't running to find a new home. All she wanted now was to find her friends and make sure they were safe. Poor Vlad hadn't wanted to come in the first place, and now it was her fault he was being chased through the woods by werewolves.

She sprinted, dodging between trees that whipped by, desperately trying to catch sight of Vlad and Lyla.

Behind her, she heard the rushing of paws in dirt gaining quickly on her. She jumped over a log, then scurried backwards and pressed herself beneath it.

Just in time too. As soon as she had, three wolves leaped overhead and cleared the log in a single bound.

Eve held her breath as they stopped before her and sniffed the air.

They were unlike any wolves she had ever seen: long and sinewy, with hand-like paws and muscular limbs.

There was a howl somewhere in the distance, and the three rushed off like shadows in the night.

Lyla's potion had worked, Eve realized. They hadn't even so

much as caught a whiff of her. She made a mental note to thank Lyla when she saw her—turns out her cauldron magic *was* better than her normally unreliable spells.

Shouts of "Spread out!" and "Find them!" echoed throughout the trees, and Eve's stomach dropped as she realized they were closing in from every direction.

A bush rustled nearby, and Eve turned just in time to see the leaves explode in all directions. Out from it burst Peaty.

Her heart swelled.

"Good boy!" she said, unable to contain her relief. Quickly, she grabbed his reins and deftly hopped into the saddle. Now she just needed to find Vlad and Lyla, and then get all three of them as far from here as possible.

Eve dug in her heels, and Peaty launched through the woods like a bat from its cave. He ran faster than Eve had ever seen him run, even barreling over one surprised werewolf who made the poor choice of trying to block their path.

The trees began to spread out and Peaty gathered even more speed.

Eve was so busy looking for signs of Vlad or Lyla that she didn't see what was ahead until it was too late.

The tree line abruptly stopped and suddenly the ground opened before them into a jagged cavern, like the mouth of a sea creature swallowing a ship.

Peaty skidded to a halt, his hooves digging through wet earth.

But Eve couldn't hold on. She lost her grip of Peaty and was flung forward.

She fell into the cavern, rolling down the sharp incline until she landed roughly at the base.

Fighting through blurred vision, Eve attempted to stand.

Everything hurt. Her skin burned. Her head quaked as if it had been a bell too hard rung. Every bone pleaded not to be moved.

Through the narrow cavern opening overhead, Peaty had to be at least twenty feet, if not more, above her. And to Eve's dismay it was far too steep to climb back out.

She struggled to raise herself, coercing her legs to stand and hoping her wobbly knees didn't buckle.

The cavern walls around her were rocky and damp. Only traces of moonlight made it down to her, but Eve didn't need it. Even in the darkness, she knew where she was.

She was in the Cursed Caverns, beyond the forest and at the base of the mountains.

The same caves the Pumpkin King had once made her promise never to enter. *So much for that*, she thought.

In their flight, she must have gotten turned around and come out the wrong side of the forest.

Eve peered around, but couldn't see a way out. From somewhere high above, she could hear Peaty snorting worriedly.

Then something else—something breathing right behind her.

Eve spun on her heel, but nothing was there. Only darkness.

Yet . . . were the shadows moving?

No, they can't be. It was just a trick of her mind.

Something tapped on her shoulder, and Eve whipped back around.

A clouded shadow floated before her, countless more behind it. With a shapeless arm, it reached out to grab her, and when Eve pulled away, it lunged at her. Followed by all the others behind it.

Reflexes kicked in, and Eve turned and ran in the opposite direction.

She didn't know how, but she could feel their presence chasing right behind her, like a bodiless evil that wanted nothing more than to add her to its ranks.

Rocks snagged at Eve's arms, and the cavern walls tightened in on her like a vise as she ran for her life.

Her foot caught on a crevice, and she tripped forward, smacking her head against the canyon wall.

She lifted herself from the ground just in time to see the shadows pouncing down on her.

Instinctively she shielded herself with her arms—

But only silence followed.

Slowly, Eve peered over her shaking forearms, but there was nothing. No shadows. No movement whatsoever.

Then it happened, the thing Eve dreaded most. The fear she had been bottling up deep inside burst forth and spread through her like wildfire.

Everything went black.

CHAPTER FOURTEEN

Terrors in the Night

EVE WOKE TO A LONE WAYFLAME HOVERING BEFORE HER. IT sputtered with fiery wisps in an otherwise dark world, like a single sapphire in a sea of black.

"What . . . ," Eve began, pressing a scraped palm to her aching head. "Where am I?"

The Wayflame bobbed, then slowly began to float away from her, taking with it the only source of light.

"Wait, don't go—come back," Eve said with a groan. She lifted herself off her bruised knees, pursuing the Wayflame deeper into the void.

Blades of sparse grass began to rise around her feet, but whenever she stepped on one, it turned to an ash that burned her nose.

"Where are you taking me?" Eve asked, peering around for any sign of something she recognized.

The walls of the cavern she had fallen into were nowhere to be seen, just more empty world. She tried to call out for Peaty, for Vlad and Lyla, but the words disappeared into the nothingness.

She began to follow the Wayflame up some unseen hill, and in its blue light, Eve saw two curved shapes ahead.

A feeling in Eve's gut told her something was wrong. Very wrong.

She neared, and the two shapes took form before her eyes.

They were tombstones. Each rising from a mound of churned earth.

Eve didn't have to read the names to know who they belonged to. Something deep down told her that answer before she even realized what they were. She knew it in her heart. She knew in the deepest fibers of her core.

The graves were for her birth parents, the ones she had never met.

Eve's heart felt like it stopped beating.

She wanted to cry.

More than anything, she wanted away from this place.

"Why are you showing me this?" she said in a voice hardly more than a whisper. "Wh-wh-where are we?"

The Wayflame didn't answer but only sat flickering in the blackness.

Then something made Eve's ear twitch. Laughter. Familiar laughter.

"Vlad!" Eve shouted, running past her parents' graves. "Lyla! I'm over here!"

She found her friends in a strange yet familiar playground, one she had spent her childhood watching other children play on while she sat alone on the outside. Wanting away as fast as possible, she made for Vlad and Lyla, only to find she couldn't get near them.

"What's going on?" she called. "Do you know how to get out of this place?"

Her friends looked up at her, confused frowns plastered across both of their faces.

"Why would we help you?" Lyla asked.

"Huh? Maybe because we're friends," Eve said, taken aback. "Now, seriously, we need to get out of here."

"We can't be friends," said Vlad. "You're *living*. You shouldn't be here at all."

Eve's heart was pounding now, to the point she thought it was going to explode from her chest. "This isn't funny. What's wrong with you two? We've been friends since the Pumpkin King adopted me. Don't you remember?"

They both gave Eve puzzled looks, and then Vlad lifted a pale finger and pointed over Eve's shoulder. "The Pumpkin King is dead," he said. "The sun went missing, and he died along with the rest of his farm."

The playground dissolved into nothing, taking Vlad and Lyla with it.

Eve felt something looming over her shoulder that wasn't there before.

Every ounce of her was screaming to not look. To ignore whatever new awfulness was behind her. Yet she couldn't help herself.

Turning, she found a third tombstone, giant in size and towering over her.

THE TOMB OF THE PUMPKIN KING was scratched into the face of it.

"No . . . ," Eve said, panic rising like bile inside of her. "No, please no! Make it stop! I want to go home! I want to—"

Something grabbed her by the shoulders, something unexpectedly warm in the otherwise cold void. Around her, the world began to blur, the tomb turning to a smear of gray before fading entirely.

Eve felt herself lifted from the blackness, and suddenly she was back in her own—real—bed, surrounded by familiar blankets.

Outside, a yellow moon peeked through the drawn-back curtains of her bedroom window.

Before her, two triangular eyes stared down at her, each glowing with concern.

"Eve, you were having a nightmare," the Pumpkin King said. "You are safe now."

The Pumpkin King! He was awake!

Eve went to lift herself up, but every part of her hurt. Her muscles ached, and her skin felt raw.

She scanned the room, making sure the tombstones from her night terror were gone. The effort caused her head to throb.

Her eyes landed on someone unexpected, and her fear spiked once more. Quickly she pulled away from the Pumpkin King, pushing herself against the head of the bed. Whatever joy she felt from seeing the Pumpkin King awake and moving was quickly wiped away.

"What's *he* doing here?" she said, pointing at the werewolf in the corner.

The Pumpkin King stepped aside, revealing a weary-looking Harlock. His hair was combed roughly back, and where the top buttons of his shirt spread open to accommodate his barreled chest, Eve saw a vial swinging from a necklace, full of glowing moonlight: one of the amulets Lyla had said werewolves wore to control their transformations.

"Hrmph," the Pumpkin King grumbled. "*He* is here because he saved your life."

Eve looked up at him, her face twisted in disbelief.

"My pack pulled you from the Cursed Caverns, Princess," Harlock said, stepping cautiously forward to the edge of Eve's bed. "I brought you back here myself as soon as I realized who you were."

"Your werewolves were the reason I was in the cavern in the first place!" she accused. "You were hunting me!"

"No," Harlock assured her softly. "We were trying to protect you. As soon as we realized you were children, we spread out, trying to find you and bring you back. The Grimm Pine Woods are no place for the Pumpkin Princess or her friends."

Her friends. She turned to look at the Pumpkin King. "Vlad, Lyla! Are they okay?"

"Harlock brought them back as well. Peaty too, though the poor horse hasn't stopped shaking. Everyone is safe, despite your efforts otherwise."

Eve stared back at him, unable to decide if she was more confused or hurt.

"We were trying to save *you!*" she said defiantly.

"Yes, yes," the Pumpkin King grumbled. "Your friends told us all about your little mission in the woods, and I've been apologizing to Harlock ever since."

Apologizing? Eve couldn't believe her ears.

"But the werewolves are behind it all!" she protested, fighting to not look at Harlock as she accused him so openly. "We heard them plotting the night of the Harvest Festival, then what Fenrik said at the Council, and they were going to perform a ritual last night! Something Moon Thistle is used for!"

The Pumpkin King's eyes shifted from orange to a dangerous

red, and she saw anger boil into his pumpkin features. "What does any of that—"

"If I may?" Harlock interrupted, waiting for a curt nod from the Pumpkin King before continuing. "What you saw last night was my son attempting to overthrow my rule of our pack. He does not believe I am doing enough for our people. Had he been successful, there *would* have been a ritual to signify the change of leadership, but one that involves moonlight, not Moon Thistle. As for what you heard that night at the clock tower, that was him voicing his frustrations against me and only me. The night of the Harvest Festival was him creating his plot to force me out. A plot that didn't work."

Eve faltered. "But all that stuff Fenrik said about the moon and not needing the sun? And—and that older werewolf last night talking about repercussions?"

"Us werewolves worship the moon, yes, but for the role it plays in nature. A role that must yield to the sun. Without it, life in our forest would come to a halt. Fenrik knows better, but he is hotheaded. The repercussions the elder referenced were exile of whomever lost last night's bid for pack leader. Exile I must now enforce on my own son."

Eve's theory was crumbling around her and with it, her confidence.

She was stunned. How could she have gotten it so wrong?

"I—I don't know what to say. I'm . . . so sorry."

He nodded solemnly before turning to face the Pumpkin King.

"I'm afraid I must take my leave now. After last night, my son will be looking to splinter his supporters from my pack, and I must make sure that doesn't happen. But before I leave, I must know that you understand the impact these accusations could have had if the town latched onto them. We are just now making progress—"

"I understand," the Pumpkin King growled.

Harlock's face turned even more serious and worrisome. He looked to be choosing his next words carefully.

"It does not help that the accusations came from . . . the living."

"Hrmph," the Pumpkin King rumbled, and Eve could tell he had heard enough. "You should get back to your pack."

"I should." And with that, Harlock departed, leaving Eve alone with the Pumpkin King.

Eve stared down at her palms, skinned and bruised from her fall. She found herself unable to meet his glowing eyes.

It was the first real time she had upset him. But that was nothing compared to the disappointment she could feel radiating off him.

"What did he mean?" Eve finally asked into her sheets. "Why does it matter the accusations came from the liv—me?"

After the nightmare she had experienced, Eve couldn't bring herself to say the word. To point out what made her alone here and so different from everyone else.

251

The Pumpkin King sighed heavily.

Eve saw his shoulders sag and his legs wobble.

He must still be weak, she realized. He was only acting strong while Harlock had been there, putting on airs that everything was normal.

The Pumpkin King lifted a stack of books from a chair before settling into it.

"Long ago, the first werewolves were revenants of fallen criminals," he explained. "They were reborn from their sin as undead, cursed to once a month transform and be reminded of their violent pasts.

"Over time, they grew to control their transformed states, and even rehabilitated themselves against violence and crime. Their kind began to spread naturally, but they were forever persecuted by those who couldn't see past their wrongful origins."

"The . . . living?"

"Hrmph, yes. They were being hunted mercilessly when I found them. I brought them here, carved out a home for them in the woods myself, and promised them sanctuary from the reach of the living. But even here they have struggled to shake the prejudices put on them. Something Harlock has worked tirelessly to change.

"Then you, as both someone living and as the Pumpkin Princess, immediately pointed at them when something was amiss."

Eve's gut sank.

"But I didn't know any of that," she argued, and whether she was trying to make herself feel better or him, she wasn't sure.

"It matters not," he answered. "All Harlock saw was the Pumpkin Princess, someone who is supposed to represent Hallowell, persecute his kind further. Naturally, he would have concern."

Eve swallowed down her shame. Painfully, she shifted in the uncomfortable weight of the Pumpkin King's disappointed eyes.

"I don't know what to—"

"And that's not even the worst of it," the Pumpkin King continued. "You put your friends and yourself in danger. Do you know what could have happened to you in those caverns if the werewolves didn't save you? You could have been captured or possessed. Or worse, lost in there forever."

Eve had no response.

She could feel his anger mounting once more and was smart enough to know how in the wrong she was at this point.

"So," he continued, "we're going to try a parenting trick that Lyla's mother told me about. Something called *grounding*. You are not allowed to see your friends for a week. Seline is doing the same with Lyla. As for Vlad . . . well, he'll most likely escape punishment, because neither Seline nor I want to talk to the baroness."

Eve looked up at him, confused.

"What?" he grumbled. "Hrmph, I didn't do anything wrong. Why should I be punished and have to talk to her?"

Eve nodded. Being grounded was only fair. She was sad she

wouldn't be able to see her friends but took solace knowing that they were safe. A week wouldn't be too bad; she had faced much longer punishments at the orphanage, beginning after her third escape attempt.

Her head was throbbing, and she could feel her heartbeat in the bump from where she had tripped and slammed against the cavern wall.

"May I rest?" she asked quietly.

The Pumpkin King nodded, and Eve watched as he used the back of the chair to help lift himself, then gingerly made his way from her room and out into the Hall.

The door closed softly behind him just as tears began to well up in Eve's eyes.

She grabbed the nearest pillow she could find and buried her head in it. Then she cried.

She had endangered her friends. She had upset the Pumpkin King. She still didn't know what had caused the sun not to rise. And worst of all, her nightmares were back.

Eve spent the remainder of the night nursing her injuries alone in her room. She watched from the window as scarecrows toiled across the homestead, until eventually the moon began to fall and the dim light of morning began to rise.

The Pumpkin King brought her thirdmeal and silently dressed her cuts and applied a salve to her bruises.

He asked after the redness of her eyes, but Eve played it off as being tired.

She watched under the crack of her door as the blaze in the hearth died to a smoldering ember, and eventually the snores of the Pumpkin King filled the Hall.

Standing from her bed, she tossed back the window drapes, letting in as much of the day's sunlight as possible.

It was still weaker than normal, but it was enough.

She dragged a chair and a book next to it, where she spent the entirety of the day desperately doing whatever she could to not fall asleep.

She knew what waited for her on the other side of sleep: a nightmare.

Eve could feel the fear in her bones even now, just as she had as a child. It was constant, unable to be chased away, like a monster had taken up residence in her stomach, then built a vacation home in her brain.

So instead, she read, trying as hard as she could to get lost in one of the books scattered about her room.

To her relief, it worked, and after successfully managing to stay awake all day, the moon finally rose over an increasingly exhausted and still quite sore Eve. That night, she soon found herself in a grove of maple trees. Next to her was Scrags, each of them going quietly about checking the syrup taps to make sure they were all in working order. The Pumpkin King was still upset with her, and Eve couldn't help but notice that he skipped out on all her lessons that night.

He had never been mad at her like this before. She wanted so badly to fix it, to make it right, but didn't know how.

Maybe, had she had a clear mind, she might have been able to think of something to say to him, something that would make him forgive her. But all she could think about was her fears: how scared she was to go to bed, how scared she was that she had lost the Pumpkin King's faith, how scared she was that the sun would go missing again and that she'd lose him for good.

She had already tried all her old tricks that helped her get rid of her fears back at the orphanage: telling herself fear wasn't real, just a needless emotion; rewriting the nightmare she'd had with a happier ending, one where the Pumpkin King burst from the tomb and offered her an apple pie; picturing each fear being placed in a box and locked away—then when that didn't help, picturing each fear being placed in a box and smashed repeatedly with a hammer. None of it was working.

Instead, that morning she stumbled tiredly back to her bedroom, where she once again waited patiently for the Pumpkin King's snores to fill the Hall. When she heard the slow rumbling of his sleep, Eve then snuck downstairs and into the kitchens to make herself some coffee.

Which she then mixed with their strongest tea.

Only to dump in as much sugar as she could find.

And then did jumping jacks as she drank it.

Sleep would not find her, not if she had anything to say about it.

The week of her grounding began to blur. Nights and days, days and nights, all melded together in her sleep-deprived mind.

It was a mash-up of tending trees and working in soil, bottling preserves and feigning attention during her lessons. She could hear Scrags teaching her about aging spices but couldn't find meaning in the words. She could tell the Pumpkin King was still angry with her but found herself no longer able to process it. Food was placed before her, and she ate it. Or at least she thought she did; she didn't remember tasting anything. Somewhere in another room she could hear the Pumpkin King grumbling that all the coffee beans were gone.

That day—or was it night?—she shuffled blurry eyed through the pages of an adventure novel, trying to position herself as uncomfortably as possible in her reading chair.

Her eyelids began to disobey her and slowly started to drift closed.

No, she thought. *Not now. I can fight it.*

Her chin fell listlessly to her chest.

Please, no.

The book drooped in her hand. . . .

Joy shot through her as a knock echoed at her door before she had the chance to fall into a nightmare.

"Evelyn," the Pumpkin King said through the door. "Get dressed. It's time to go."

Wearily, Eve rose from her chair and went to open the door. She didn't need to change, she was still wearing her working clothes. Her pajamas she had long since hidden from herself; there would be no need for them until the threat of nightmares went away.

"Where are we going?" she asked, opening the door with a yawn.

Behind him the Hall was quiet, and the hearth below lay empty and cold.

That's weird, she thought. Usually the first thing he did every evening was start a fire. The Hall was always welcoming and warm, except for now. Now it felt cold and dark.

"I'm taking you back to the orphanage," the Pumpkin King growled.

Eve's heart shot into her throat.

"What? Why?" she said, dread taking her.

"Adopting you was a mistake," the Pumpkin King answered, reaching out to grab her with one of his strong arms. "You hid your nightmares from me. The Pumpkin Princess should be fearless. Formidable. You are neither."

Eve's breath turned to lead in her chest. Every muscle in her body constricted as it felt like someone was ripping her world away.

"But this is my home!" Panicking, she pulled away from his outstretched hand. "No, I won't go!"

Eve slammed the door in his face and turned to bury her head into her pillows, but when she turned, she was no longer in her room.

The loose sheets that adorned her bedroom ceiling were gone, replaced by dingy white tile riddled with stains from years of leaks. A lonely cot sat where her bed should be.

Eve went entirely and completely cold. Pinpricks ran up her fingers and down her spine.

She was back in the orphanage.

Instantly a thin layer of sweat spread over her. She felt nauseous. She wanted to retch.

No matter how hard she tried, or how far she got, it seemed she would never escape this place, not even here in the Hallowell Valley.

She opened the door behind her, hoping the Hall of the Pumpkin King would still be there, and if not, to run and find her way back.

What she found instead were the yellow beams of two searching flashlights, held by men who were trying to reach out and grab her, to drag her back to her old life.

"No, no! I escaped you already," yelled Eve, backing away from them. "You can't take me back!"

"It's okay. You're home," a voice echoed around her.

"No!" Eve shouted back. "I got away from here!"

The voice grew louder, and around her the room began to spin like water in a drain.

"Eve, it's okay. You're safe! Wake up!"

The two approaching lights grew and morphed, and Eve found herself staring into the face of the Pumpkin King.

Around her the orphanage dissolved, and Eve saw that she was back in her reading chair, a book hanging loosely from her hand.

"I could hear you shouting from my chambers. You were having a nightmare," the Pumpkin King said. He was knelt down on one knee beside her, both hands resting on her shoulders.

Eve pulled herself from him, pushing his hands away.

"You were going to send me back!" she accused, fighting back tears.

His eyes grew in surprise. "Hrmph!" he grumbled, appearing insulted. "You are my daughter, the Pumpkin Princess. I would never send you away."

"But you did!"

He paused, and slowly the insult of Eve's accusation melted from his jack-o'-lantern features, replaced by something else, something paternal.

"This is your home," he said firmly. "It will always be your home."

"Do you—do you promise?"

"Of course I promise," he answered. "Now, tell me what is going on."

Eve stayed cowered back in the chair, still reeling from the nightmare she had just woken from.

The burning in his eyes softened. "I cannot help you if you do not let me."

Finally, after a week of fighting it on her own, Eve broke— and it was like a dam had been let loose, everything she had been bottling up since arriving in Hallowell flooding through her.

Tears burst forth and she threw herself into the Pumpkin King.

He hesitated but for a moment, then wrapped her in a wide embrace, enveloping her in his arms.

She told him everything: about the unbearable fear she had felt as a child, about the disabling nightmares that plagued her when first arriving at the orphanage. How she thought she had finally beat her fear and convinced herself she would never be scared again. And how wrong she was, when after falling into the Cursed Caverns it all came rushing back, bringing the nightmares that Eve so dreaded.

He listened silently, never once letting go of her.

"Why have you never told me of this?" he asked, after several moments of quiet.

"I didn't . . ." Eve hesitated, not wanting to say. But at this point it didn't matter; she had no will left in her to fight it. "Because no one ever wanted to adopt me when they learned about my night terrors—the headmistress told them I was . . . told them I was broken. And . . ." Eve could hardly get out the words. "And I worried that if I told you, then you wouldn't want me either. That you'd be like all the others."

Eve pulled back, staring up at him through tear-soaked eyes. "But it doesn't matter because I *am* broken! Just like she always said." Eve angrily wiped at the tears streaming down her cheeks. "I can't be the Pumpkin Princess! You chose wrong. You picked a broken daughter."

He stared down at her, his eyes cooling to a liquid amber.

For some time, he was silent, and Eve found she was unable to break the silence herself.

"No," he said finally.

"No?" Eve didn't understand.

"I did not *choose* wrong. Nor do I believe I chose at all. To me, you were my daughter the moment we met, a daughter who is perfect in every way, night terrors or not. And, hrmph, *I* do not believe you to be broken. But if this is how having these nightmares makes you feel, then I shall do everything in my not-so-limited power to get rid of them. And, should you like, I can pay this *headmistress* a little visit as well, and show her what it feels like to be scared."

The thought of that cheered Eve up considerably. She wiped

262

a stubborn tear from her face. "No, it's okay." As much as she wanted to see that happen, she didn't want him to leave her. "Are you sure you don't want to take me back? Now would be your chance," she asked, feigning a pathetic smile.

The Pumpkin King let out a grunt. Or a chuckle, she couldn't quite tell. "Eve, there are no powers possessed by undead or, hrmph, the living, that could take you from me."

"But what about the sun?" Eve asked, reality coming back to her. "It almost took *you*, and we still haven't figured out what stopped it from rising."

"You let me worry about that. I am the parent," the Pumpkin King said. "Your only concern should be feeling better."

His mouth formed into a jagged yet warm smile, and once more she buried her face into one of his shoulders.

He held her till she fell asleep, and then long after.

No nightmares came to her then, for none could reach her while she was wrapped in the safety of the Pumpkin King's arms.

CHAPTER FIFTEEN

Smoke and Chains

Not for the first time, Eve woke to two mismatched buttons staring back at her.

"Hi, Scrags," Eve mumbled, rubbing at her eyes.

"Good evening, Prin'sis," Scrags croaked. "How are yous feeling?"

"Better, thanks," Eve answered truthfully. Whatever sleep she had finally managed to get worked wonders, and she felt more rested than she had in nights. "Where is the Pumpkin King?"

"Errand. Should be back soon," Scrags explained. "Would yous like something to eat? I can make some secondmeal?"

Secondmeal? Eve peered through her bedroom window. She

could see the moon peeking out from behind thick clouds, already high in the night's sky. She must have overslept.

"No, it's okay. I'm not hungry," Eve said, lifting the covers from herself.

"I's have something made up anyway. It'll be good for yous to eat."

Eve tried to protest, but Scrags was having none of it. Like a mom on a mission, Scrags had her washed, dressed, and at the table in the matter of an hour.

"See, don't yous feel better?" he asked, basically force-feeding stew down Eve's throat.

"Ye'm, mu' be'er," said Eve, attempting to gulp down a spoonful.

The fire burned in the hearth, and between the warmth, the food, and actually getting some sleep for once, Eve was beginning to feel a little closer to her normal self. Her hand still trembled as she held her spoon, and she knew the fear was still there in the pit of her stomach, but at least it was packed under what had to be at least several inches of stew by now.

She was fending off another bowl when the door to the Hall swung open, revealing the Pumpkin King and someone else unexpected.

"Ms. Shroud?" Eve said, waving off Scrags as he attempted to feel her forehead. "Scrags, I'm fine, really," she insisted.

The hunched-over ghost author barely came up to the Pumpkin King's waist as she made her way through the door and toward the table.

The Pumpkin King pulled out a chair for her beside Eve, which she hopped onto, hovering over the seat ever so slightly.

"Hello, Evelyn. The Pumpkin King told me about what happened," said Ms. Shroud briskly, jumping right to the matter at hand as old ladies have a tendency to do. "I gathered from his grumbling on the ride over that he'd probably like me to apologize for my part in the matter, encouraging you on and all. But seeing as you did what I would have done, and because I don't speak grumble, I'm not going to."

Eve bit down a smile that attempted to creep out.

"Hrmph," the Pumpkin King growled, taking a seat across from both Eve and Ms. Shroud, and Eve caught him eyeing her second bowl of untouched stew.

She pushed it over to him.

"Missed firstmeal," he mumbled. "Cecilia, would you like anything?"

"I's can go make ghost pepper tea?" Scrags offered.

"No, thank you, I'm okay," Ms. Shroud answered, resting her cane across her lap. "Besides, I don't believe you brought me here for tea."

"Brought you here?" Eve asked, confused. "I didn't even know you two knew each other."

"Of course I know Cecilia!" said the Pumpkin King. "Who do you think found the water wheel for her to hide away in?"

"Me and the big brute here go way back," Ms. Shroud added.

"Oh, I didn't know—wait a second." Eve rounded on the Pumpkin King. "You knew this whole time that my *favorite* author lived nearby and you never said anything?"

"I—she—hrmph—" he stammered before finally composing himself and shifting back toward Ms. Shroud. "Well, Cecilia. You have seen her, as requested. What is your professional opinion?"

"My opinion is that Eve and I could use some privacy," she quipped back. "Why don't you and the straw-man here go busy yourselves in the dirt and leave me with the Pumpkin Princess? I've met shadows less clingy."

"Clingy!" said an affronted Pumpkin King and Scrags simultaneously.

"Yes, now tuk-tuk." Ms. Shroud got up and began shooing them both away. (But not before a hungry Pumpkin King grabbed the bowl of stew on his way out.)

"Good, just the two of us," she said once the door had closed. "Now us gals can talk."

"Talk? About what?" asked Eve, feeling increasingly confused. Why did the two of them need to be alone? "What's going on?"

"Your father tells me you're suffering from nightmares, and not for the first time?"

"Huh? Oh . . ." Eve was caught off guard. They weren't something she found herself wanting to think about, let alone talk about. "Kind of. . . . Well, I mean, yeah—yes. But how come he told you?"

"He thinks us chatting could help. And please, don't be upset

267

with him for confiding in me. He's a new parent who sees a problem. Right or wrong, he's going to try every solution he can. The way he sees it, his daughter feels sick. But not a sickness brought on by germs, one brought on by fear. Which, naturally, is why he saw the need to drag me from my writing. To look at your fears and tell you what I see."

Eve frowned. "You can see fears?"

At this, Ms. Shroud smiled.

"As a matter of fact, I can. You see, when most ghosts are starting out, they struggle to know how to haunt. So they resort to the basest of tricks: knocking the occasional thing over, shouting *boo* when people aren't expecting it, that kind of thing," Ms. Shroud explained. "But when a ghost has been undead as long as I have, they learn to read fears, to see where those fears come from and to use them to haunt. It's how I know the scarecrow, Scrags, is worried you will leave Hallowell, it's how I know the horse that pulled the cart is terrified someone will forget to feed him, and it's how I know the Pumpkin King is scared of—well, I probably shouldn't say. Haunter-Hauntee confidentiality and all.

"Which leaves you, Evelyn. What is it you think I see?"

Eve tried to think back to when her nightmares had started again. It had been shortly after falling into the Cursed Caverns, but, now that she thought about it, that wasn't when her fear had first come back to her. No, it was the night at the clock tower. When the Pumpkin King fell.

"Losing the Pumpkin King?" she offered, unsure.

"Yes, definitely that. Fear of loss is written over you plain as the moon. No doubt losing your parents and winding up at the orphanage didn't do you any favors there. But, Eve, I also see the nightmares themselves. You're just as scared of them as anything else.

"But as long as you are scared of them, you will continue to have them. It's a terrible little loop you've got yourself stuck in, and one only you can break."

"How?" Eve asked, never wanting an answer to a question so badly in her entire life.

"You have to take away their power over you," Ms. Shroud explained. "Being afraid of them only gives them more strength. You've met vampires, trolls, werewolves, all posing just as great a risk to you as any night terror, yet you were fearless in the face of them. I encourage you to show your nightmares that same resolve. You might be surprised to see what they do in turn."

Again, Eve wanted to ask Ms. Shroud how she expected her to do that, when nothing Eve had done ever seemed to be a permanent fix, but before she could, the door to the Hall flew open.

In stomped the Pumpkin King, clutching a letter in his glove and followed closely by Scrags.

"A letter came from Harlock," the Pumpkin King announced, grabbing his traveling cloak from the coat stand and throwing it over his shoulders.

"It's urgent its said," added Scrags, appearing worried.

The Pumpkin King turned to face Eve and Ms. Shroud.

"Hrmph, I apologize, but I must go to the Grimm Pine Woods at once." He sighed, and Eve could tell how much he didn't want to. "Cecilia, Scrags will take you home." His gaze fell on Eve. "Will you be—"

"I'll be fine. Go," Eve said, sounding shorter than she meant to. She wasn't angry, but rather felt exposed and desperately wanted to disappear to her room. Besides, she knew for something to call him away like this, it had to be important. Hopefully it was a clue about what had happened to the sun.

The Pumpkin King hesitated, shifting undecidedly on his boots. His eyes fell back to the letter, and he sighed another deep sigh before then storming from the Hall.

"Everything will be all right," Ms. Shroud said, lifting herself from her chair. "Trust me when I say your father has dealt with far worse and come out unscathed. You just take it easy and try and get some rest."

With that they left, Ms. Shroud following Scrags out through the door as the scarecrow cast Eve a worried look.

Some time later (Eve wasn't sure how long, just that she had read about a hundred pages), a *tap tap tap* came from Eve's bedroom window.

Startled, Eve looked up from her reading, only to be more surprised when she saw who it was.

Staring back at her through a tiny opening in the curtains were two lilac eyes floating up and down.

Eve rushed over to open the window for Lyla.

Outside, a gray drizzle was building across the farm, heralding the wet gloom of an early spring.

"What are you doing here?" Eve asked. "We're still grounded."

"Are you going to let me in?" Lyla asked back. "Witches aren't waterproof."

Eve stepped aside and helped pull Lyla and her broom through the window and into the room.

Lyla stomped her pointy black shoes dry and shook off the bristles of her broom, sending water droplets everywhere.

"Is Mr. P. home?" she asked, rather urgently for someone who never seemed rushed.

"No, he left a while ago for the Grimm Pine Woods. A letter came for him. I'm hoping that maybe Harlock found out something about what happened to the sun."

"That's why I'm here!" Lyla shouted, grabbing Eve's coat from the dresser and tossing it at her, then practically dragging her to the window. "Mother Morrigan contacted me! She thinks she found out something about who's behind it."

"Whoa, slow down," Eve said, pulling away. Meanwhile,

271

Lyla was already halfway out the window. "Did she say who? Shouldn't the Pumpkin King come with us?"

"That's why I was hoping he would be here, but there's no time!" Lyla said, and it was one of the few occasions she looked legitimately flustered. "Mother Morrigan said she thinks they plan to do it again soon! Like tonight!"

Eve hesitated. She thought of the Pumpkin King and how upset he might be if she ignored being grounded and went with Lyla. But then, Eve had a different thought, one that scared her to her core: If she didn't go, if she had the chance to solve what was going on and didn't even try, then it would be her fault if it happened again. And in that case, there'd be no Pumpkin King to be mad at her at all. . . .

Lyla must have sensed her dilemma. "Eve, we're going to see my greatest-grandma, not sneak into a werewolf camp," she said reassuringly. "The worst that can happen is she makes us stay for thirdmeal afterward. All she ever eats is bog fish."

"Okay," Eve said with a nod, coming to a decision. "But let me tell Scrags first. He can get a message to the Pumpkin King." She rushed over to her door and shouted for the scarecrow, but no answer came. The Hall was entirely deserted.

"Eve, Mother Morrigan said we need to hurry!" Lyla pressed.

"All right, fine," said Eve, running back into her room. She tore a page from one of her lesser-liked books and scribbled a note onto it for either the Pumpkin King or one of the scarecrows to find. Tossing the note on the bed, Eve then pulled on her coat and climbed through the window with Lyla. Together, they leaped onto Lyla's broom and flew out into the night.

The Misty Moors swept beneath them, droplets of rain rippling through the violet of its fog-encircled hills. And although the rain never became more than a faint drizzle, that didn't stop Eve and Lyla from becoming completely covered in glistening water by the time the fires of the coven grew near.

Lyla angled them lower until finally their feet touched down onto sparse, muddy grass. Huts and hovels spread out around them, so covered in earth and moss that they practically looked like mini-hills themselves. In fact, had it not been for the orange and green glows emitting from their tiny windows, Eve wouldn't have known they were homes at all.

Ahead of them, one of the huts opened, and a familiar figure bathed in green light waved them over.

"That's Mother Morrigan!" Lyla said, grabbing Eve's hand and leading her out of the rain.

Mother Morrigan held the door for them as they entered into a wide and circular hut. In its center was a large cauldron steaming with a strange green liquid, beside which stood a wooden pedestal currently home to an ancient-looking tome. Lining the walls were glass cabinets, each stuffed full of tiny vials containing all manner of ingredients. The air was heavy and humid, like the inside of a rotten log, and save for the cauldron glowing in the center, there was very little light.

"Hello, greatest-grandmother," Lyla said, squeezing the rain from her witch's hat.

"Evening, you two," Mother Morrigan said with a smile. "Glad you were able to come on such short notice. Here, dry off." She held out an old towel that was barely holding itself together.

"I'm okay," Eve said, waving it off. If Mother Morrigan's news truly was urgent, she didn't want to waste even a second. "Lyla said you found something?"

"Ah, right to it, then," she said, tossing the towel over a crooked chair. "Lyla, can you be a dear and add some knotvine to the cauldron?"

"Sure thing!" Lyla said happily, no doubt excited to show off some witchcraft she knew she was good at.

Lyla carried a chair to a nearby cabinet and riffled through a series of vials before pulling the stopper from one and tossing its contents into the cauldron. Then Eve watched as she began making wide circular motions above the cauldron with her wand, and slowly the brew began to spin.

Dense green smoke poured out, carrying with it a bitter herbal scent.

"Thank you, Lyla. Your brewing has always been quite good," Mother Morrigan complimented her. "Your cauldron-craft might eventually rival my own."

Lyla beamed. It wasn't often she was complimented on her skills as a witch.

"Now, why don't you go visit your greatest-aunt Agnes next door? I'm afraid I need to talk to the Pumpkin Princess alone."

"Why?" Lyla asked, looking taken aback.

"It's okay. She can stay," Eve said. "We don't have secrets."

"Yeah," Lyla agreed. "She'll just tell me whatever you say anyway."

"What I have to say is delicate and is meant for the Pumpkin Princess only," Mother Morrigan said meaningfully.

Lyla looked as if she were about to protest, but after a significant look from her greatest-grandmother, she grabbed her broom and dragged it sullenly across the floor and out into the night. The door closed quietly behind her.

"What's so important that Lyla couldn't be here?" Eve asked, offended for her friend.

"We'll get to that," Mother Morrigan said, beginning to mash something on a knotted table littered with broken leaves. She tossed whatever it was in the cauldron, then pointed to a glass container near Eve containing a prickly plant with a black flower. "First, can you grab me that plant?"

"Yeah, sure, I guess," Eve said impatiently. She hurried to reach for the jar, but just as she did, she faltered. . . .

There, in tiny writing across the front of the glass, were the words:

"Mother Morrigan, why do you have the—" she began to ask, not understanding, when suddenly the room started to spin around her.

Smoked continued pouring from the cauldron while Mother Morrigan threw in what appeared to be broken animal bones. A pungent odor began to fill the hut.

"Yes, yes," said Mother Morrigan, as if she were explaining something to an infant. "I was the one who stole the Moon Thistle. Though Annabelle was never supposed to be there when I did. I do feel bad about the Forgetfulness Hex I had to cast on her after. The last thing that pathetic girl needed was more memory issues."

Annabelle ... Forgetfulness Hex ...

Eve's mind was becoming dizzy. Each thought felt like trying to grab a wisp of wind. She struggled to remain standing, grasping onto a nearby shelf to stay upright.

"Mother Morrigan, what's happening to me?"

"Better have a seat, dearie," Mother Morrigan said, pulling out a chair for Eve and sitting her down into it. "We wouldn't want you to fall and hurt yourself. You are far too valuable." Grabbing the jar of Moon Thistle, she emptied it into the cauldron, which hissed at the touch.

The door to the hut swung open, and in entered half a dozen cloaked and shadowed figures. Eve's vision was beginning to blur, making it difficult to discern their faces. Beneath their dark hoods she saw warts and wrinkles, large noses and missing teeth.

Slowly they circled the cauldron, tossing in bones and leaves as they chanted and prodded at it with their wands.

It steamed and bubbled, frothing at the rim.

"The Forever Night spell is finally ready once more," one of the shadows breathed. "We just need . . ." All the hoods turned from the cauldron and stared at Eve. *"Her."*

The fumes seemed to be seeping into Eve's mind, clouding it and obscuring her thoughts. Slowly, like a bubble through syrup, a memory fought to the surface.

A faint recollection of sitting across from Ms. Shroud at the Wailing Water Wheel, talking about who would have the most to gain if the moon replaced the sun. The werewolves, the vampires, and . . .

The coven, where the witches still practiced an old magic that relied on the moon.

"It's been you this whole time?" Eve said disbelievingly. She attempted to stand, but Mother Morrigan flicked her wand and spectral ropes bound Eve tightly to the chair.

"Of course, child," Mother Morrigan spat. "Who else is powerful enough to stop the sun?"

"But how? Why?" Eve asked, still not wanting to believe it.

Mother Morrigan was supposed to be a friend. Supposed to be *her* friend.

"To return to our former, terrible glory, that's why," Mother Morrigan hissed, her normally gentle demeanor melting away. "Do you have any idea what it's like to be feared? It's a hunger that can't be satiated. To be feared is to be powerful, and long ago, we were *all-powerful*. Everyone feared us, terrified of our magic and our spite. Yet now we live on the outskirts of Hallowell like wretches as even our own laugh at our ways, calling them old and forgotten.

"But no longer! Once we summon the Forever Night, the moon will be imprisoned in the sky, and we will be able to draw magic from it endlessly. No one will be able to dispute our power after that. And it's all thanks to you." Her face split into a sinister smile, outlined in the venomous green glow of the cauldron.

Cackling laughs erupted from several of the nearby witches.

"Me?" Eve asked, confused. "What does any of this have to do with me?"

"It has *everything* to do with you," Mother Morrigan answered. "The Forever Night spell requires life, and not just any life—trust me, we spent years trying them all." She shook a jar with a hoof in it. "But a special kind that we've never been able to get our hands on in Hallowell. That is, until you arrived. Little does the Pumpkin King know that on the night he adopted you, he brought about his own demise."

Eve's inside turned to ice.

They were going to use her against Hallowell.

If she had never come here, her friends . . . her family . . . would never have been in danger.

Then something else dawned on Eve.

"That's why you made sure I wasn't banished," Eve said accusingly. "So that you could use me for this Forever Night spell—" Comprehension flooded over her. "You lied! Back at the clock tower, you knew it wasn't a ritual, but you made us think it could be anyway."

"Well done, right on both counts, I'm afraid. A spell would have been too easy to trace back to witches. As for you being banished, obviously I could never allow that to happen. Your arrival here was the answer to all of our prayers to the Dark. All we needed was a drop of the blood that contains your life—or so we thought—until the drop we did have failed us."

"Drop you had?" Eve asked, feeling her confusion start to turn to anger. "When—how did you get my blood?"

"Technically, I didn't," Mother Morrigan answered with a devious smile. "In fact, I worried myself over how I might without arousing suspicion. But then on the night of the Harvest Festival, I saw my opportunity, when a certain skeleton had a needle mere breaths away from your skin. The magical nudge I gave Ellie was even easier than swiping the needle from her afterward.

"We used the blood from that little pinprick in our first attempt at the spell, the day the sun didn't rise, and the Pumpkin King summoned the Council to the clock tower. But as soon as we cast it, we knew something had gone wrong. The spell was weak, hardly even visible, let alone strong enough to permanently bind the moon. We thought we'd tipped our hand, that the Pumpkin King would be onto us after that and end our plot before it ever stood a chance. Then something entirely unexpected happened. He fell. And our little miscalculation gave rise to a realization that we had not known. That with no sun, there *is* no Pumpkin King. Meaning the only one who could stop us wouldn't be able to once we cast our spell correctly."

A loud gurgle came from the cauldron as a bubble surfaced and popped, hissing more steam into the hut. Eve shook her head, not wanting to believe anything she was hearing, hoping she had somehow fallen into a new nightmare instead. Yet, deep down, she knew this was far too elaborate to be anything other than reality.

"But without the Pumpkin King, without his crops, Hallowell will starve!" Eve pointed out angrily. "Lyla said that you knew how important his land is! That Hallowell needs him and his farm! What good does endless magic do you if no one can survive here?"

"Oh yes, the valley would be in trouble," Mother Morrigan agreed. "But with an infinite supply of moonlight, we'll be more powerful than ever before—able to conjure our own fields, grow our own food with magic. Those who bow to us will be fed, and those who don't . . . well, we'll see how long those ones last."

Something in Eve flared alive, sending her anger to new heights. She wanted to break her bonds and throw herself across the room at the witch.

"But we trusted you!" Eve shouted. "*I* trusted you!"

"Funny, isn't it?" said Mother Morrigan. "The trick kindness can play? I didn't even need to use magic to blind you to the truth, I just had to be your friend. And then, with the Pumpkin King weakened and you off chasing werewolves—yes, I knew you would go digging. You're a clever girl, and worse, a persistent one—we were left with all the time needed to brew the spell once more. And now, after nights of stirring, it's ready. We just need your—"

The door to the hut opened once more, and Eve's hopes shot up, expecting the Pumpkin King to burst in and save her at that very moment.

Instead, her heart sank.

In entered Baroness La'Ment.

"—blood," Mother Morrigan finished.

Instinctively, Eve tried to edge her chair back and away, but to no avail.

"Hello, *Princess*," said the baroness, smiling vehemently. Her wicked black eyes fell on Eve, and her red lips parted, revealing the pointed teeth in her grin. "As Mother Morrigan is no doubt explaining, the Forever Night spell needs life from the living. What you may not realize is just how much life it actually needs."

Wide-eyed, Eve looked to Mother Morrigan.

"You don't have to do this," Eve said desperately. "Please, it's not too late! You don't have to kill me!"

"Kill you?" Laughter echoed throughout the dark hut. "Child, if we wanted to kill you, we wouldn't need the baroness. After the first attempt at the spell failed, we realized not only did we need a lot more of your life, but a steady supply of it if we want to keep the spell from fading and the moon in the sky forever. Unfortunately, we don't have anywhere to stash you, not without risking someone finding you. Thankfully for us, the baroness has access to some particularly well-hidden dungeons and is rather skilled in making blood last. So that night after the clock tower, she and I came to a mutually agreeable accord."

"They promised me stewardship over all of Hallowell once the Pumpkin King is no more," Baroness La'Ment said with an evil grin. "They get infinite power, and I get to rule. It's quite the trade. And to think, I almost had you banished. Had I known what that precious blood of yours could be used for, I would have thrown you a welcome party instead."

Two witches stepped forward and grabbed Eve from the chair, pulling her to the side of the cauldron.

Eve struggled, but they were too strong.

One of the witches forced Eve's hand open over the frothing

green liquid, and before she could do anything, Mother Morrigan drew a line of blood across Eve's palm with the sharp edge of a knife.

The witches shoved her hand into the cauldron.

The pain was searing. Eve felt as if her life were being drained from her and out through her hand. Around her, the room began to spin.

"The Pumpkin King will realize I'm gone. He'll stop all of you," she gasped defiantly.

The cauldron crackled violently.

Then, in a sudden burst, translucent green chains erupted from the cauldron, tearing through the ceiling and rocketing into the dark sky with terrifying speed.

Mother Morrigan turned to face Eve; the spectral chains whizzing by her face cast an ominous glow over her.

"Oh, dearie, by then it will be too late."

The chains flew high above Eve in a blur. Through the hole in the roof above, she watched in terror as they coiled around the moon. Not flickering or weak like they once were, but ghastly and terrible.

Her vision blurred, then faded, and no longer able to fight it, Eve fainted.

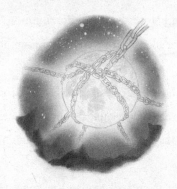

CHAPTER SIXTEEN

The Gift of Life

EVE STRUGGLED IN AND OUT OF CONSCIOUSNESS, DRIFTING back and forth between nightmare and reality.

Visions swirled around her; what was real and what wasn't, Eve had no idea.

Through a rainy night sky, she saw a moon wrapped in ethereal chains as she was carried and tossed into a wagon. A door closed and she was suddenly back in the orphanage, the headmistress sitting across from her.

Darkness.

The wagon jostled side to side, rain beating down on it. The headmistress smiled with pointed teeth.

Darkness.

Eve peered out an orphanage window and Castle Dracula peered back.

Darkness.

Passageways and stone tunnels became painted corridors with fluorescent lighting. Faceless orphans stared back at her, watching as she was brought to the headmistress's office. Something clinked shut, and a heavy metal lock latched down. Bars surrounded her.

Once more, darkness.

"Tsk. Tsk. Tsk," came a familiar voice.

Eve fought to open her eyes, but her eyelids felt immeasurably heavy.

"We warned you," a second voice said. "You should have left while you still could."

A dungeon cell began to form around Eve as she forced herself awake. Here the air was cold and damp, and smelled of rotten grapes.

She lay on a thin bedroll, drenched in sweat. Surrounding her were three walls of brown bricks and an iron gate made of rusty bars. Between which, two sets of fanged teeth smiled at her.

It was the matching images of Corina and Elisabetta. In one hand each held a torch, and in the other they held leashes to a pair of their canine-like gargoyles, each of which was sitting and growling hungrily at Eve.

"You won't get away with this," Eve said meekly, struggling to rise.

"We already did," Corina corrected. "You've been asleep for hours, and guess what? The moon hasn't moved an inch. The Forever Night is upon us."

Elisabetta sneered. "So, I guess we owe you an apology. Turns out we were wrong. Hallowell will be your home—sorry, did I say home? I meant prison."

Together the twins laughed.

"No, I'll find a way out of here," Eve said defiantly, each word sapping away what little energy she did have. "I've broken out of places before. I can do it again."

"Hah!" Elisabetta scoffed. "I'd like to see you try. No one will find you here. We'll be leeching your life out for decades. Or . . . well, however long you *living* last."

The cell swirled around Eve, and she was in detention at the orphanage, Corina and Elisabetta staring down at her from where she copied lines at her desk.

In her state, she didn't have the strength to fight off the nightmares, and they were now blending openly with the real world.

"The Pumpkin King will . . . ," Eve mumbled, falling back into her bedroll, where she once more succumbed to a feverish sleep.

She woke to the sounds of two voices arguing.

"Let me try first," said a girl.

"Your magic works like half the time," argued a boy. "What if you send out fireworks and alert the whole castle?"

"I *won't*. I need to make it up to her. It's all my fault."

"Lyla?" Eve coughed, beginning to rise from the cold dungeon floor. "Vlad?"

"Eve!" Lyla exclaimed.

"Shhhh!" Vlad hushed her.

"Eve, I am so sorry!" Lyla said, rushing the words out in muted whispers. She had her broom in one hand and her wand in another. Beside her, Vlad held a torch and a weird metal contraption with springs and thin metal prongs.

"I swear I had nothing to do with it!" Lyla said quietly. "Mother Morrigan fooled me too! Please forgive me? I should have never brought you there. Please, say you forgive me."

"It's not your fault. I forgive you," Eve said, wobbling to the rusty bars on uncertain legs. "How did you know where to find me?"

"I knew something was wrong when the baroness arrived at the coven," Lyla explained. "I spotted her through my aunt's window. When I did, I tried to get out, but that old prune Agnes grabbed me. She tried to convince me to join her and the other witches of the coven, but I said no, so she held me prisoner till after you had disappeared. Eventually, she let her guard down, and I gave her a kick to the shin and escaped. Then I flew straight here to tell Vlad everything that had happened."

287

"We figured if the baroness was involved, they might try and hide you here," Vlad continued. "No one suspects the vampires of anything yet, and nobody, not even myself, knew where to find the dungeons. It took us forever to find this place, but thankfully one of the staff I've helped was kind to me and pointed us in the right direction."

"And the Pumpkin King?" Eve asked.

Lyla's and Vlad's eyes fell to the floor.

"What?" Eve said, her fear rising.

"Well . . . ," Lyla began nervously. "This time, the coven's spell was much more powerful, and everyone in Hallowell saw the chains of the Forever Night come from the Misty Moors. The Pumpkin King arrived right when I was escaping. He was trying to find you."

"What happened?" Eve's heart was pounding in her chest.

"They were expecting him and had set a trap," Lyla said gravely. "Under the full moon, their old magic is more powerful, and when the entire coven combined their spells at the same time . . . well . . . They bound him in magic and are holding him prisoner. Any other night he'd be able to break free as soon as the moon went down and their power went with it. But the moon's not going down, is it? Not ever again. So they'll only get stronger."

"And he'll only get weaker," Vlad added. "Until—"

The cell swirled around her, and she was talking to Lyla and Vlad from back within the detention room of the orphanage.

Eve fought it off.

"We need to save him," she said. "Lyla, how do we stop the Forever Night spell?"

Lyla's face contorted in thought. "It wouldn't be easy. We'd have to brew and cast the counterspell, but you would need the spell book Mother Morrigan used and the cauldron that still has the spell in it. Wait—why?"

"Because that's what we're going to do. As soon as you two get me out of here."

"Oh, okay," said Lyla, nodding. "That makes sense."

"What! No, it doesn't!" argued Vlad. "Eve, you're barely even awake. No way. We're getting you out, then we're going to go hide till this all blows over."

"Vlad, you know I can't do that," Eve implored. "This is all my fault! It was me who suspected the werewolves instead of Mother Morrigan. It was my blood that they used for the spell. And it's because of me that the Pumpkin King is captured. I can't just sit around and see what happens. I might not have a life here if I do that!"

"We could go to the village for help?" suggested Lyla.

"What, and trust someone else like we did Mother Morrigan?" shot Eve. "Not a chance. Who knows how many others are in on this!" Mother Morrigan's betrayal still tasted like bile in her throat, and there was no world where she was going to let that happen again. "Look, neither of you has to go with me. But

I have to fix this—I have to do something before it's too late. *Please?* I can't risk losing him."

Lyla looked at Vlad, who in turn let out a begrudging sigh.

"I'd want to save my parents too if I could," he said, speaking more to himself than them. "All right, fine. But we need to hurry. Corina and Elisabetta could be back any minute. They love kicking someone when they're down."

"Step aside," Lyla said, pointing her wand at the cell door.

"Stop!" Vlad and Eve yelled at the same time, but it was too late.

There was a loud bang, and suddenly the lock started screaming like a baby crying.

"Jinxes," Lyla said.

"Lyla . . . ," Eve moaned.

Vlad rushed forward, sticking a prong from his metal invention into the lock. The lock began to suck on it like a pacifier, and the screaming stopped. Vlad pressed a switch on the device, and there was a series of clicks and ticks before the lock popped open.

Eve and Lyla stared gratefully at him.

"It's a lock-picking device," Vlad stated. "After all the times the twins threatened to bring me to the dungeons, I figured it might be good to have."

"Nice," said Lyla, lifting the lock and swinging open the gate.

Eve stumbled out, her legs weak. "We need to hurry," she said. "Someone had to have heard that."

"We passed by some sewers on the way down here. We might

be able to use them to sneak out," Vlad said, beginning to pull Eve one direction.

She resisted.

"What's wrong?" Lyla and Vlad asked at the same time. "We have to go!"

Eve's mind was spinning; the narrow stone corridor they were in kept flickering back and forth to painted hallways that didn't belong. But that wasn't what was bugging her. She thought she had an idea, but her nightmares were clouding her head.

Eve focused as best she could, trying to swallow her fear and force it away. For a moment, the hallway changed back to the correct stone tunnel it should be, and she had a plan.

"No," she said. "Vlad, we need to go to your room."

"My room? Are you crazy?" Vlad sputtered. "That's all the way back through the castle. We'll get caught."

"We need to chance it. I have an idea, I promise."

Vlad and Lyla exchanged confused looks.

"Fine," Vlad said. He wrapped one arm around Eve to support her, and with the other held the torch high and led them back in the opposite direction. "But just so we're on the same page, you owe me big time."

Lyla shrugged. "Probably for the best anyway," she said, following behind with her broom and her wand. "These dungeons are smelly enough. I would've hated going in the sewers."

They staggered on, walking through a maze of dimly lit and

damp tunnels, until finally Vlad pulled on a torch hanging from a wall, and a secret door opened, revealing the inside of the castle.

The warmth of the stale air hit Eve first, followed by its musty smell. They entered a long hallway, draped in black curtains and lined with portraits of vampires. Eve ignored all the orphan children playing on the crimson carpet. She knew they weren't real, only a figment of her nightmares.

Continuing to sneak quietly through the castle and avoiding staff and familiars at every turn, they had almost made it when a savage bark echoed behind them.

The three turned, and at the end of a long corridor were Corina and Elisabetta, holding back the orphanage hounds, Curfew and Watcher. Or were the hounds actually gargoyles?

"Oh no," Vlad breathed.

With wicked smiles, the twins let the leashes go.

The two hounds warped back into gargoyles, and they charged.

Stone paws ripped across velvet carpet, tearing down the hallway at frightening speed.

Lyla gave a snap of her wand, and to Eve's dismay, one of the gargoyles quadrupled several times in size.

"Jinxes, that wasn't right," Lyla said.

Thankfully, it became so big it filled up the entire hallway, bursting into the walls and ceiling and slamming the other gargoyle through one wall and into another corridor.

"Oh, actually it kind of—"

Eve grabbed her and the three ran, Vlad still heavily support-ing Eve.

They turned down another hallway and lunged into the din-ing chamber that was Vlad's room.

Lyla and Vlad quickly pulled a table and a cabinet in front of the door.

"Okay, we're here. Now what?" Vlad asked, turning his attention to Eve.

"Gather as many inventions as you can," she ordered.

"How is that going to help us?" Vlad fretted.

The door shuddered behind them as the massive gargoyle slammed into it.

"Trust me!" Eve said. Grabbing Vlad's pillow from his cof-fin, she ripped off the pillowcase and began filling it with every device she could find. And there was no shortage of them; Vlad had obviously kept busy while she and Lyla were grounded.

Vlad grabbed a sheet and began tossing more onto it before bundling it up; meanwhile Lyla flipped her crooked hat upside down, filling it to the brim.

The cabinet and table rumbled as the door quaked once more, and a giant stone paw burst through.

"We're running out of time! What now?" Vlad asked between shakes of fright.

"Now we jump out the window and fly away on Lyla's broom," Eve answered, bundling up the last of Vlad's creations.

"That's your plan?" said Vlad, panicking. "That won't work!"

"I'm not sure my broom can carry three of us and all this stuff," Lyla said, eyeballing everything they had grabbed. As if it heard her, the broom seemed to give a slight quiver.

"It will have to," Eve said, tossing open a window.

Outside, the rainclouds had cleared completely, and chains the size of bridges spanned the night's sky, wrapping around the moon and binding it in place.

A violent *CRACK* snapped Eve's attention away from them.

Behind them, the door they had barricaded was beginning to splinter and break.

"We need to go!" Eve shouted.

"Well, I guess falling to our deaths is better than being eaten," Lyla stated, marching over to the window and tossing out her broom.

It hovered just outside, waiting for them to hop on.

Lyla went first, still clutching her hat full of Vlad's inventions.

CRASH!

The door burst open. In ran the gigantic stone gargoyle, sniffing hungrily at the air.

Vlad helped Eve over the windowsill and onto the broom, tossing her the rest of what they had collected.

The broom wavered, dipping away from the window and leaving Vlad trapped inside.

"Jump!" Eve and Lyla shouted.

"Uh, no thanks," Vlad scoffed, like it was the most absurd suggestion he had ever heard.

Lyla pulled on the broom, managing to lift it up just enough that Eve could see into the room as the gargoyle caught sight of Vlad.

It bounded directly for him.

"Jump!" they shouted again. "You have to!"

"Oh man," Vlad fretted. "You both are the worst!"

Then he jumped.

The window frame behind him buckled and the glass shattered as the gargoyle burst through behind him.

It reached out with a stony paw, narrowly missing Vlad as he landed on the back of the broom.

Too large and heavy for its wings to support it, the gargoyle plummeted down, landing with a splash in the narrow moat that wrapped the castle far below them.

To their dismay, they weren't far behind.

The broom dropped like a rock, struggling to hold their combined weight and all of Vlad's gear.

"Lyla . . . ," Eve and Vlad urged, their panic rising as they spiraled down.

"I'm—trying," grunted Lyla, pulling with all her might on the broom. "We're too heavy!"

"Ugh!" Eve groaned, then quickly took Lyla's hat and dumped it, then did the same with Vlad's sheet full of inventions, keeping only her pillowcase's worth.

Devices plummeted alongside them, the moat itself getting closer and getting closer fast.

Yards became feet, feet became inches, and just when Eve could smell the rank water of the moat, the broom lifted, turning up and launching back into the night.

A paw shot from the water, missing the bristles of the broom by a hair.

Lyla pulled up and up, coercing as much lift from the broom as she could. It struggled, brushing over the tops of vineyards and grapes, until finally she was able to get a little more air under it.

"Now where?" she asked. Ahead, the lights of Hallowell Station stretched out before them.

Eve struggled to hear her; the adrenaline from being chased by a giant gargoyle was starting to wear off, and slowly she was beginning to drift back into a nightmare, her head falling forward onto Lyla's shoulder.

"Eve! Wake up!" Vlad said, jostling her.

Eve shook back awake.

Down in the village, she could see figures gathering in the streets and pointing up at the chain-wrapped moon, no doubt wondering what was happening.

"We need to go back to the coven," Eve said as they flew over the clock tower. "We have to cast the counterspell to the Forever Night and save the Pumpkin King."

Behind her, Vlad let out a nervous groan.

The rolling knolls of the valley drifted by as Lyla's poor broom worked to keep them in the air. Meanwhile, Eve once more drifted into a nightmare, and it wasn't until the broom lurched and dropped several feet that she suddenly woke back up.

They were above the Misty Moors, the huts of the coven not far in the distance. And just in time too, because Lyla's broom had apparently gone as far as it could take them.

They descended, and with a not-so-gentle landing, crashed into a muddy hill on the outskirts of the witches' dwellings.

The exhausted broom collapsed into the dirt, and when Lyla went to grab it, it rolled away from her hand.

"How rude," Lyla said, offended. "Well, I don't think we'll be flying any time soon."

"That's okay," said Eve, rallying all the energy she had left and hefting her pillowcase full of Vlad's gear over her shoulder. "Follow me."

The three snuck down into the hollow, where the huts of the witches lay scattered before them. Together, they hurried behind the back of a circular, mud-clad dwelling. Eve peered around it and into the center of the camp.

There in the middle, wrapped in ropes of shimmering green shadow, was the Pumpkin King.

Dozens of coven witches surrounded him, wands pointed and conjuring the bonds that held him.

Mother Morrigan and several others laughed and danced around him.

"What now?" Vlad whispered.

Eve emptied her pillowcase onto the ground behind the hut.

"Now we see how many of these work," she answered. Eve ignored their confused stares, grabbing a device that looked like a large wooden spider. She turned a crank on it, and the legs began to move.

"Lyla, I'm going to throw this over. Can you hit it with a spell while it's in the air?"

"Probably. What spell?"

"Surely your plan isn't based on Lyla getting a spell right?" Vlad asked, bewildered. "Her spells never go the way she means them to! No offense, Lyla."

"Some taken," said Lyla, pulling her wand from her sleeve and getting an angle over the roof.

"You're right, Vlad," Eve said, and Lyla frowned. "And I'm counting on it."

Slowly, Lyla's frown faded, and comprehension dawned on her face.

"Ready?" Eve asked.

Lyla smiled. "Ready."

Eve pulled back and lobbed the wooden spider into the air like a grenade. As it flew over the roof of the hut, Lyla hit it with a spell. . . .

And it multiplied into dozens more of itself.

What landed on the other side of the hut was not one simple toy, but rather an army of rampaging, gear-powered spiders, scampering up the witches' robes and breaking through the windows of their huts. Shouts and cries broke out amongst the coven.

"Vlad, start another and toss it to me," Eve ordered over the noise. "Lyla, get ready."

Catching on, Vlad flipped a switch on something that resembled a jewelry box with wings and tossed it to Eve. Eve took aim over the roof and threw it toward the gathered witches. As it crested the roof, Lyla cast another spell.

Fireworks blasted in all directions, followed by more screams.

Next, Eve threw over a wooden catapult, and Lyla hit it with a spell that made it grow teeth and bite the wand hand of a witch.

"It's working," Eve encouraged them. "Keep going."

Invention after invention flew over the hut, each hit with one of Lyla's unpredictable spells.

The devices caught fire, exploded, turned to hungry slime, came to life, strobed with flashing bright lights—and chaos rained down on the witches.

Eve peered around the hut to assess the damage.

The witches struggled to keep their wands pointed at the Pumpkin King as they fought off inventions gone mad.

Mother Morrigan was barking orders, but they were falling on ears too distracted to hear.

Finally, a group had to drop their wands and dive out of the way when a giant gear almost rolled over them.

The ropes began to fade away from the Pumpkin King's chest.

Eve watched Mother Morrigan turn and try to point her own wand at him, but it was too late.

The Pumpkin King rose from the ground, looming over all around him. He gave a mighty roll of his shoulders, and what remained of the bonds around him snapped.

In the dark shadows of the moors, his eyes lit the night with a blazing fury.

Mother Morrigan and the other witches all froze, fear rising across their faces.

Slowly, the Pumpkin King's jagged mouth twisted into an evil smile, and Eve realized why others feared him. And why *he* was the king of Hallowell.

Witches attempted to cast ropes back at him, but this time he was ready for them.

Thorned vines erupted from the earth.

Hundreds of them.

They burst forth, twisting around everything they could, pinning witches to the ground and crumbling their huts.

Eve saw her chance.

"Follow me!" she shouted. "We need to cast the counterspell!"

She sprinted out from their hiding spot and directly into the fray.

They dodged around witches and vines, spells and falling huts, making a mad dash for Mother Morrigan's cauldron and the source of the spell.

In the chaos, Eve lost track of the Pumpkin King. What little energy she had left was focused on ending the Forever Night.

She ducked under a grasping vine and jumped over a witch's spell before slamming through the door and into Mother Morrigan's hut.

The floor sparked with angry smoke, and in its center bubbled the raging green cauldron. On the pedestal beside it, Eve found the spell book that Mother Morrigan had used to cast the Forever Night. Quickly she tossed it to Lyla.

"Wait, *I'm* doing it?" Lyla asked, looking confused.

"Of course you are. Who else would?" Eve said, equally confused. Around her, the room began to shift in and out of focus. Darkness formed around the edges of her vision, and for a brief moment Eve thought she saw a familiar tombstone rising from the cauldron.

Not yet, she told herself, fighting off the nightmares that once again tried to take her. She just needed to stay awake a little longer.

"You've seen my magic," Lyla pointed out. "I'm no Mother Morrigan."

"Sure, you are," Eve said, forcing a smile. "Brewing cauldron spells is your specialty, remember? Even Mother Morrigan said so."

"Oh, so now we're trusting Mother Morrigan?" Lyla quipped.

"Lyla . . . ," Eve moaned.

"You can do this," Vlad encouraged her. "We'll help you."

Lyla nodded. "Guess I don't really have a choice, do I?" She began to flip through the pages of the book, when suddenly there was the flash of a spell just outside the window.

"Maybe hurry a little, though," Eve urged.

"Okay, okay," Lyla said, rushing over to the cauldron. "Here we go. . . .

"*Should this spell need to break,*

In the cauldron you should make—

"Blah, blah, blah, okay here it is. Um, I need:

"*Hair of spider and beak of crow,*

Barb of bramble and black cat's toe."

Vlad and Eve quickly set to raiding Mother Morrigan's cabinets.

"Here you go!" Eve shouted, tossing her a vial.

"Found it. Catch!" copied Vlad.

"All right, good," said Lyla, catching the ingredients and mixing them. She floated her wand across the surface, and the potion shifted from swamp green to a murky blue. "Um, burn and bubble, yada-yada. Okay:

"Cream of henbane and beetle's horn,

Wrap of mummy and rose's thorn."

Exhausted, Eve's vision blurred, but between her and Vlad they tossed Lyla what she needed.

"Last bit," Lyla said, sounding far away.

The room around turned into the yard at the orphanage until Eve shook her head and brought the hut back.

"For the sever, a sharpened knife,

And last of all, the gift of life.

"Oh, uh-oh," Lyla mumbled. Both she and Vlad looked at Eve.

"How much life do you need?" Eve asked.

"Um, how much do you have?"

"Lyla!" Vlad blurted. "Look at her! She's barely standing."

Eve smiled at him through tired eyes. "It's okay, Vlad. Don't worry, I'm fine," she lied.

She unwrapped the bandage from around her palm, revealing the red line Mother Morrigan had cut.

"Will this work?" Eve asked, walking over to the edge of the cauldron.

"Should," Lyla said hesitantly. "Eve . . . I'm sure there's another—"

The door to the hut shattered into a thousand pieces as the

Pumpkin King was blown through. He stumbled to the floor, the chest of his coat smoldering.

His fiery eyes fell on Eve, and surprise and shock spread across his face. "What are you doing here? Run!" he growled, and she could hear the fear in his voice.

Over the splintered door stepped Mother Morrigan, her wand fixed dangerously on the Pumpkin King. She surveyed the room like a cat looking for a mouse, and her eyes fell on Eve, her hand just above the cauldron. She saw the spell book in Lyla's hands, and all the vials littered around their feet. The anger on her face turned to panic.

"What are you doing!" she spat. "The counterspell will take what little life you have left!"

The Pumpkin King struggled to lift himself from the floor. "Eve, don't," he pleaded.

Without warning, the hut drifted out of focus, and Eve was surrounded by blackness. Before her loomed the tombstones of her parents . . . and the one marked THE TOMB OF THE PUMPKIN KING.

Please, not now! she screamed at her nightmare. *I need to finish it! I need to break the spell!*

Except this time, it didn't fade. In fact, it only seemed to grow stronger and more real. Eve tried to will it away once more, but at this point she was beyond exhaustion. She wanted to pass out. She wanted to quit.

But then, somewhere in the darkness, a small memory

surfaced, and with it the words of Ms. Shroud—telling her to take away its power.

Eve forced her eyes closed, desperately trying to think of a way to show the nightmares she wasn't scared of them. But . . . she was. Not only did they bring her so much fear, but they had plagued her since she was a child, keeping her from ever getting adopted—

Eve's eyes shot open.

Those nightmares, the same ones she was so scared of, were what put her on the path toward the family she had now, the family she had always dreamed of. They might have brought her pain and fear, but they had also given Eve her greatest gift: a home unlike any other.

Before her, the tombstones faded away, and Eve found herself back in the forest where she had first encountered the Pumpkin King. His glowing gaze was before her, surrounded in the dark brambles from the night they'd met—the night he adopted her and she became the Pumpkin Princess.

"Listen to him," Mother Morrigan's voice raged, snapping Eve back to reality. "It will kill you!"

Eve found the Pumpkin King's eyes. And she smiled.

"Then maybe I'll become undead. Just like my dad."

Eve plunged her hand into the cauldron.

Shouts of "No!" filled the room, and everything went white.

CHAPTER SEVENTEEN

The Pumpkin Princess

A RAVEN TAPPED ON A NEARBY WINDOW.

"Shoo, shoo," said a familiar voice.

Slowly Eve opened her eyes, waking to a strange room. It resembled the nurse's office back at the orphanage, with a small bed in the middle and a cabinet full of unfamiliar vials and cloth bandages. For a brief, disorienting moment, Eve panicked that she had woken still in a nightmare, but then she spotted the assortment of bat wings, crow feathers, and flasks of smoking liquids lining the shelves, and she felt herself relax. She was somewhere in Hallowell.

Beside the bed, early morning sunlight was pouring in through the window.

The sun...

It was back! They had stopped the Forever Night! But . . .

How was she still alive? She was sure breaking the spell would be the end of her.

"Ah, you're awake," said the woman's voice. A gentle hand reached out and felt her forehead.

Something large stirred in the corner, and Eve looked over to see the Pumpkin King beginning to wake in a chair that was far too small for him. A book was strewn loosely across his lap: *Parenting Your Monster through Good and Evil* by Twill Creaksly.

Eve looked at the face beside her, immediately recognizing the dark brush strokes beneath deep green eyes. It was Dr. On'Jure.

"'Ello, Evelyn. It's quite the pleasure to see you finally awake," she said, the sleeves of her black coat rolled back and revealing the symbols sketched onto her arms.

Eve opened her mouth to say hello back, but found her throat far too sore and her voice nothing more than a whisper. Instead, she pushed herself higher up the bed, causing the sheet covering her to roll off.

Instantly she panicked.

Translucent yellow leeches were covering her arms and legs, pulsing with a faint luminescence.

Eve hurriedly tried to swat them off, but both the Pumpkin King and Dr. On'Jure reached out and grabbed her, holding her back.

"Eve, it's all right," the Pumpkin King growled. "They're to help you."

"They're spirit leeches," Dr. On'Jure explained, slowly releasing her grip on Eve. "Please, you must leave them on."

Eve looked between both of them in alarm. Once more she attempted to say something, but found herself unable to do more than cough.

"Why can she not speak?" the Pumpkin King asked worriedly. "Is that a side effect?"

Dr. On'Jure checked Eve's pulse at her wrist, then looked into each of her eyes through a series of mechanical, strangely colored lenses.

"It is 'ard to say." Dr. On'Jure frowned. "Honestly, I'm not sure if I understand how she's alive at all. But, still, it looks like she is through the worst of it."

"Worst of what?" Eve finally managed to croak, causing both to sigh with relief. "What are these things?" she asked, still not fond of being covered in whatever spirit leeches were.

Dr. On'Jure glanced over at the Pumpkin King, and Eve saw him give her a nod before explaining.

"Well, Evelyn, they are the reason you're still with us. Whatever 'appened in that hut to counter the spell, it drained you of almost all your life. In truth, you shouldn't 'ave survived. The fact that the Pumpkin King made it back here with you alive in his arms was a miracle in itself. Even then, there was very little I could do for you on my own. We really only 'ad one option, and it was a bit of a long shot."

"What was it?" Eve asked, seeing the trepidation build on the Pumpkin King's face.

"A . . . transfusion," Dr. On'Jure answered hesitantly. "You desperately needed blood after the cauldron took most of yours for the counterspell. The only problem is that you're living and 'ave human blood. Something 'allowell doesn't really keep stocked."

"So what did you use?"

Dr. On'Jure exchanged another look with the Pumpkin King.

"Well, against my better judgment, I let your father convince me to use whatever blood we could get. I explained the repercussions could be worse than death, they could 'ave been torture and extremely pain—"

"Hrmph!"

"My apologies. Anyway, we spread the word, and anyone in 'allowell who 'ad blood to give, we took. The Pumpkin King was the first, and when you survived that, Vlad and Lyla were next. Lyla's mother as well, and many others that knew you from her bookstore. Even Mayor Brumple."

"Harlock too," the Pumpkin King added meaningfully.

"Unfortunately . . . ," Dr. On'Jure continued, shifting uncomfortably in her seat. "No matter what I did, it didn't seem to be working. So, we, erhm, *broadened* the pool of donors. We put spirit leeches on everyone willing, hoping something might take. Bone marrow from Ellie; ectoplasm from Ms. Cecilia Shroud; tallow from the candle-spirits; honestly, if there was an undead with something to give, we took it. The leeches have been transferring all of it to you for nights now."

Eve didn't know what to say.

She hardly even knew what to think.

Hallowell did that for her? *And it worked?*

"Wait—" Eve said, her mind reeling. "Doesn't having vampire blood or werewolf blood make me one of them? What about witch's blood?"

"No, it doesn't quite work like that," Dr. On'Jure explained. "The vampiric curse is transferred via their bite, as is the werewolf's. And witches from their pact with the Dark long ago. Regardless, an undead-to-living transfusion 'as never been done, and it was far from easy on you. Your body 'as been fighting to make sense of itself for almost a week. I've been trying every spell, ritual, and potion in the book to keep you breathing."

Eve looked at her hand that wasn't heavily bandaged, half-expecting to see something different . . . something changed. Instead, her normal palm stared back, the same as it had ever looked. Yet . . . was there a tingle in her fingers? Or was she imagining it?

More importantly, what did that make her?

"So . . . am I undead now?" Eve asked abashedly. "Or am I still living?"

At this, Dr. On'Jure hesitated, her forehead creasing. "To be honest, we're not sure. You might be a bit of both, or a bit of neither. This early on, it's 'ard to tell. I'll want to monitor your condition for a few more nights if that's okay with you?"

Eve didn't answer. Her mind was too busy playing catch-up. She could hardly believe she'd survived the cauldron in the first place, and now this?

"We will stay," the Pumpkin King answered for her, settling back into his rather small chair.

Dr. On'Jure took her leave, and Eve barely waited for the door to close before blurting the other questions that had been fighting to get out.

"What happened to Mother Morrigan and the coven? Are Vlad and Lyla okay?"

"Hrmph? Ah yes, Vlad and Lyla are safe and well. As for Mother Morrigan—" She could see the anger still blazing behind his eyes. Eve didn't blame him; just the thought of Mother Morrigan and her betrayal made Eve's blood boil.

"I have banished her to a place where she can do no harm," the Pumpkin King explained. "As well as any others who still wish to follow her. Anyone who wants to remain must renounce her cause. Hallowell thrives because we work together for the common good of all. Those who have only their own interests at heart do not belong."

Eve's brow furrowed, wondering how many would follow

Mother Morrigan and how many would stay. Eve doubted if she'd ever trust a coven witch again, not after what they and the baroness had done.

At the thought of the vampire, the rotten smell of the dungeons came rushing back to Eve, almost causing her to retch.

"What about Baroness La'Ment?" she asked, fighting down the urge to vomit.

"Hrmph! Neither she nor her daughters could be found after that night. No doubt they heard what had happened and knew I would be coming for them next. So they ran."

"And as for the vote regarding you staying in Hallowell," he went on, "that too is finished."

Eve shot up as high as she could in the bed.

"The Council met, and convinced by all the undead trying to save you, Mayor Brumple changed his vote to being in our favor," the Pumpkin King explained with the edges of a smile. "Of course, the baroness didn't show, so we decided the next in line for the castle should temporarily vote in her place."

"Vlad?" Eve asked, feeling a rush of excitement.

"Vlad." He nodded. "You can imagine how that went. And, hrmph, for what it's worth, Harlock took back his vote and instead abstained. It's as close as he can get to supporting you without upsetting his pack. He's still not happy about your accusation, but he respects what you did for Hallowell. Either way, it is done. Mother Morrigan's vacant seat matters not, as you have your three votes. Hallowell has accepted you. This is your home."

Relief washed over Eve. She felt like she had finally come up for air after being underwater for far too long. If she hadn't been so dehydrated, she might have even shed a tear of joy. Still, she just had one more question.

"When can we go home?"

"Soon," he answered.

Over the next couple of nights, undead streamed in and out of the doctor's, waking Eve from her sleep to visit until the Pumpkin King or Dr. On'Jure would chase them off. Ellie came by, leaving a number of new pants, shirts, and jackets behind with the claim that "a new outfit could cure anything." (Even by Hallowell standards, Eve doubted if that was true.)

She was surprised when the reclusive Ms. Shroud visited, bringing with her an advance copy of one of her new books, *Shadows of Doubt*—but not nearly as surprised as she was when she saw the dedication page: "To the Pumpkin Princess, a welcome breath of life."

At one point, an army of scarecrows poured in, and it took all the Pumpkin King's tricks to get them out and back to the farm.

Throughout it all, Eve thanked everyone she could for what they had done. The idea that Hallowell had come together for her, a *living*, made Eve feel more welcome than she previously thought possible. For the first time, she felt truly accepted, and the idea of being the Pumpkin Princess seemed less daunting than it ever had before.

Often, the doctor's assistant, Annabelle, would pop in to check on Eve and bring her another pudding cup. Eve had enjoyed them at first but, after what had to be her hundredth, thought she would be okay never having pudding again.

The more Eve got to know Annabelle, the more she realized the Pumpkin King had been right and there wasn't an ounce of anything suspicious about her. She was blissfully cheerful and transparent to a fault. She had also been quite relieved when Eve told her the reason her memory had been extra spotty lately was because Mother Morrigan had cast a Forgetfulness Hex on her. Still, that didn't explain why Annabelle kept forgetting whether or not Eve had taken her medicine, and it usually fell to the Pumpkin King to keep her from doubling up.

Ultimately, though, the two people Eve wanted to see more than anyone were Vlad and Lyla, who showed up together, accompanied by Lyla's mom, Seline.

To Eve's relief, both Dr. On'Jure and the Pumpkin King let them stay far longer than anyone else. They stayed by Eve's side, laughing and chatting. Vlad showed off the improvements he had already made to his lock-picking device, and Lyla informed them that her broom was thankfully starting to forgive her. Whether because they were told not to, or just didn't want to, no one brought up what had happened during the Forever Night.

Finally, after more checkups and tests than Eve could keep track of, she had a clear bill of health from the doctor. Thankful to be able to leave, she and the Pumpkin King made their way out and to the wagon parked out front, where Gleysol and Peaty stood waiting. As soon as she saw him, Eve rushed forward to give Peaty a hug (and the two puddings that she had snuck out for him).

Turning down the Pumpkin King's offer to help her into the cart, Eve climbed in—far less gracefully than usual—but ready and excited to return home all the same.

The cemeteries and twisted trees of the Haunted Hollows rolled by, until finally the northern fields of the Pumpkin King's land came into view, fields of grain and trees as far to either side as the eye could see. A damp wind combed through them, shaking the recent rain from their leaves in an otherwise clear, refreshing night.

As soon as the wheels of the wagon crossed into their land, Eve felt safety wash over her. She was home.

If she had her way, she'd never leave the homestead again. (Not counting trips to the bookstore obviously.)

Eve looked for Scrags—or any of the other scarecrows—but didn't see a single one as they made their way back to the barn.

They weren't in the maple trees, nor the berry bushes, nor the greenhouse.

In fact, the farm was silent save for the bats fluttering out from the barn to hunt for the night.

They unhitched Peaty and Gleysol from the wagon, and the Pumpkin King walked slowly beside Eve to make sure she was all right. She felt breathless after climbing the hill covered in all its vines. She was still weak—and rather hungry after almost a week of only pudding to eat. What she wouldn't give for some scarecrow cooking.

Her mind flashed back to her first night in Hallowell, and to all the food the scarecrows had excitedly prepared for her. How confused she had been, her first time hearing one of them talk (and her second, third, fourth, and fifth times). Now, a conversation with Scrags felt as normal as waking up. To be fair, the two often went hand in hand.

The door to the Hall of the Pumpkin King opened, and what little breath Eve had after climbing the hill was taken away.

WELCOME HOME banners were hung all across the ceiling, from the banisters to the chimney. The tables were laden with every one of her favorite dishes. Herb biscuits, potatoes with rosemary, oats with cinnamon and berries, fresh cheeses and milk, and every cookie, pie, and dessert imaginable. Scarecrows beamed at her from smiles torn into burlap sacks.

Vlad, Lyla, and Seline were there as well, holding their own

Welcome Back sign (theirs spelled far more correctly than the ones the scarecrows had made).

"It was Scrags's idea," the Pumpkin King growled. "He insisted on it."

Eve beamed, and before Scrags knew what was happening, Eve had found the blue-and-white-eyed scarecrow and tackled him in the biggest hug she could muster.

"Welcome homes, Prin'sis," he rasped. "We's missed yous."

"I missed you too, Scrags."

Something grumbled loudly behind her, and it wasn't the Pumpkin King speaking—but . . .

"Was that your stomach?" Eve asked, eyes wide in surprise.

"What?" the Pumpkin King said, looking embarrassed. "All I've had is the same pudding you've been eating, and it's not exactly filling, is it?"

Eve laughed. "It really wasn't."

And with that they all set to eating. And eating. And eating. Until Eve was convinced that she was going to need to write to Ellie for larger pants.

The Pumpkin King alone ate half a table's worth.

The scarecrows had outdone themselves and kept bringing more and more food to the table. They'd even prepared special food just for Vlad using the blood carrots they had grown in the greenhouse.

Eve was glad to be around the scarecrows again, despite

Scrags insisting that she looked like she was wasting away and needed to keep eating more.

At some point, Seline made her way over to her, Eve's mouth half-full of fresh-made applesauce.

"You know, I can't remember the last time I saw his Hall this cheerful," Seline said. She nodded toward the Pumpkin King. "All he and the scarecrows used to care about was their harvest. You've changed this place, and for the better."

Eve smiled, not knowing what to say.

As the evening drew on, the scarecrows made their way back out to see what small chores they could squeeze in before the night's end.

Lyla, Vlad, and Eve all exchanged hugs, none wanting to part.

"Are you going to be okay at the castle?" Eve asked Vlad. "Who's going to be in charge now that the baroness is gone?"

"The vampires will elect someone else, I guess," Vlad said with a shrug. "But don't worry about me. Whoever takes over can't be worse than the La'Ments, right?"

"I suppose." Eve nodded, though she was still worried about her friend.

"You should do it," said Lyla. "It's your name on the castle."

Vlad frowned and shook his head. "I'm probably still too young. Besides, I have way too many inventions to make. Not sure you remember, but you two dumped half mine in the moat, then destroyed the rest."

"It was Eve's idea," quipped Lyla.

"And your magic," Eve pointed out.

"That's true," said Lyla. "My magic did kind of save the day."

"Literally," Eve said with a laugh. "But we couldn't have done it without you, Vlad. I promise to help you make more."

"Help?"

"Meaning I'll read beside you," she teased.

"Oh, gee, thanks," Vlad said, laughing.

Soon her friends had left, and Eve attempted to help Scrags clean the dining table before getting shooed off and told to take it easy.

After several pies' worth of sugar, Eve didn't feel quite ready to turn in for bed, and instead headed down the hill and across the farm.

She let her mind wander in the gentle evening, enjoying the soft breeze and watching as her shoes left wet footprints in the mud.

Whether deliberately or by accident, she found herself at the bench that she and her friends had sat on during the Harvest Festival, the one looking out over the farm.

Nearby, a torch blazed, and Eve felt herself shying away from it. It seemed brighter than usual. In fact, the whole farm seemed clearer to her than it normally did this time of night. Perhaps the moon was brighter than normal, or perhaps . . .

Was it something else? Was it . . . *her?*

The sound of footsteps interrupted her thought, and up the hill came the Pumpkin King.

"Hrmph, there you are," he rumbled. "Is everything okay? Do you feel all right?"

"I feel—um—fine," Eve answered, unsure. She closed her eyes as hard as she could and when she reopened them, the darkness of the farm seemed to return to normal, the torch now less blinding.

The Pumpkin King nudged Eve over and took a seat beside her, causing the bench to sink heavily to one side.

"Something troubles you," he said.

Eve hesitated. Something *was* eating at her.

"It—it was all my fault," she finally said. "If I never came here, none of this would have happened. Me being living almost destroyed Hallowell."

"No," said the Pumpkin King. "The coven almost destroyed Hallowell. You being living is what saved Hallowell."

"But—"

"I have been in Hallowell longer than anyone. In that time, it has seen troubles and dangers even without you here. But you know what it hasn't seen?"

"What?" asked Eve.

"A Pumpkin Princess like you," he rumbled. "You have brightened this place. Do you think Vlad would have acted so bravely without you? Or Lyla trust in her magic? I even heard

Ellie made Franklin start their own Winter Solstice tradition after hearing about our Christmas. And as much as it annoys me, even the scarecrows are different. Hallowell is best when it comes together, and what you did only brought it closer. Your blood is now proof of that. A mix of you, of me, of all the undead here."

"But I still don't understand what that makes me," Eve said, frowning. "If I'm not undead, but I'm not fully living, what am I?" She had worried so long about whether or not Hallowell would accept her for being living, that she couldn't help but wonder what it meant now that she was . . . whatever she was.

"Eve, your best friends are a witch and a vampire, and hrmph, a scarecrow was so excited you were okay that he threw you a welcome-home celebration. It is not *what* you are that matters, but rather *who* you are. And you showed Hallowell exactly who you were when you were willing to sacrifice yourself for it. Yet, if you still insist on an answer to your question, I have one for you."

"What?"

The glow of the Pumpkin King's face warmed.

"You are the Pumpkin Princess."

Eve considered this for a moment.

She *was* the Pumpkin Princess. And now equal parts her and Hallowell itself. Even then, she felt she was just now learning what it truly meant to hold that title. She knew she had a long path before her to fill the Pumpkin King's massive boots, a path she promised herself would start with gaining the werewolves' forgiveness. But as long as she had her friends, as long as she had him . . .

"I am," Eve said meaningfully. "But don't forget your promise to help me. I still have a lot to learn."

"Hrmph, of course. So long as you remember your promise to teach me how to be a good father."

Eve paused, looking up at him. "I don't know, Dad. You're pretty good at it already."

The night lit up in his smile, and he rested a heavy arm across her shoulders.

Eve snuggled closer, and together the two sat there long into the night, staring quietly out over their land.

This was her home. The scarecrows her family.

And the Pumpkin King was her father.

And nothing was going to change that.

Acknowledgments

First and foremost, to you, the reader: Thank you for being such an important part of Eve's ongoing story. This book is and always will be immensely personal to me, and I can only hope that reading it brought you even a fraction of the joy that writing it brought me.

Secondly, to all those who supported my little tale of the Pumpkin King adopting Eve, and who helped to transform it into a book:

My agent, Lauren Galit; editors extraordinaire Liz Kossnar, Lauren Kisare, Lily Choi, and quite literally everyone else at Little, Brown Books for Young Readers; the world's most talented illustrator, Matt Rockefeller, for bringing just as much life to Hallowell as Eve did; my incredible friends and family; and finally, the person whose support is beyond words, my first reader and amazing wife, Ashley.

Scrags looks forward to seeing you all in Book 2, where he sincerely hopes, for his own sake, that Eve has a much easier time. . . .

SARA PRYDE

STEVEN BANBURY

grew up surrounded by farmland before eventually moving to a part of California with notably fewer cows. Somewhere along the way he married his legend of a wife, adopted their annoyingly cute dog, and developed a penchant for writing he hasn't seemed to shake. *The Pumpkin Princess and the Forever Night* is his debut novel.